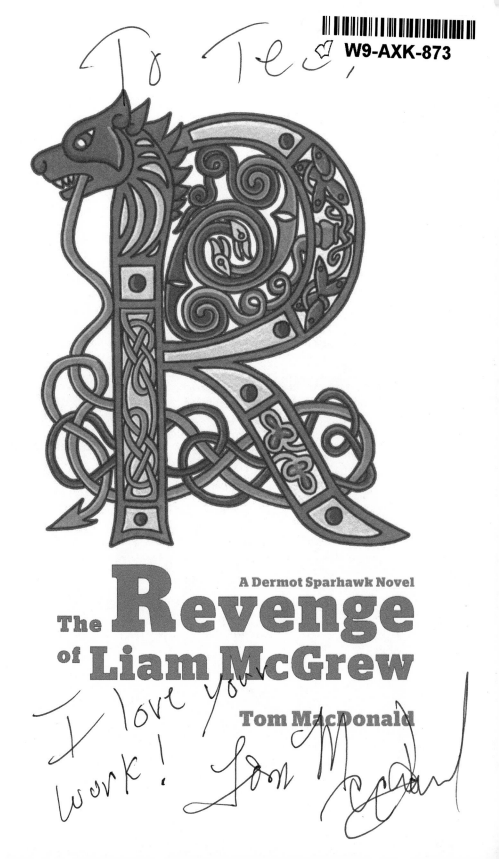

To Ted,

I love your work!

Tom McDonald

A Dermot Sparhawk Novel

The Revenge
of Liam McGrew

Tom MacDonald

Other Books by Tom MacDonald

The Charlestown Connection
Beyond The Bridge

Hardcover: 978-0-9967332-0-5
Softcover: 978-0-9967332-1-2
ebook: 978-0-9967332-2-9

Published in the United States of America by
Sparhawk Press
Braintree, Massachusetts

1 2 3 4 5 6 7 8 9

Interior artwork ©Heidi Hurley
Cover concept by Joanne Coughlin
Book design by Robin Wrighton

Printed in the United States of America

This book is dedicated to my father

Thomas J. MacDonald

June 25, 1931 - September 15, 2014

In gratitude to Saint Padre Pio
The great healer

ACKNOWLEDGEMENTS

It all starts with my wife, Maribeth, whose loving support and ruthless story analysis are unmatched. Without Maribeth, none of this happens.

A special thank you goes to Heidi Hurley, the talented artist who drew the illustrations, al a comic noir. Heidi's creative diligence brought the pictures to fruition and to life. Heidi translated my sketchy ideas into first-rate sketches, and she was quick to make modifications on the fly. Another special thanks goes to Robin Wrighton, who designed the cover and formatted the text and sketches for print. The collaboration with Robin was easy and professional, and her ideas and suggestions were always on the mark. Thank you to Joanne Coughlin for her contributions to the book cover.

I am grateful to the following story consultants: Dick Murphy, whose Charlestown sensibilities and literary intuition bring an element of realism and believability to setting and dialogue in this fictional tale; Chris Hobin, whose ability to deconstruct a scene, diagnose the pieces, and reassemble the parts, enhanced the clarity on each page; John Malkowski, Rhodes Scholar extraordinaire, whose proficiency in grammar constructs and word usage are unrivaled; Colin McKenzie, my talented nephew, whose insights to story structure and character development are expert.

I thank Kate Victory Hannisian of Blue Pencil Consulting for applying her editing skills to the manuscript.

Also…

Joe Hobin, Joe Matthews, Michael McKenzie, Carman Ortiz, Sharon Hanson, Maureen Preskenis, Cookie Giodarno, Tom Coots, Paul Martin, Rene Menard, Richard Murphy, and Al MacPherson.

I am grateful to Scott & Tara Savitz and Dennis & Sharon Hanson for buying character names for charity. Their proceeds went to Harvest on Vine emergency food pantry in Charlestown, Mass. The same goes for Kenny Bowen, who bought a character name. Kenny's proceeds went to the Stonehill College football program.

Lastly, I'd like to recognize the following master grammarians, who honed their craft in parochial school, with a smiling nun tapping a ruler in her hand: Patricia MacDonald, my mother; Frank Carney, my uncle; Olly Beaulieu, my father's classmate at Stonehill College, class of 1953.

THANK YOU

We are grateful to our friends and family for helping us launch Sparhawk Press through our Indiegogo drive. We couldn't have done it without you!

With Gratitude,
Maribeth and Tom

Tommy Amaral
Eliot Andler
Al and Diane Barese
Patrick Barnes
Clarence and Carol Bass
Olly and Claire Beaulieu
Debbie Biggins
Jack and Marianne Boyce
Dick Bowen
Leo Breen
Keith and June Buckley
F.S. Burns
Judy Burton
Caffé Bella, Randolph, MA
Grant Cambridge
Peggy Caron
Eileen Casey
Michael Cawley
Steven Codd
Irene Costello

Paul Cummins
Jane Curran
Mickey DeCosta
Mary DeLorey
Vernon Dent
Francis X. Dooher
Chris Dolan
Ginny Doyle
Dan Duff
Effie's Oatcakes
Bryan Gillis
Kathleen 'Cookie' Giordano
Stephen Griffin
Dr. Craig 'Skeeter' Gruskowski
Dennis and Sharon Hanson
Fred Hanson
Bill and Carol Hayward
H. David Hennessey
Joyce Hogan
Bob Irgens

Tom Kadzis
Rich 'Ratt' Kennedy
Dave and Nancy Kormann
Dave Lauria
David Lear
Pete and Donna LeCam
Debbie Leppanen
Diane MacDonald
Patricia MacDonald
Joan MacIsaac
John Malkowski
Frank McDermott
John McDermott
Tom McDermott
Bob McGann
Martin McGovern
Richard McGuan
John Moore, Navy Yard Bistro
Tom Motley
Dick Murphy

Rich Murphy
Billy Nelligan
Jeff Nord
Donna and Jim O'Brien
Michael O'Connor
Johnny Palmer
Steve Partridge
Kevin Patts
PJ and Maureen Preskenis
Bill Quinn
Julie Quinn
Chuck and Marilyn Race
Florence 'Lornie' Rawls
DeAnn Foran Smith
Eve Spangler
Bill Sullivan
Deidre Sullivan
Judy Sweeney
Bette Task
Diane Yee

PROLOGUE

The radio crackled inside a police cruiser idling in front of Lauria Trattoria on Hanover Street in Boston's North End. The dispatcher said, "Operation for Alpha-103."

Officer Paul Simpson, broad-shouldered and blond-haired, sitting in the passenger seat of a two-man squad car, pressed the button on his collar mic and answered with a cop's certainty. "Alpha-103 responding."

"Alpha-103, we received a call reporting that a man has been shot. The location of the incident is Saint Jude Thaddeus Church, 55 Vine Street, Charlestown."

"Alpha-103, we're on our way." Simpson punched the siren and turned to his partner. "Hit it, Steve-o."

"You got it."

Officer Steve Partridge, long-limbed and sandy-haired, shifted into drive and sped over the Charlestown Bridge into City Square. He raced past Kormann & Schuhwerk's Brat House, a known cop hangout, and swerved under the Tobin Bridge onto Vine Street. He slowed the vehicle, killed the siren, and pulled into an unlit lot behind Saint Jude Thaddeus Church, a small parish abutting the projects. Partridge shifted into park and shined a spotlight down an arched alleyway. A sign on the wall read "Joe Boyce Food Pantry." A chain-link fence barricaded the far end of the alley. There was no way out. He aimed the light lower, and the cone-shaped beam cut through the fog and illuminated the bodies of two motionless men lying flat on the blacktop.

"Looks bad," Simpson said.

"Mucho bad," Partridge agreed, and radioed for an ambulance.

The cops got out of the car and drew their weapons, listening for danger, hearing nothing but the traffic on the Tobin Bridge. They inched toward the bodies, taking every precaution they'd been trained to take, proceeding like the professionals they had learned to become. They assessed the scene, all seemed tranquil. Partridge studied one of the downed men.

"No ambulance needed for this guy. His head is cratered." Partridge holstered his Glock pistol and shined a flashlight on the area. "Look at the blood on the rock next to him. I'll radio for Homicide."

Simpson examined the other body. "This one's alive, but the bus better get here soon. He's bleeding like a bastard, bullet wounds."

"Bullet wounds," Partridge said. "The yuppies will freak when they hear this. One man shot, another with his head caved in, all within blocks of their luxury condos."

"It's almost enough to make you feel bad for them," Simpson deadpanned.

Partridge joined Simpson and looked at the hemorrhaging gunshot victim. "Hey, I know this guy. I gave him a ride once to see Hanson."

Simpson gloved his hands. "Superintendent Hanson?"

"Yup, Wyatt Earp himself."

"If Hanson wanted to see this guy, he must have clout." Simpson studied the body more closely. "No wonder he's alive, look at the size of the son of a bitch. You'd need a moose rifle to put him down."

"A Remington 700 would get the job done," Partridge said.

"A Remington 700?" Simpson checked the wounds as he spoke. "You hunt?"

"Every fall at a lakeside camp in Maine, up there in uncharted territory," Partridge said. "You should join me next time. We can drink some beers, smoke cigars, do a little male bonding."

"Male bonding?" Simpson grunted. "Like hippity hop to the barbershop?"

"Forget it, Simmie." Partridge shook his head. "I'll get the crime-scene tape."

Part One

Belfast, Northern Ireland

CHAPTER ONE

I.

O'Byrne hobbled along the Falls Road, head down, gait slow, limping like a balding Irish Frankenstein. At the Garden of Remembrance he made the sign of the cross and kissed the plaque of the Tullyverry Four: Madden, Casey, Francis, McBrine. Four brave soldiers martyred for freedom. O'Byrne blessed himself again and trudged ahead. He went into Slattery's Pub and sat at the bar away from the windows, keeping his back to the wall and his eyes on the door. One can never be too careful, even in times of declared peace. Old gray Slattery himself rapped his knuckles on the scarred mahogany surface, a judge calling for order.

"What'll you be drinking today, O'Byrne?"

"A glass of Guinness would suit me fine," he said.

"'Tis a fitting choice on this gloomy afternoon." Slattery poured a pint from the tap and placed it on the bar in front of him. O'Byrne sipped the black beer and licked the froth from his mouth. Though the pub was mostly empty, Slattery leaned in closely and whispered, "Liam called earlier." He wiped the bar as he spoke, barely moving his thin blue lips. "He'll be in the back room tonight at ten o'clock."

"Ten o'clock." O'Byrne sighed. "And I suppose he wants me to be there."

"I'm afraid attendance is mandatory."

"Aye, like Easter Mass." O'Byrne's stomach churned, churning the way it had in the Long Kesh blanket protests, when the IRA inmates refused prison uniforms, wearing blankets instead. He touched the gun in his waistband, and his stomach settled down. O'Byrne muttered to himself. "Proud to be a blanket man."

"What was that you said?" asked Slattery, ever the nosy one.

"It was nothing." O'Byrne moved his hand from the gun and palmed his smooth scalp. "I'll be needing something stronger, Mr. Slattery. Be a good man and fix me a jigger of Jameson, the twelve-year-old."

Slattery reached high to the top shelf for the good stuff.

"I don't blame you at all, O'Byrne, not at all." Slattery poured O'Byrne a glass and then poured himself one, too. He toasted, "May you never be without a drop."

O'Byrne finished the drinks and left the pub to address a matter.

§

He advanced to Saint Malachy's Church on Alfred Street. With its turrets and gables and steeply pitched roofs, it looked more like a Tudor castle than a Catholic house of worship, as if the Protestants themselves had designed it. O'Byrne stepped inside the church and admired the vaulted ceilings. He listened to the peal of the great bell, the largest in Belfast, and perhaps the largest in all of Ulster, and it clanged the six o'clock Angelus. He walked up the side aisle and stopped at the statue of Saint Angus MacNisse of Connor, baptized by Saint Patrick himself, and he whispered a plea to the ceramic figure.

"MacNisse, it's me, O'Byrne from West Belfast. Are you listening? Aye, you're listening, saints are obliged to listen. I know I'm not good enough to be talking to the Almighty directly, so I'm talking to you instead, no offense." He looked over his shoulder and then back at the icon. "Liam sent word that he wants to see me. Aye, I know, it's very bad to be sure. Can you help me, MacNisse? Can you get me out of this grand mess I'm in? A miracle of yours would be most charitable at this time, most charitable indeed."

O'Byrne waited. Nothing happened. He raised his massive head and shouted to the rafters on high, "I need you, MacNisse!"

II.

At ten o'clock O'Byrne entered the back room of Slattery's Pub, a windowless cavern with low ceilings and worn floors. A lone bulb cast a dim beam, scarcely enough to chase the shadows. At a shaky round table in the center of the room sat Liam McGrew, a burgundy birthmark staining half his face, an oxygen tube pumping air into his nostrils, fuel to feed the fire. The only instinct that kept Liam alive, it was said, was an unmitigated rage and an unquenchable thirst for violence. And those who knew him best said that he would never die until he savored every atom of anger in his vacant soul.

Resting next to Liam was his blackthorn walking stick, a symbol of power, a Gaelic gavel, though some in Belfast saw it as a crutch and nothing more. The stick leaned hard against the oaken chair, at the ready in case a wayward lad needed a swift lathering. A shillelagh shampoo with splinter conditioners, Liam would say.

Liam McGrew cleared his throat of phlegm and in a wheezing burst said, "It is good of you to come by tonight, very good indeed. I rely heavily on you, O'Byrne, more heavily than a man has a right, hmm." His voice grew hoarser with each forced utterance. His dewlaps shook as if adding vibrato. "I have the utmost gratitude for your loyalty, and the greatest trust in our comradeship."

"We go back a long ways, don't we now, Liam?" O'Byrne said, hoping his casual reply might keep the conversation light and innocuous.

"We do indeed, we do indeed. We've endured the Troubles together, you and I." Liam turned the knob on his tank. "I require more oxygen this time of evening. I believe the Belfast air thins at night." He regained his wind. "I see where you visited Saint Malachy's earlier today."

"Yes, yes." Was Liam following him? "I lit a candle for Kathleen."

"Ah, your lovely wife, Kathleen. A dreadful loss, most dreadful indeed. We must pray for the repose of her soul, for it is our duty to do so." Liam bowed his head in apparent earnest, and then in a huffed cadence he spit out, "Now to business. We have a big job in Boston, bigger than the museum heist I'm told."

"Bigger, you say?" O'Byrne hadn't been to Boston in two decades, which was fine with him after the way they cocked things up last time. "How much?"

"Two million." Liam rubbed his hands together. "Two, I say!"

"Sterling or dollars?" asked O'Byrne, perhaps too eagerly. "I'm merely curious."

"Green American dollars. The exchange rate no longer favors us in these ghastly economic times. Still, it's a great deal of money." Liam took a lungful of air followed by a mouthful of drink. He poured a glass for O'Byrne and picked up where he left off. "It's a simple job, fantastically straightforward, a task we can do in a snap."

"Working for Mr. H again?" O'Byrne asked.

Liam nodded, saving his breath.

Another deal with Mr. H. This was dire news indeed as far as O'Byrne was concerned. "You're in no condition, Liam. You shouldn't be making a trip to America, the shape you're in."

"On that we must agree. Old age has caught up with me and left me in its cruel wake, so we'll be needing a different approach this time, a new line of attack. That is why I called you here tonight, to tell you of my idea." Another twist of the knob, another gasp for air. "This particular job calls for fresh blood, an infusion of youth, so I'll be sending my grandson, Alroy. The time has come for Alroy to learn the family trade, to cut his eyeteeth so to speak."

"Alroy?" Did O'Byrne hear him correctly? "Did you say Alroy?"

"I'll be sending McAfee, too. He's a nasty head-banger, McAfee, the perfect gunman to flank Alroy on his first international job." Liam sucked oxygen. "A brilliant pairing they'll be. Brilliant, I tell you!"

"You're calling on Alroy to go to Boston?" O'Byrne couldn't believe what he was hearing from Liam.

"I am indeed." Liam answered.

"Are you sure Alroy is up to the challenge?" O'Byrne asked. "He is terribly young." *And terribly dimwitted, not the full shilling.* "With every due respect, Liam, the boy isn't ready for a job like this."

"No, no, Alroy is ready." Liam stuck to it.

"Liam, he's a kid."

"I said the boy is ready. He's as goddamn ready as he'll ever be. Alroy is shipping up to Boston, for it is time the lad became a man. You *yourself* were but a teen when you started out." A darting look escaped Liam's eyes, and O'Byrne knew there was more to come, probably something unpalatable. Liam pointed a shaky finger at him and said, "I'll be needing you to go with Alroy and Mac to America."

"What was that you said?"

"And then I'll have peace of mind, knowing you are at Alroy's side. He can learn from you, O'Byrne. I want Alroy to learn from the best, and you are the best in Belfast, and perhaps the world. The job will go bang-on with you in Boston."

"I'm too old, Liam," O'Byrne said, stalling for time, thinking of a way to get out of this mess. "I'd only slow the lads down."

"Nonsense, man." Liam barked with confidence. "I have faith in you, and the job is easy besides. We just walk in, take the loot, and walk out." Liam leaned forward as if pleading. "You know Boston, you know it well."

"The city has changed since I was there last."

"Come now, it hasn't changed *that* much." Liam forced a smile. "It will be fine."

"I'm not so sure about that," O'Byrne said.

"What do you mean?"

"I'm not talking about Boston, per se. I'm talking about Mr. H." O'Byrne massaged his temples with his thumbs as he thought about the previous Boston job and the problems that arose from it. "This job could be a feckin' set-up, Liam."

"A set-up?" He scoffed. "Do you honestly believe I'd put my own flesh and blood at risk? Alroy is my only family, my only remaining kin. I would never place him in jeopardy."

Liam grabbed the jug and topped his glass. O'Byrne slid his glass over for a refill. God knew he needed it.

"I know what Alroy means to you," O'Byrne said, "but I think you're placing too much faith in Mr. H. He got screwed the last time out, and he got screwed by us!"

"Oh, for Christ's sake, O'Byrne, Mr. H knows we had nothing to do with that fake Vermeer."

O'Byrne tried a different angle, anything to avoid babysitting Alroy in America. "Boston is a tricky town, no place for a youngster. I'd rather do the job myself."

"No!" Liam leaned closer. "Alroy is going to Boston." Liam grabbed his walking stick and shoved himself up from the chair, his face throbbing and red. "Tomorrow night, same time, same place, you, me, Alroy, and McAfee. Understand?"

"Aye, understood."

O'Byrne walked to the door. He was ring-fenced and he knew it.

§

O'Byrne left Slattery's Pub for his Divis Street flat, a tiny efficiency above a fancy café. He lit a gas burner under a copper kettle and waited for the water to boil. He steeped two teabags in two cups of Belleek china, placed the cups in matching saucers and carried them to a pine table that had been a wedding gift from Bridie. He set one cup in front of an empty chair and pulled out another chair for himself.

O'Byrne said to the vacant seat, "How was your day today, Kathleen? That's grand, just grand. My day? Oh, I hate to be complaining. Yes, 'twas Liam again. He wants me to go to Boston for yet another job. I know I shouldn't be going and Lord knows I don't want to go. What was that you said? Have I gone to confession? No, I haven't, but I'm working my way up to it." He took a swallow. "You're quite chatty tonight, Kathleen, not that I mind. It helps with the loneliness. Please don't say that about the brigade. We're not just a bunch of crooks. We're fighting for something important. No, no, that's okay. I want you to speak your mind. Get some sleep now, for I'll be turning in myself shortly. Oh, all right, I'll stay up a wee bit longer."

O'Byrne went to the stove and made two fresh cups of tea and continued the monologue with his long-dead wife, Kathleen.

III.

The following evening at ten o'clock O'Byrne entered the back room of Slattery's Pub. He found Liam McGrew in the same chair at the same table, his rosy birthmark beaming brightly, a near-empty bottle of whiskey in front of him. Next to Liam sat his grandson, Alroy McGrew—young, skinny, redheaded, reckless—a boy destined to do something stupid. Sitting beside Alroy was McAfee, who by comparison looked cerebral. His white complexion, orange mustache, and green eyes reflected the tricolors of the Irish flag. McAfee possessed a toughness that made him valuable on jobs, so long as the job wasn't too intricate. O'Byrne sat down. Liam leaned forward and cast a long shadow across the round table, bringing to mind a sundial—Liam at twelve o'clock, Alroy at three, McAfee at six, O'Byrne at nine.

"Well now, lads!" Liam harrumphed, his words scratchy but not yet slurring. "I thank you all for joining me on this most auspicious occasion. We are gathered here tonight to discuss a promising opportunity, an opportunity that will yield the cause abundant funding for future maneuvers. And, I might say, a venture that will add a few coins to our own purses as well."

O'Byrne wondered about the money from the museum job two decades ago. On what maneuvers was it spent? He couldn't recall the purchase of ordnance or intelligence. As for his purse, O'Byrne wouldn't have minded a few more quid.

"How much coin, Papa?" asked Alroy.

"We'll get to that soon enough. Show a bit of patience." Liam tapped the knob of his stick on the table, each tap getting louder. "I can tell you this much, and this much alone. It is a straightforward robbery. Mr. H, for security reasons, won't divulge the entire plan until you get to Boston—much safer that way."

"Boston!" McAfee leaned forward. "When do we go?"

"We must act quickly, Mac, for timing is of the essence," Liam said, not answering the question.

"When?" Mac pressed.

"Your flight leaves tomorrow." Liam adjusted the oxygen tube and turned the knob. "I only wish I could join you lads myself, but I can't for my worsening health."

"You don't need to go, Papa." Alroy patted Liam's shoulder. "I can handle the robbery."

"Aye, that's true, Alroy, I have great faith in you," Liam said. "I have no doubt you will handle the robbery. I'm not worried about the job, for the job is in good hands. I want to go to Boston for another reason. I have unfinished business over there."

"What kind of business?" asked Alroy, with a child's rapt gaze.

"A few years back a feckin' half-breed named Dermot Sparhawk insulted me in an ungodly manner. He is a lowlife mutt from Charlestown, this man." Liam sucked air and his eyeballs bulged. "I wanted to teach him some respect with my stick, but I was called off him at the last moment."

"Who called you off, Papa?" asked Alroy.

"A man named Mr. H reined me in." Liam nodded as if that explained it. "Mr. H stopped me from teaching Sparhawk respect. He stopped me because of a museum heist we pulled twenty years prior. Mr. H didn't want to draw attention to it."

"What heist?" Alroy's eyes fluttered.

"It was well before you were born, son."

"How did Sparhawk–"

"Sparhawk happened after the fact, Alroy, after the feckin' fact." Liam paused for oxygen. "He had nothing to do with the art heist, but I had reason to visit him when I was last in Boston, and that's when the scummy feck ridiculed me."

"He ridiculed you!" Alroy shouted.

"He did." Liam nodded. The wattles on his throat squeezed like fish gills. "I had hoped to return to Charlestown one day and kneecap the sorry bastard, and someday perhaps I shall."

"We have a good man over there in Charlestown," O'Byrne said.

"I am well aware of that, my friend, well aware indeed. You needn't remind me." Liam leaned against the wall and mumbled, "Dermot Sparhawk, filth of the earth."

O'Byrne studied Liam's face. For the first time since the Sparhawk affair, he knew why Liam never avenged the "ungodly" affront of the Charlestown strong boy. Liam was afraid of him.

"Sparhawk!" Liam regained his energy and whaled the table with his stick. His face beamed so brightly the blotch disappeared. "I'd double kneecap him if I had the chance. I'd put the boots to him, kick him to a red wad shod. Then I'd cyclops the swine with a bullet to his forehead, the dumb-ass mongrel." He doubled over gagging. "That's what I'd do to him, damn it, that's what I'd do."

"Whoa, Liam," O'Byrne said. "Easy now."

Liam laid his stick on the table and sat with his head up and his mouth agape, sucking like a trout on a pier. Ten minutes passed before he caught his breath, during which time the mood calmed. Liam nodded, ready to resume, now that he had regained his composure.

"Let's move on to the business at hand." Liam placed four cell phones on the table. "Disposable phones, they cannot be traced to any person or address. I have saved the necessary contact numbers in each one. C1 is for me, C2 is O'Byrne, C3 is Alroy, C4 is Mac. All the numbers have a Boston area code and a US country code. We will use these phones and only these phones to communicate. Is that clear?" Liam stared at his grandson. "What are you writing, Alroy?"

"I'm making a list so I don't forget. C1 is Liam McGrew, C2 is O'B–"

"Jesus, Mary, and Joseph, boy. Secrecy! That's the reason for the codes to begin with. And don't go calling your friends, either. No one is to use these phones except on robbery business. Do I make myself clear?"

"I get it, Papa." Alroy crumpled the paper. "Secrecy."

"Christ almighty in heaven." Liam shook his head and then gazed at O'Byrne. "I'll be needing to speak with you before you take leave."

McAfee interrupted. "Guns?"

Liam said, "No guns will be needed on this job, no weaponry at all."

Soldiers without guns? They looked at each other but said nothing. Alroy and McAfee left the back room, and once they were gone, Liam took hold of O'Byrne's arm.

"I'm counting on you. I am hoping this job goes as smoothly as the museum job." Liam released O'Byrne and cranked the tank. "On your cell phone is contact C5. C5 is for Mr. H. He'll be expecting your call once you've landed in Boston. Now pour us a good glass, would you?"

O'Byrne filled two glasses. "C5 goes directly to Mr. H?"

"Not directly, no. It likely goes to his front man. I cannot remember the lad's name for the life of me." Liam rolled the walking stick in his hands like a pool shark before a tough shot. "I need you to do one more thing for me. Keep a close eye on Alroy. He may be raw, but the lad shows potential."

Potential? God save us, Saint MacNisse.

§

Early the next morning, well before the scheduled flight to Boston, O'Byrne cabbed to Sailortown, or what remained of it after the Parliamentary purges. He walked along the docklands to the now-shuttered Saint Joseph's Church, the Chapel on the Quays, and looked up to its mighty steeple as he spoke.

"Do you remember our wedding day, Kathleen, right here in this very church? Aye, 'twas a splendid morning indeed. You in your mam's dress, me in my rented suit, Father Monaghan performing the nuptials." His eyes lowered. "Why did you leave me, Kathleen?"

He read a plaque that honored two Catholic school girls who were murdered by an Ulster Defense Association car bomb. The feckin' UDA, homicidal cowards killing innocent girls. O'Byrne stopped himself from getting angry, for anger did him no favors, and he screamed to the Ulster sky, "Will ye no come back again, Kathleen?"

O'Byrne heard no answer, not even a dismissive echo. He lumbered down Pilot Street to Barrow Square and went into the Teagueland Inn, a friendly tavern where a man could imbibe a peaceful drink. A stiff bracer was needed before the flight to Boston, and a stiff bracer he had. As he was sipping a tall glass of whiskey and ice, a thought came to him: When a man tells you that you don't need a gun, you'd better bring one that's loaded.

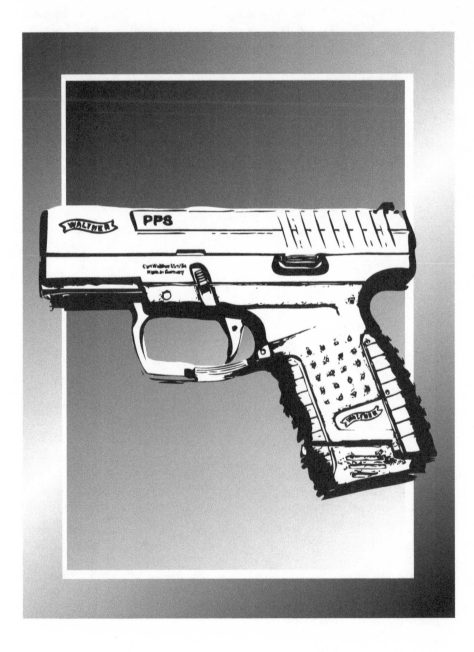

CHAPTER TWO

I.

The plane traversed the Atlantic and landed at Logan Airport with nary a bump. With trumped-up passports, Alroy, McAfee, and O'Byrne passed through US Customs as smoothly as the jet had touched down on the tarmac. A customs agent named Emmett O'Burke, known to be a Wexford man and an IRA sympathizer, nodded to O'Byrne as he went through the gate. The three Belfast men crossed the concourse to the curbside drop-off area. O'Byrne watched the baggage handlers greeting taxis and stacking luggage, toiling the way Sailortown dockworkers once toiled on the waterfront.

A black Chrysler 300, sporting darkly tinted windows and a short chrome antenna, pulled up in front of them. The driver got out with the car still idling and wiped the windshield with a Kelly green handkerchief, a signal to let O'Byrne know this was the car. The plan was working. O'Byrne, Alroy, and McAfee got into the big Chrysler, with O'Byrne poised behind the wheel, and they pulled away from the curb into the afternoon traffic. Driving on the right-hand side of the road didn't unnerve O'Byrne any, though his untraveled passengers seemed thrown by it. They drove out of Logan Airport and into Boston via the Ted Williams Tunnel. Tonight they would billet in a safe house in a section of Jamaica Plain once known as White City. He had taken refuge in the house before, courtesy of Mr. H.

O'Byrne motored along the Arborway to Forest Hills. The area hadn't changed much since his last visit. Boston had changed, but not Forest Hills. He turned onto Eldridge Road and looped White City twice, making sure he wasn't being shadowed. He circled again and found their destination on Meyer Street.

Tall hedges, eight feet or higher, bordered the lot and secluded the house. O'Byrne clicked a gizmo on the visor and the driveway gates swung open. The gates promptly closed once the car entered the property. In front of them sat a gray Victorian house with an attached garage. Another click and the garage door opened. O'Byrne pulled into the garage and killed the engine, and the door rumbled shut behind them. The three men got out of the Chrysler and entered the house through a breezeway sided with frosted jalousie slats. Nobody could see the lads in the car, getting out of the car, or walking into the house. All was going as planned.

Alroy opened the refrigerator and like a soldier on leave he said, "Three shelves of Guinness. Welcome to America, eh lads?"

"Give me one," McAfee said, exhausting his daily word allotment.

McAfee and Alroy poured mugs of beer and toasted with a tap of the glass. O'Byrne excused himself to lie down in one of the large bedrooms.

II.

O'Byrne awoke at twilight and walked into the living room, where he saw McAfee and Alroy slumbering on couches—Mac snoring, Alroy slobbering. O'Byrne looked at Alroy, already deemed a dolt by most, and wondered how the boy would bollix things in Boston.

In the kitchen O'Byrne saw dozens of the empty Guinness bottles and an empty liter of Newfoundland Screech rum, which explained the sleeping slugs in the living room. Screech rum? He went to the garage and started the Chrysler and drove to Charlestown. Thirty minutes later, he pulled into the driveway of his old friend's house on Chappie Street. O'Byrne hitched up the backstairs and reached for the doorbell, but it was painted over solid. He knocked on the wooden door. A man with a lion's mane of dark hair answered the door; 'twas Jackie Tracy himself.

"Been expecting you," said Jackie, a retired longshoreman whose face bore the marks of his youthful occupation, that of a professional boxer. "Come in, O'Byrne. It's been too long."

"'Tis a perfect evening outside, isn't it?" O'Byrne said.

"Yeah, it's a perfect evening for the Red Sox to take another beating, especially with that chump on the mound tonight."

O'Byrne followed Jackie into the house.

"We have no professional baseball in Ireland, I am troubled to say, but I can understand your passion for the game."

"I wish I could understand it." Jackie sat down and slapped his knee. "I shouldn't complain. They won the World Series, twice no less."

"Even in Belfast we heard about that."

"You know what it is?" Jackie went on. "We got so used to complaining about them it became a habit. Now if they don't win it all, we think they failed."

"Indeed." O'Byrne kept the banter going. "I loved *The Natural*, Robert Redford and that other fella, the old coot from *Cocoon*."

"Wilford Brimley."

"Aye, him." Actually, Kathleen loved the movie. O'Byrne never cared for the theatrics of Hollywood, never cared much for idle chatter, either, and he decided to get to the point. "I hate to be so forward so quickly, Jackie, but I need a gun."

"You IRA guys are always in a rush for guns."

"And you Charlestown guys are always glad to furnish them."

O'Byrne remembered a gun shipment to County Down. Literally a shipment, the boat's hold filled with armaments, courtesy of Jackie Tracy. He also remembered the disaster at Tullyverry, a disaster that Jackie had somehow escaped.

"And here I thought you were stopping by to talk about the national pastime." Jackie laughed. "So you need a gun, doesn't surprise me, I guess. As I understand it you're working for the man again."

"Let's just say I need a gun," O'Byrne said, wanting to sidestep Jackie's tack.

Another laugh from Jackie filled the room.

"Okay, hypothetically speaking, let's just say you're working for the man again, and let's say the man told me that no guns were needed for the job. In fact, he was a little concerned about guns." Jackie leaned forward. "A botched robbery is one thing. A killing, well, that's another matter altogether."

"I understand your concern," O'Byrne said. "But it's like this. A man never knows which tools he might need to get a job done."

"I suppose a man needs his tools," Jackie allowed.

"It's a bit like a game of chess. The goal is to capture the king, but along the way a pawn or two might get knocked off."

"I get nervous when I hear about pawns getting knocked off." Jackie went to the kitchen and came back with two cans of Budweiser and handed one to O'Byrne. "Sorry, no Guinness."

"Bud is a fine brew." He drank some. "The gun?"

"I have guns on the way, but they won't be here until the end of the week." Jackie opened the beer. "You wouldn't believe the profit in guns nowadays, and the demand for them is crazy. Every gun I get flies out of here the second it comes in."

"Sounds like you have a good supply chain," O'Byrne said, "and a ready customer base."

"I have a gig going that keeps me overflowing with the stuff, but my man won't be back 'til Friday night."

"Not 'til Friday night, you say."

"He drives an eighteen-wheeler, Boston to Seattle and back, does a run a month. When he's out west, out there in Montana and Idaho, he goes to gun shows. Cowboy country, it's wide open. No background checks, nothing. But even if they had background checks, most of the deals get done at the back door."

"He sounds like a good contact."

"They sell everything out there. Pistols, rifles, ammo, whatever you want. You want a Kevlar vest, no problem. Night goggles, piece of cake. My guy buys all he can haul, and then I buy it from him, but he won't be back until Friday night."

"Can't wait that long, I'm afraid," O'Byrne said.

"Yeah, I know you can't. You have to move fast, because everything's on a timetable. That's what I heard anyway." Jackie paused for a swig. "I probably shouldn't even say this."

"Say what?"

"I have a gun, but it's no good."

"Is it jammed?" O'Byrne asked. "I'm good at fixing weapons."

"The gun works fine, but it's, ah–"

"It's what?"

"Well, it was used in a bank robbery over there in Hyde Park," Jackie said. "The robbers shot a cop with that gun. It was a bad scene, real bad, what I heard."

"I see." O'Byrne took it in.

"It wasn't my job, Hyde Park, word of honor. I came by the gun after the fact, and I should have dumped it the minute I got it, but I hate to throw away good merchandise."

"What about the garda?" O'Byrne asked, and noticed Jackie's confusion. "The policeman, how is the lad faring?"

"He's hooked to life support, not doing so well. As for the gun, there could be ballistics on it, probably are, and because of ballistics, I'm a little uneasy even having the damn thing. Do you see the position I'm in?"

"I do indeed." O'Byrne understood.

"A bad history comes with the gun, but it's the only gun I have at the moment."

"I'm not worried about a bad history," O'Byrne said. "I grew up in the land of bad history. What type of weapon are we talking about?"

"A Walther PPS nine millimeter with a five-round clip." Jackie's face came to life when he talked about the Walther. "The gun is a gem except for the baggage."

"I prefer a revolver to a pistol, a personal preference of mine," O'Byrne said. "Don't get me wrong, I want the Walther."

"Why a revolver?" Jackie asked.

"You don't have to pick up the brass afterwards."

"You're worried about fingerprints," Jackie concluded.

"I have to be careful in the North," O'Byrne said. "I might be on the right side of history, but I'm on the wrong side of the law."

"You've been warned," Jackie said. "I'll get you the piece."

"I'd appreciate it if this stays between us."

"Between us?" Another roar of laughter burst from Jackie's gut. "It better stay between us, or we'll both be wearing shackles in front of a federal judge."

III.

O'Byrne left Jackie Tracy's house and drove under the Tobin Bridge to the Charlestown Navy Yard. He parked on First Avenue near the old Marine barracks and took out the disposable cell phone that Liam McGrew had given him in the back room of Slattery's Pub. He couldn't believe it had only been a day since the meeting at Slattery's. O'Byrne pressed C5 on the contact list and it rang. 'Twas a valid number.

A man answered with a monotone drone. "What do you want?"

The terse greeting threw O'Byrne, until he remembered he was in Boston. That's the way Yanks talk in Boston.

"I suppose you could say I'm in want of a job." He poured on the brogue.

"Yeah."

"And I was told you might know of a job, a particular job that might require my particular skills."

During the prolonged pause that followed, it struck O'Byrne that the pause lasted longer than the man's words.

"Meet me at McGreevy's in an hour," the man said. "It's on Boylston Street across from the Hynes."

The man hung up.

"Aye," he said into the dead line.

O'Byrne drove alongside the Charles River, looped onto Boylston Street and stepped on the gas, driving like a native Bostonian, cutting in and out of traffic, swerving into lanes. He regained his senses and slowed when he saw McGreevy's on the left. 'Twas his lucky night. He found a parking space on Dalton Street, directly across from Bukowski Tavern. He turned off the engine and walked to McGreevy's.

Sitting on a barstool and listening to the familiar sounds of a bustling saloon, O'Byrne felt at home. He ordered a draught beer, drank a gulp and ordered a shot of top-shelf Jameson. A young lassie placed the whiskey in front of him. With her black hair and taut figure, she could have been the Rose of Tralee. O'Byrne scrutinized her backside as she walked away, and he thought of Kathleen, and he felt shame for his gawking. O'Byrne chugged the shot of Irish and tried to forget about his lewdness. Before he could slump into further despair, a ruggedly built man with gorilla hands sat on the stool next to him. Looking straight ahead, the man said, "Can I buy you a drink?"

"Aye." O'Byrne recognized the man's flat voice from the phone. "'Tis most generous of you. I believe I'll have a Bushmills, a single malt whiskey distilled in the north of Ireland, as you must know."

"I know it now." The man ordered a beer for himself and Bushmills for O'Byrne. "It's noisy in here."

"But it's a pleasant noise, don't you think?" O'Byrne raised his glass and looked at the amber liquid. "You represent Mr. H?"

"I do," the man murmured.

"We're off to a good start, meeting like this." O'Byrne waited, but the man said nothing more. "You're not much for talking, I see. As we say in Ireland, a silent mouth is sweet to hear."

"What was that?"

"I've seen it too often that a man's tongue broke his nose, which is no concern of yours, I suppose."

"Witty."

"At times." O'Byrne sipped the Bushmills. "Ah, that's fine stuff."

"I have to go." Gorilla-mitts pushed away his nearly full beer. "I'll meet you tomorrow at noon, your house. We will review the plans at that time. Make sure the other two aren't around, just you and me."

"I'll see to it." Something occurred to O'Byrne. He had never met this man before. "Have you a name?"

"Call me K." He dismounted the stool like a cowboy.

"K, as in the letter between J and L?" O'Byrne asked.

K left McGreevy's without answering.

"Nice to meet you, K," O'Byrne said to himself.

IV.

K showed up the next day at noontime, carrying a long leather tube under his bulging right bicep. He looked even more formidable in daylight, despite the Oxford getup, which was highlighted by a pink polo shirt, tan slacks, and a lavender belt with little white whales. Americans are a strange lot, hooligans wearing pink shirts and lavender belts, O'Byrne thought.

"Are we alone?" asked K.

"Aye, I'm on me tod." O'Byrne answered, and saw K's confusion. "The lads are enjoying a splendid tour of your grand city."

"Can't you just say we're alone?" K scoffed. "Okay, now to important matters."

From the leather tube, K removed a lengthy roll of bound paper. Blueprints, K said. He flattened the sheets on the kitchen table and anchored the corners with empty beer bottles.

"This is the Hynes Convention Center, the location of the job," K said.

"The building across the street from McGreevy's," O'Byrne correctly noted.

"That's why I met you there." K smoothed the drawings with his large hands. "The plans show the layout of the entire building. Every floor, door, and room is outlined on these pages. Exits and parking and roof accesses, too. We've marked every alarm, camera, heat sensor, and motion detector. We've detailed security rounds to the second. We know everything there is to know about this building and this event."

"What event?" asked O'Byrne.

"We'll get to that in a moment." K flipped the charts and stopped at one. "These are the fire doors facing Dalton Street. That's how you'll get in, Dalton Street. The Hynes will be buttoned tight except for those fire doors, which will be unlocked and unalarmed for ten seconds." He flipped to another page. "Once you're inside, you go to Exhibition Hall A. That's where the loot is on display."

"What loot?" O'Byrne asked. "You've given me a grand tour of the Hynes, and a grand tour it has been, but you've told me nothing of the nuts and bolts."

"Not nuts and bolts, O'Byrne, bills and coins. You and your crew will be making a withdrawal from the World's Fair of Money tomorrow night." K ran his finger along the blueprint to a small rectangular figure in Exhibition Hall A. "This right here, this is the case you want. Inside it you will find three sheets of $100,000 bills. You'll know they're $100,000 bills because President Woodrow Wilson will be staring back at you. Each sheet has thirty-two bills, ninety-six bills in all, for a total of $9.6 million. Not a bad night's pay."

"And I suppose the case will be unlocked and the alarms will be off and the guards will be in an alley smoking a fag." O'Byrne became skeptical. "We simply slide down the rainbow and grab the money the way a leprechaun grabs a pot of gold."

"Speed and timing are of the essence." K raised his head from the blueprints. "It's a smash and grab, except nothing gets smashed." K then straightened up and poked O'Byrne in the chest. "Do not, I repeat, do not take anything from any other case, not that you'd be able to open them anyway. But you'll be tempted for sure, seeing all that money on display. Every case will be locked and alarmed except the one I just specified. Now pull up a seat and we'll go over the details. Any questions before we begin?"

"I suppose not."

"Let's review the plan."

V.

In the early hours on Monday morning, Alroy, McAfee, and O'Byrne left White City in the Chrysler 300 to rob the money show. They turned onto Massachusetts Avenue in the South End, and because roads were empty, it took O'Byrne a second to realize he had to keep to the right. They passed Symphony Hall and the Christian Science Church Park and turned onto Boylston Street.

The time was 3:00 a.m., the streets were quiet, the Fenway crowd long dispersed. A truck horn blared from the Mass Pike underpass, a deafening sound in a sleeping city. O'Byrne rolled to a halt on Scotia Street, where the plan called for them to park.

He flicked the high beams twice as he was told. A black van drove away from the curb with its flashers blinking, and O'Byrne parked in the vacated space. His cell phone read 3:12. At 3:30 they were to be stationed at the fire doors of the Hynes Convention Center on Dalton Street. Don't get there too early, he was told, don't attract attention to yourselves. Dalton Street was twenty yards in front of them. They were in mighty good shape indeed.

The three men waited in the car, nobody saying a word. O'Byrne patted his side and felt a sense of serenity at the heft of the Walther PPS. To the right sat a church named for Saint Cecilia herself, she of divine music and betrothed to an angel. He slid his hand away from the gun and thumbed the rosary beads in his pants pocket. He prayed to Saint Cecilia, praying that the heist would go glowingly and that nobody would get hurt. O'Byrne had never prayed to her before, and not wanting to be presumptuous, he petitioned Saint Angus MacNisse of Connor to intercede, to talk to Saint Cecilia up there in heaven, to assure her that his request was indeed valid. It didn't strike O'Byrne as odd, asking one saint to ask another saint to abet him in a crime.

The Belfast men stepped out of the car and crossed Dalton Street.

O'Byrne, McAfee, and Alroy waited at the fire doors. The time was 3:29. When it struck 3:30, they would have ten seconds to open the door and get inside. Thank the good Lord in heaven for satellites or the timetable would be impossible to keep. The clock hit 3:30. Something clicked. Mac pulled the door open and they stepped into the Hynes. Alroy tripped and would have fallen down the stairs if O'Byrne hadn't caught him.

"Calm down, Alroy," O'Byrne whispered. "Pull it together."

A second click and the door locked behind them. It happened that fast. They descended the concrete stairs to a dark corridor and began their journey through the bowels of the building. McAfee shined his flashlight in front of them, leading the way as they walked in the direction of the X on the map. The fact that it was literally an X on an actual map made O'Byrne feel like an Irish pirate.

"Light the chart," O'Byrne said, and then he pointed to a spot on the map. "We're standing here, we need to get there, so we best turn left up ahead, just past the firebox."

The red dot on the firebox marked the first leg of the trek. The men turned left at the firebox and continued on the map route, a map given to O'Byrne by K himself. Alroy hadn't said a word all evening. Would the boy hold up? O'Byrne had his doubts, especially after Alroy had nearly fallen down the stairs.

A fluorescent bulb flickered behind them. The three men froze in place, and the bulb sputtered out. They moved ahead, navigating the underground maze. Time crawled, their eyes adjusted to blackness. They came to a stairwell that led up to street level, according to the map. The Belfast soldiers ascended the stairs.

O'Byrne opened the door a crack and glimpsed inside. 'Twas the main lobby indeed. He said to Alroy and Mac, "We're bang on, right where we're supposed to be."

Alroy still hadn't said a word. They walked across the lobby to an escalator that led to the Plaza Level. Not surprisingly, the escalator was off. They scaled the metal risers to the next story, an open space that looked like a mezzanine. O'Byrne's adrenaline was pumping now. He didn't limp a bit, the pain totally gone. They made it to the top, Exhibition Hall A, a colossal space with high ceilings and unlit chandeliers. Rows and rows of glass cases lined the gallery floor. The aisles between them were long and wide, offering plenty of room to operate. Alroy remained mum. Mac nodded toward the chart. O'Byrne held it up and said, "The leftmost row about halfway down, that's the case we want."

O'Byrne was relieved to see no security guards on duty, just as K had promised. Many people had made many promises to O'Byrne over the years, and given his experience, he put no stock in them. Still, he was glad to see no security. He didn't want to shoot anybody tonight if he didn't have to.

Wandering down the middle aisle, gawking at the various cases, Alroy said the first words he'd uttered all night. "Look at the silver dollars! They're big and shiny!" Maybe the boy was thawing out, O'Byrne thought.

"Get over here, Alroy," O'Byrne said in a loud whisper. "We have a job to do, so let's get to it. Mac, give me the light. You two, follow me."

O'Byrne walked to the case that contained the loot, with Alroy and McAfee trailing behind him. He tried to lift the glass lid, which lay flat on the case, but it didn't budge. The case was ten feet long, six feet wide, two feet deep. Inside it O'Byrne saw the money, sheet after sheet of $100,000 bills, just as K had said. But there were four sheets, not three, and a $5,000 bill, too.

His cell phone read 3:50 a.m. At 3:55 the lock would deactivate. They waited. The five minutes felt like five years, like O'Byrne's sentence in Long Kesh Prison. A click sounded from the case. O'Byrne hoisted the hinged lid an inch. With its thick glass and steel frame, it must have weighed two or three hundred pounds.

"Alroy, Mac, lift it from the sides. I'll grab the sheets." Alroy and McAfee raised the lid. O'Byrne grabbed three sheets of $100,000 bills and looked at the remaining sheet. *Oh, for the love of Pete, take it.* He took the fourth sheet. Alroy stuck his hand in and snagged the $5,000 bill as they lowered the cover shut.

"Let's move," O'Byrne said. "We go out the way we came in."

They retraced their steps out of the building and headed back to White City. As O'Byrne was driving along the Jamaicaway toward Forest Hills, one pesky thought gnawed at him: It had been too damn easy.

CHAPTER THREE

I.

The next day O'Byrne turned the Chrysler 300 onto Hillside Street in Milton and swung into the parking lot of Houghton's Pond. He watched the young mothers in bathing suits as they frolicked with their children on the shoreline, laughing and splashing and spreading maternal love. He thought of Kathleen.

He parked at the snack bar as directed by K, who was sitting at a table under an overhang in the picnic area. O'Byrne ordered coffee at the stand and joined K at the table. Neither of them said anything for a moment and then K spoke.

"The job went well?"

"A schoolboy could have done it," O'Byrne said. "And a schoolboy would have done it for less than two million dollars."

"Overpaid?" K munched on a donut. "I never heard that complaint before."

"Not a complaint." O'Byrne dropped the car keys on the picnic table. "The loot is in the trunk, three sheets of $100,000 bills, ninety-six bills in all."

O'Byrne didn't mention the fourth sheet since he wasn't asked about it. He delivered what he was paid to deliver, and that was enough. The fourth sheet was a gratuity of sorts, a perk for a job well done. K dropped a different set of keys on the table.

"They go to the green Avalon at the end of the lot," K said. "How long are you staying in Boston?"

"Not long at all," O'Byrne said.

"Mr. H doesn't like people hanging around after a job is done, that's why he hires crews from out of town. You said a schoolboy could have done the job. The way we set it up, a schoolboy could have done it, but Mr. H doesn't like the idea of locals working for him. They drink, they brag, they screw up. That's why he hired you, and that's why he overpaid you, because it's worth it to him. You could call it peace of mind. So I ask again, when are you leaving?"

"Tomorrow evening."

K dropped an envelope on the table. "Have a good time tonight and be on that plane tomorrow. As for the Avalon, leave it running in departures. What flight?"

"Lufthansa 7974, 4:45 p.m."

"Our man will pick up the car." K put the keys to the Chrysler 300 in his pants pocket and said, "Mr. H is a very cautious man."

O'Byrne counted the money in the envelope, two thousand dollars in hundred-dollar bills. 'Twould be a memorable time in Boston tonight.

II.

Back in White City, inside the kitchen of the Victorian house, O'Byrne opened a bottle of Guinness and thought about the robbery. The job couldn't have been easier, a job a stooge could have done, and yet Mr. H called in the IRA to do it. Why? O'Byrne concluded that it didn't matter why. Mr. H had wired the money to Liam McGrew, two million dollars for a two-bit heist. The job was done and the contract fulfilled—still, O'Byrne didn't like it.

McAfee and Alroy walked into the kitchen and helped themselves to Guinness. O'Byrne removed the envelope from his pocket and counted the money again. Two thousand dollars in hundreds. He fanned the bills.

"Two thousand divided by three is $666 each, but they're all hundreds. I'll take six. You two get seven. K told us to have a good time tonight and to be on the Belfast plane tomorrow."

"All right!" Alroy said. "Let's meet some Boston girls."

"Did K say anything about the fourth sheet?" Mac asked. "Did he ask about the $5,000 bill?"

"No," O'Byrne answered flatly, no singsong lilt in his voice this time, no hint of joy for their unexpected jackpot. His suspicions about the robbery grew stronger. He became anxious thinking about it, and the anxiety bordered on paranoia. Something was wrong, but he couldn't figure out what it was. He said to his mates, "Let's get a drink."

"Yeah, let's!" Alroy cheered.

"I know of a pub in Dorchester called the Blarney Stone," O'Byrne said. "They serve a hearty drink and cater to the neighborhood lassies, who are terribly interested in meeting lads from the old sod. They find it romantic, I'm told, having a chat with a *boyo* from the Emerald Isle."

Alroy and McAfee left the kitchen to shower and shave. O'Byrne opened another bottle of beer and slowly drank it. He thought about the job, the simplicity of it, and his mind drifted. He looked at the bottle and it was empty. He didn't remember drinking it. He cracked another one and sipped it with care, not rushing, taking deliberate swallows to make it last longer. Again his mind drifted to a distant place.

Another empty bottle sat in front of him on the table. How long had it been sitting there empty? He took the Walther PPS from his jacket pocket, ejected the magazine, cleared the chamber, and placed the weapon and ordnance in the flatware drawer. The sound of Alroy uncapping a Guinness startled O'Byrne. He hadn't heard him come into the kitchen. Then McAfee strutted down the hallway, showered and shaved, wearing white pants and an Irish rugby shirt. Time had gotten away from O'Byrne.

"The Blarney Stone," O'Byrne said. "We have an Avalon now."

He watched as Mac checked his moustache in the reflection of the kitchen window, and Alroy primped his messy hair to no avail. The cowlicks and sprouts couldn't be combed out.

"I'll be in the garage." O'Byrne walked down the breezeway.

III.

They drove to Fields Corner and pulled up at the Blarney Stone and went inside. It was five o'clock and the place was almost empty, reminding O'Byrne of Slattery's back home. O'Byrne chose a table. They had no sooner sat down when a cocktail waitress, a plump, brown-haired woman named Delia, set napkins in front of them.

She pointed at Alroy. "You look young."

"He's of age," O'Byrne said, and palmed her two hundred dollars. "I'll keep an eye on him."

"What'll ya have?" she asked.

As Delia was writing the order, McAfee shamelessly ogled her. His pupils ballooned and blackened his green irises. Delia blushed but didn't seem to mind the attention. They placed the order, Delia served the drinks, and the lads imbibed with vigor. Every few rounds they handed Delia a hundred and told her to keep the change, which kept Delia smiling and coming back for more.

It was now half seven, and the lads, save O'Byrne, were in their cups. McAfee had all but proposed marriage to Delia, and Delia had all but accepted. Alroy was scoring points with a local girl at the bar, who apparently found him charming. All was coming up aces for the Belfast boys. O'Byrne mulled over the robbery, and a bad feeling churned in his gut, the same churning he felt in the blanket protests. He was thinking about Long Kesh Prison when McAfee bumped into the table, with his pasty face flushed red.

"Delia gets off at ten," he said. "I'm taking her out for drinks."

"Make sure you're back by one o'clock tomorrow. We've a flight to catch in the afternoon." O'Byrne didn't see Alroy at the bar. "It seems that Alroy is gone. And so is the girl he was talking to."

"Aye," Mac confirmed, saving his words for Delia no doubt.

"Don't forget about the flight."

O'Byrne stayed until midnight and drove back to White City.

§

O'Byrne's eyes opened in the morning. Daylight poured through the framed windows and painted a shadow grid on the plaster walls. The grid was skewed by the angle of the sun, not like the square grid of the Maze prison bars. In the kitchen O'Byrne boiled water for tea and toasted bread and sat at the table to eat breakfast. Despite the previous evening's whiskey, he felt good, even energetic, a positive sign indeed. He walked around the house and found nobody home.

The front door opened and McAfee bounded down the hallway and into the kitchen. He looked like a disheveled rogue with a hangover, in other words, a man who got laid after a night of heavy drinking. Mac raved about his dalliance with Delia. O'Byrne feigned interest. Mac asked, "What's wrong?"

"Alroy isn't here," O'Byrne said.

"Ah, he'll be back soon enough," Mac said. "He met with good fortune last night, just as I did. Alroy will be here any second now."

"I suppose you're right," O'Byrne said. "Did you actually see him leave with her?"

"I saw him at the bar with her. The next time I looked they were gone."

"That's the way I remember it, too." O'Byrne tried to sound confident. "They must have left together."

It was noontime and Alroy still wasn't back. O'Byrne punched C3 on his cell phone, the contact number for Alroy, and he heard a muffled ringing. Was Alroy in the house? Aye, he must have come home undetected and taken a nap without telling them. Yes indeed, he was taking a nap.

The faint ringing continued and O'Byrne followed it to the kitchen. He opened the flatware drawer and saw Alroy's phone inside it, but the gun was gone.

"Mac, get your ass in here," O'Byrne snapped.

"What's wrong?" McAfee rushed to the kitchen.

"Alroy's phone is in the drawer," he said, "and my gun has gone missing."

"You had a gun?"

"I put it in the drawer when the job was done." O'Byrne slammed it shut. "What did that feckin' eejit do with my gun?"

IV.

It was one o'clock and still no sign of Alroy. O'Byrne called Belfast, pressing C1 for Liam McGrew. Liam answered and wasted no time talking about the heist.

"Well done, O'Byrne, well done!" he exclaimed. "I knew I could count on you."

"I'm afraid we have a problem," O'Byrne said, cutting into Liam's gust. "Alroy isn't home yet, and our flight leaves in a few hours."

"Where is he?" Liam asked.

"He met a girl last night."

"I see, a girl," Liam muttered over the phone. "Well, I suppose that's not the end of the world."

"I hate to miss the flight, but I think we should wait for Alroy," O'Byrne said.

"I agree." Liam coughed into the phone. "Stay in Boston and wait for the lad."

"There's something else," O'Byrne said. "A small fortune came our way."

"I got the wire." Liam assured him. "And there was nothing small about it."

"I'm not talking about the wire," O'Byrne said.

"What are you talking about?" asked Liam.

"Perhaps I should wait until we get back to Belfast."

"Nonsense, man. Tell me now."

"I'm concerned about the phones, Liam."

"The phones are safe, damn it. I told you that at Slattery's already." Liam quieted his tone. "Tell me about this small fortune."

Thinking the house could be bugged, O'Byrne went out to the backyard and walked to the tall hedges. He spoke in a low voice.

"Mr. H directed us to steal three sheets of $100,000 bills, which we did in fact steal, but the case contained four sheets. We grabbed the fourth sheet for ourselves, $3.2 million."

"Damn skippy, O'Byrne!"

"Once Alroy is back, we can get the next flight to Belfast," O'Byrne said. "We can book it in a day or two."

"You could do that I suppose." The tone of Liam's voice shifted and took on an air of authority. "I have changed my mind. Come home on the scheduled flight."

"What about Alroy?"

"Instruct McAfee to wait for Alroy." Liam ordered. "I want you to come home immediately, and bring the money with you."

"I'll have to tell Mr. H what's going on."

"Why?" Liam asked.

"We'll be needing the house and car for a few more days." O'Byrne explained.

"Right, right, I didn't think of that." Liam paused. "Tell Mr. H, but make it fast. You have a plane to catch."

V.

O'Byrne called K using contact C5, hoping that K hadn't discarded the phone. O'Byrne was relieved when K answered, even though he sounded ticked off.

"Yeah?"

"A problem came up," O'Byrne said. "We need the house and car for another day or two."

"Another day or two?" K roared. "That's totally out of the question. You were hired to do a job and to get the fuck out of Boston. The job is done, go home."

"I understand how you feel," O'Byrne said. "But it's not that simple."

"It's not that simple?" K grumbled. "What's that supposed to mean?"

"It has to do with our mutual friend with the half-pink face," O'Byrne said. "His grandson assisted in the job and now he's gone missing."

"Gone missing?" K sounded incensed.

"Last night he met a girl." O'Byrne explained. "I'm sure the lad will turn up soon, but not in time for the flight."

"This better not be a fuckin' problem," K said. "I'm not happy about this and Mr. H won't be, either."

"It will be a bigger problem if we leave the lad behind," O'Byrne said. "The boy isn't exactly worldly."

The two men continued to talk. K finally relented. He told O'Byrne he could have the house and car for two more days and not a second longer. O'Byrne told K that he'd be flying back to Belfast that afternoon, and that McAfee would be staying behind to wait for Alroy.

After they hung up, O'Byrne cursed Liam under his breath.

"Let Alroy cut his eyeteeth in Boston, my arse!"

§

The sheet of bills formed a rectangular grid, four across lengthwise, eight down height-wise. O'Byrne folded the sheet in half, top to bottom, careful to fold it on the edge of the bills, and not across the bills themselves. He halved it again, left to right, with the same care to detail. He creased the sheet flat with his thumbs and squeezed it into a manila envelope. He tucked the envelope into his pants against the small of his back and checked himself in the mirror. 'Twas unnoticeable. If he could avoid a strip search at Logan Airport he'd be fine, and with Emmett O'Burke on duty in US Customs, O'Byrne was convinced he'd get through without incident. The Belfast end was already taken care of, that he knew for sure.

CHAPTER FOUR

I.

The plane departed from Logan on time and arrived in Belfast ahead of schedule. After sailing through airport security unscathed, O'Byrne exited the terminal and hailed a cab for his Divis Street flat. Except for Alroy's disappearance, everything had gone as planned—better than planned, considering the bonus sheet of banknotes. Alroy would turn up tomorrow, and when he did, both he and McAfee would share their tales of conquest, and they would catch the next flight to Belfast, and they would revel in the bounty of a successful venture. All would be fine again, not a thing to worry about.

Inside his flat O'Byrne took the manila envelope from his pants and removed the $100,000 bills. He smoothed the sheet on the kitchen table and admired his American pot of gold, $3.2 million. Thirty-two portraits of Woodrow Wilson, wearing pince-nez glasses, stared back at him from the currency, staring like a judge. O'Byrne thought about Judgment Day, and then he thought about his wife. Kathleen, eyeing him from heaven, looking down with disgust, the stolen loot on their pine table, a wedding gift from Bridie herself, and the joy of triumph turned to the shame of betrayal. He had smacked Kathleen's cheek with a Judas kiss when he stole all that sordid money. And at that very moment something shifted inside him. A sense of doom engulfed his soul, and he was now certain beyond a doubt that he would go to hell. Yes, he would bypass purgatory and go straight to the netherworld, the eternal abyss.

The idea of hell didn't bother O'Byrne much. He had friends down there. But the idea of never seeing Kathleen again, because Kathleen was in heaven, *that* bothered him. In fact, the prospect of never again seeing Kathleen made him morose.

"Is it too late, Kathleen?" O'Byrne got on his knees. "Pray for me."

He blessed himself and went to the counter and poured whiskey into a glass. He gulped it down with neither ice nor mixer, guzzling it like a pig at a trough. The intoxicating burn befogged his betrayal, a deliberate sellout that disgraced the memory of his wife. O'Byrne poured another glassful and dwelled on his sins and his lack of character. Would he ever get to confession? Would he ever utter an act of contrition? He drank more and kept drinking until he was drunk.

Drunk, he vowed to get rid of the money. Drunk, he promised to give it to Liam McGrew and be done with it. He would dispose of his thirty pieces of silver, yes indeed, that's what he would do. The very thought of dumping the money eased his pain. His eyelids lowered and his eyes closed shut.

He awoke from a recurring nightmare, or was it post-traumatic stress disorder? He never knew which, didn't really care. The dream played out the same way every time, reenacting a horror from the days of the resistance, when the British Army had kidnapped O'Byrne and forced him into a helicopter.

In the dream the Brits soar a thousand feet above Ulster, up into the wispy clouds. They open the hatch and push him toward it. The roar of the rotors thumps his ears, the blistering wind blinds his eyes. They tie a hood around his head, nearly choking him, and pretend to shove him out. They laugh at his shrieks and pretend to shove him again.

And then they shove him out.

He is airborne, falling toward earth, flailing his arms, and his screams awaken neighbors. But unbeknownst to O'Byrne, the pilot has dropped the copter to a foot above ground. And when O'Byrne lands, he lands softly on the grass, physically unharmed but psychologically shattered, and the scorn of their laughter never leaves his ears.

Morning came and O'Byrne walked to Slattery's Pub to meet Liam McGrew. Slattery nodded toward the back room. O'Byrne went in and found Liam sitting at the same round table he always sat at, his blackthorn walking stick at his side, a satisfied smirk on his face.

"You did well, soldier, very well indeed." Liam cleared his throat. "Have ye the goods with you?"

O'Byrne slid the manila envelope across the table. Liam removed the sheet and unfolded it. The sorry fool nearly drooled on the $100,000 bills while staring at them, and then he giggled. O'Byrne watched Liam and something occurred to him. Liam never mentioned Alroy's name, never showed an ounce of concern for his grandson, his so-called flesh and blood. O'Byrne thought further and decided to leave well enough alone. At least Liam didn't blame him for Alroy's disappearance.

"Any word on Alroy yet?" O'Byrne asked, fishing.

"Alroy will be fine, just fine." Liam inhaled through his mouth, never taking his eyes off the money. "McAfee is awaiting his return as surely as we are sitting here. The boy will soon be back from his carnal affair, full of manly knowledge. Ah, for the love of youth. Who knew the lad had it in him?"

"Did Mac call?"

"Mac will call when Alroy gets back and not a moment sooner," Liam said. "All is fine, O'Byrne. The boy is having a wee fling, so let him enjoy it."

II.

Each day at noontime, which was 6:00 a.m. on the East Coast of America, O'Byrne logged on to the computer and read the Boston dailies. On the third day he saw it, a newspaper item he feared he might see: a composite sketch of a man's face. The caption read, "Do You Recognize This Person?" The person in the sketch was Alroy McGrew.

"Feck!"

O'Byrne pressed C4 on his disposable cell phone, but no one picked up. He pressed C4 again and this time McAfee answered.

O'Byrne said, "Did you see the newspapers?"

"Huh?" McAfee grumbled, sounding whiskey sick.

"There's a picture of Alroy in the paper." O'Byrne waited, but McAfee didn't respond. "Alroy is probably dead, Mac."

"Dead?" Mac cleared his throat. "What do I do?"

"Don't do a bloody thing until I call back." O'Byrne hung up.

Using his regular cell phone he called Jackie Tracy, the Charlestown gun dealer who had sold O'Byrne the Walther PPS. Jackie picked up. O'Byrne made no attempt to exchange pleasantries.

"We have a problem, Jackie," O'Byrne said. "In today's *Boston Globe* there's a sketch of a man, and in all likelihood the man is dead."

"I saw it," Jackie said. "And you're right, the man is dead. What's the problem?"

"The kid in the sketch is Alroy McGrew."

"Is he related to our friend?"

"His grandson," O'Byrne said.

"His grandson?" Jackie Tracy sighed. "You're not going to like this, O'Byrne, and neither will Liam. The kid was killed *by* Dermot Sparhawk."

"Dermot Sparhawk?"

"Your boy wandered into the projects and shot Sparhawk, and Sparhawk retaliated." Jackie sipped something, maybe coffee. "He picked up a rock and killed him. What was the kid thinking?"

"Alroy was never much on thinking," O'Byrne said. "I didn't want him in Boston in the first place, but it was out of my hands." O'Byrne couldn't believe it. Dermot Sparhawk had killed Alroy McGrew. *Liam would go wild when he heard this.* "You won't like what I'm about to say, Jackie, not a bit."

"It can't be any worse," Jackie paused. "Can it?"

"Alroy shot Sparhawk with the gun you gave me, the Walther PPS," O'Byrne said.

"What?"

"I was careless." O'Byrne could see the whole thing unraveling. The money-fair heist, the shooting of Sparhawk, the killing of Alroy, it could all lead back to Belfast. "Is the gun a problem?"

"Hell, yeah, it's a problem, but how big a problem remains to be seen." With a muffled laugh, Jackie said, "You know something? This might turn out okay."

"How do you mean?"

"Maybe it won't be a problem at all," Jackie said. "The Sparhawk shooting could be a godsend, depending on how it plays out."

"I fail to see the upside."

"A cop got shot with that gun—remember I told you about the cop in Hyde Park? Now Sparhawk was shot with the same gun. This will be interesting."

"I still don't see the upside, Jackie."

"I'm speculating, playing out the scenarios in my head. Alroy, Sparhawk, the gun, everything might be okay."

"You lost me," O'Byrne said. "Can you find out what the police think about the Sparhawk incident?"

"I plan to learn everything I can," Jackie said. "I'll call you when I know what's going on."

III.

Two hours later Jackie Tracy called O'Byrne back.

"You've got yourself a big fat problem, O'Byrne. Your boy Alroy had a $5000 bill in his pocket. The feds are all over it, so are the locals."

"This is a problem."

"If they identify Alroy McGrew, you're finished, and so is Liam. I can see only one hope for you."

"And what hope is that?" O'Byrne asked.

"The police still haven't identified Alroy," Jackie said. "If they can't identify him, they won't look at Belfast."

"Ah."

"There's another thing working for you," Jackie continued. "The police made an arrest in that bank job I was telling you about, the one over there in Hyde Park where the cop got shot."

"And that's good how?" O'Byrne asked.

"They arrested a Charlestown man for it and he's not talking," Jackie said, "which is good for you guys."

"And why is that good for us, Jackie?"

"It has to do with ballistics. The police compared the slugs from Sparhawk with the slug from the cop and obviously they matched, so the cops think a member of the Charlestown crew shot Sparhawk." Jackie stopped. "But no one's talking. The cops think it's the code of silence, but it's not. The Townie they arrested really doesn't know Alroy. How could he possibly know him?"

"What about the $5,000 bill?" O'Byrne asked.

"I'll get to that," Jackie said. "Alroy had no identification on him, so the cops are assuming he's a member of the Charlestown crew. And since Alroy had the $5,000 bill, the cops are also assuming that all the incidents are connected: the Hyde Park bank robbery, the cop shooting, the money-fair heist, the Sparhawk shooting, the Alroy slaying. They think it's a Charlestown thing. And since they think it's a Charlestown thing, you Belfast guys are off the hook."

"As long as the police don't identify Alroy, we should be in the clear," O'Byrne surmised. "Thanks, Jackie."

"Sure thing." Jackie hung up.

IV.

Alroy was dead at the hands of Dermot Sparhawk, a man Liam McGrew despised. How to tell Liam this news? It wouldn't be easy. O'Byrne contemplated the killing and the law of unintended consequences. Liam's rants had incited Alroy to kill Sparhawk, but it backfired, and now Alroy was dead, killed by Dermot Sparhawk. The irony of it.

O'Byrne walked into Slattery's Pub and ordered a Guinness stout on draught and a double Jameson neat. He didn't futz around, he drank. And when he finished the first pair, he ordered another pair, and drank them down, and he did it again. At five o'clock, three hours after O'Byrne first sat on the stool, Liam McGrew came into the bar rolling his oxygen tank behind him.

"We need to talk, Liam," O'Byrne said.

"Why the grim face?" Liam smiled and slapped O'Byrne's back. "You fetched home a fortune."

"I'll tell you in the back room." They went out back, and after closing the door firmly, O'Byrne said, "Alroy is dead."

"What did you say?"

"He was killed in Boston."

"No, he can't be dead." Liam dropped his walking stick. "Killed how?"

"Dermot Sparhawk fractured his skull with a rock, killing him instantly."

"Sparhawk!"

Liam leaned down to crank the knob, but he was too late. He crashed to the floor. The tank tipped over and smashed the bridge of his nose. Blood spurted from his nostrils and into the plastic nasal openings. The air tube flooded red, as if Liam were donating blood. O'Byrne called an ambulance and waited beside Liam McGrew.

V.

The next day O'Byrne visited Liam at Musgrave Park Hospital, where Liam was convalescing from a broken nose, but the hospital was more concerned with his pulmonary condition than his snout. A respirator aided his breathing. Monitors tracked his pulse and blood pressure and oxygen levels. His cheeks showed yellow bruising that would soon turn purple and black. O'Byrne rested his hand on Liam's bony shoulder.

"I'm sick about Alroy."

Liam leaned up and rasped, "Call McAfee. Tell him to kill Sparhawk." He slumped down to the pillow. "That's an order."

Revenge, that's what got Alroy killed in the first place. But O'Byrne didn't debate Liam on the issue. He said he would make the call.

O'Byrne didn't like it, putting a hit on Dermot Sparhawk. Executing Liam's orders no longer appealed to him. Earning Liam's praise for acting the obedient soldier seemed childish now.

VI.

O'Byrne carried two pints of Guinness to an empty table in Slattery's Pub. He drank one down, got out the disposable cell phone, and pressed C4. McAfee mumbled into the phone, most likely on a rum toot.

"Mac, it's me," O'Byrne said. "Liam wants Sparhawk killed."

"Why?" Mac asked.

"Sparhawk killed Alroy," O'Byrne told him.

"He killed Alroy?" Mac's voice came to life. "Where can I find Sparhawk?"

O'Byrne gave him the address, which he found, simply enough, on the Internet. He hung up and signaled Slattery for a double whiskey, drank it in a gulp, and waved the empty glass for another.

What had he done?

He prayed to Saint Angus MacNisse of Connor. Praying to a saint in a pub? Praying to a saint after ordering a man killed? He prayed to Kathleen, his wife of holy virtue, his only love. What had he done? Liam had ordered the hit, but O'Byrne had made the call. O'Byrne fingered Dermot Sparhawk for Liam McGrew.

Feeling like a lackey, he drank more whiskey. Why did he feel so guilty? He didn't even know Dermot Sparhawk, never met the man in his life. O'Byrne was following orders. Like a priest who takes a vow of obedience, O'Byrne didn't question his superiors. You can't be a renegade within a renegade group like the IRA, not a breathing one at least, and you don't question orders, no sir, you execute them. He went to the bar and asked for another drink and told Slattery to keep them coming. Slattery looked at him askance but smartly poured the booze.

O'Byrne awoke in his flat at midnight, still groggy from the binge, but coherent enough to judge his actions. He'd been out for five hours, maybe longer, scuttered on Bushmills. Despite the flood of liquor he'd consumed, the guilt remained with him, except now it was worse. What to do about Dermot Sparhawk?

He crawled out of bed and went to the toilet but didn't throw up. At the sink he filled the kettle and waited for the water to boil. He brewed a cup with three teabags, hoping to snap out of it with a caffeine blitz. He drank it black and the fogginess began to lift. Midnight in Belfast meant 6:00 p.m. in Boston. He called Jackie Tracy in Charlestown.

"Jackie, it's O'Byrne."

"Two calls in ten minutes from the IRA, it must be my lucky day."

"Right, indeed, your lucky day." Another IRA man had called Jackie Tracy? O'Byrne's mind scrambled for an answer, and an answer soon came. Liam must have called him. "Could you understand him with his wheezing and coughing?"

"Not well, but yeah, I understood him."

"Did you take care of that thing he was calling about?" O'Byrne fished.

Jackie didn't answer right away and the delay unnerved O'Byrne, and then Jackie said, "What's going on?"

Jackie must have seen through O'Byrne's charade. How to handle it? But before O'Byrne responded, Jackie said, "You know me better than that. Of course I took care of it. It was a minor request. Everything is set."

"Good, that's very good."

"Are you okay?" Jackie asked. "You don't sound yourself."

"I have to tell you something." O'Byrne's mouth overruled his brain. His conscience came to the surface. "Liam put a hit on Dermot Sparhawk."

O'Byrne couldn't believe the words he spoke. He didn't decide to say them, they just came out. He had never revealed anything before, never left himself open. What was happening to him? Was it the prayers? Did Saint Angus MacNisse and Kathleen get word to God? Maybe God had intervened to save his soul.

"I called in a hit on Sparhawk."O'Byrne continued. "On Liam's orders."

"I know Dermot Sparhawk, known him since he was a kid," Jackie said. "The hit man you called, was his name Mac?"

"Aye, McAfee," O'Byrne answered.

"Red hair, green eyes, pale face, quiet?"

"That's him."

"Liam told me to give Mac a gun, but he didn't say why," Jackie said. "If I knew it was to kill Sparhawk, I would have said no. Murder is where I draw the line. I have ethics, you know."

An ethical gunrunner?

"You sell guns to the IRA, Jackie," O'Byrne said, perplexed.

"I sell them to freedom fighters, to soldiers in arms, not murderers." Jackie paused. "I'll admit that I sell guns to criminals, too. But they're legitimate criminals, bank robbers and hold-up men, not murderers."

O'Byrne thought it over, and the idea of an ethical gunrunner didn't strike him as absurd, not at all. The more O'Byrne thought about it, the more he could relate to it, the degrees of morality.

"I always saw myself as a soldier," O'Byrne said, and then he changed direction. "I want you to warn Sparhawk."

"You didn't have to tell me to warn him," Jackie said. "I'm going to give him a heads-up, but I'll have to be careful."

"Yes, you must be careful." O'Byrne agreed. "Be very careful, Jackie."

"If Liam finds out you told me to warn Sparhawk, you're dead. You know that, don't you? And I'm dead too if I follow through on it."

"Maybe Sparhawk can leave town for a while." O'Byrne downed the rest of the tea. "Maybe he can clear out until this matter blows over."

"Yeah, maybe." Jackie didn't sound convinced.

The conversation died down, with both men turning silent. O'Byrne thought about what he had just done, contacting Jackie Tracy and asking him to warn Sparhawk that there was a hit on him. What had he done? Was he going soft in the head perhaps? But before

O'Byrne could contemplate his newfound compassion, Jackie broke the silence.

"What's going on with you, O'Byrne?"

"No more killings, Jackie. I've killed people, too many people if truth be told, but I killed them as a soldier. We stood for something back then."

"I thought you still did."

VII.

During the day O'Byrne took refuge in the Clonard Monastery, where he knelt and prayed and begged for forgiveness. In the evening he stayed at home and slept, sometimes for twelve hours in a row. Each morning before leaving his Divis Street flat, O'Byrne would read the Boston newspapers online, searching for stories on Sparhawk's murder. After two days had passed, he went to Musgrave Park Hospital to visit Liam McGrew. Liam waved him over when he entered the room.

"'Tis good of you to come by today," he said.

"How are you feeling?" O'Byrne asked him.

"Better, much better indeed. I'll be getting out of here tomorrow, should the doctors see fit." He sat up. "Did you make that call to Boston?"

"I talked to Mac straightaway," O'Byrne answered.

But Liam already knew this, of course, because he had called McAfee himself. He had also called Jackie Tracy and told Jackie to give Mac a gun. Liam's question wasn't a question at all. It was a test.

"Very good, my friend." Liam's coloring had returned to his face, rendering the red blotch less jarring. "Sparhawk will soon be dead, and I will be able to die in peace, and Alroy's murder will have been avenged."

They talked awhile longer, an informal conversation on the face of it, but guarded under the surface, fencing more than chatting. When O'Byrne left, an uneasy feeling came over him. Did Liam blame him for Alroy's death?

§

The next morning O'Byrne checked the Boston papers. He read a story about a bus driver who'd been brutally beaten by a gang in Dudley Station. The driver, a woman who was a week from retirement, was rushed to Boston Medical Center where she was treated for cuts and contusions and then released. In Dorchester's Bowdoin-Geneva neighborhood, the police arrested a ring of Cape Verdean heroin distributors after eighteen months of surveillance. In Brookline, an armed man fired into a group of mourners at a cemetery and escaped on foot. No casualties were reported. The gunman remained at large.

He saw nothing on Dermot Sparhawk.

What could he do to save Sparhawk? Jackie Tracy might warn him, but he might not. And even if Jackie warned Sparhawk, it might not be enough to save him, because McAfee was a top hand, an apt killer armed with a gun. There had to be more that O'Byrne could do.

An idea came to him, a treacherous idea that could cost him his life, but he decided to go ahead with it. He opened his cell phone and pressed C4 for McAfee. Mac finally answered, but it took four rings before he did. O'Byrne cut in before Mac could speak and said, "Don't say a word. Just listen. The hit is off, Mac. Forget about Sparhawk and come home."

O'Byrne rang off before Mac could dispute him.

He returned to Clonard Monastery and continued to pray to Saint Angus MacNisse of Connor and to his wife, Kathleen. At sunset he went home and drank a tall glass of whiskey with ice and fell asleep on the couch. At noontime the next day he woke up and logged on and browsed the Boston dailies. He read a story about a fatal shooting at a South Boston garage. In self-defense, a man wrestled a gun from an assailant and killed him with it. No names were mentioned in the article. Something about the story bothered him, and he read it again. O'Byrne was reading it for a third time when his personal cell phone rang. The caller ID said Main-e-ack, the codename for Jackie Tracy. O'Byrne answered it.

"How are the Red Sox doing, Jackie?" O'Byrne said, trying to sound upbeat.

"You're asking about the Red Sox?" Jackie unloosed a boom of laughter. "The hitters can't hit, the pitchers can't pitch, the manager can't manage, and the fans can't take it. But that's not why I called."

"I know it's not."

"Your man Mac is dead," Jackie said.

"I thought you were going to say that."

"He shot Sparhawk, but Sparhawk was wearing a vest." Jackie sighed into the receiver. "Sparhawk took Mac's gun, the gun I furnished, and shot him dead with it."

"I cannot feckin' believe this." O'Byrne turned off the computer and leaned back in his chair. "This cannot be happening."

"Believe me, O'Byrne, it happened," Jackie said. "Sparhawk grabbed the gun from Mac and killed him with it, supposedly by accident." There was a pause on the line. "I think it was an accident. Sparhawk wanted McAfee alive so he could question him."

"I imagine the police wanted him alive, too," O'Byrne said.

"But now Mac is dead, and I am hoping like hell that Liam calls off the hit on Sparhawk, because things are getting messy over here."

"Have the police identified McAfee?" asked O'Byrne.

"He had no wallet, nothing on him at all," Jackie said. "Does he have a criminal record in Belfast?"

"I believe he does, but on trivial matters." O'Byrne thought for a moment. "He's a young guy, never took a felony charge to my knowledge."

"The way I way see it, the cops will assume he's local, just like they assumed Alroy was local. Why would they think otherwise?"

"I hope you're right."

"Get back to me on Sparhawk. You guys are getting sloppy, and I want to know if I have to cover my ass."

Jackie hung up.

It occurred to O'Byrne that there could be an upside to McAfee's death. Liam would never know that O'Byrne had called Mac to cancel the hit on Sparhawk. O'Byrne thought further. Ach, probably not.

Mac could have called Liam after O'Byrne had called him. Yes, that was quite possible, likely even, because McAfee went ahead with the hit. 'Twas a mire of shite O'Byrne had got himself into.

VIII.

O'Byrne walked into Slattery's Pub and sat at a corner table. Slattery made a phone call, looked at O'Byrne, and flipped a towel over his shoulder. Fifteen minutes later Liam McGrew came into the pub with his oxygen tank in tow. He joined O'Byrne in the crook of the barroom, not in their usual spot in the back room. O'Byrne allowed Liam a moment to gather his strength, and then he told him the news from Boston.

"McAfee is dead," O'Byrne said.

Liam grabbed the edge of the table, his nostrils sucking, his lips quivering. O'Byrne told Liam the rest of it, that Dermot Sparhawk had killed McAfee in the parking lot of a South Boston garage. Liam nodded his head, showing neither rage nor rancor. He tapped his knotty shillelagh on the old oaken tabletop and waved O'Byrne away with his free hand. O'Byrne left Slattery's without saying another word.

§

O'Byrne awoke in his room. His bed was rumpled and his mind was a mess. A sense of disaster swirled in his head. He made a cup of tea and sat at the pine table and went through a stack of mail. He came across a letter from his godmother, Bridie, and opened it at once. Bridie had always called him Tossy, a playful nickname for his Thomas. She began the letter with "Dear Tossy," a greeting that brightened his mood. Bridie wanted to see him and soon. This brightened his mood even more. Yes, he would visit Bridie in Dundalk today, and he called her to tell her of his plans.

Elated, he toasted two slices of soda bread to go with his steaming tea. Oh, how he loved Bridie. Oh, how he loved Dundalk. He loved all of County Louth for that matter. O'Byrne bathed in warm water and dressed in suitable clothing. He took a cab to Belfast Central and boarded the Irish Rail for Dundalk Clark.

Dundalk, a border town in the Republic of Ireland, was sometimes called El Paso for its easy entry to the North, and vice versa. It sat equidistant between Belfast and Dublin, a telling feature of a strategic town. O'Byrne enjoyed the ride south, especially the rugged vistas of the Mountains of Mourne and the subtle ripples of Carlingford Lough. He got off the train at Dundalk Clark and took a taxi to Seatown Ward, where Bridie O'Hanlon lived in a house that had been in the family for six generations.

She was waiting for him at the door when the taxi pulled up, her hair wavy and white, like frosting atop a wedding cake. They embraced in the open doorway and stepped inside the house. His spine tingled and his skin prickled with tiny bumps. He was home.

"Thank you for coming down so quickly, Tossy," Bridie said, "but I found the tone of your telephone call rather foreboding. You have much on your mind, yes?"

"I do indeed." He agreed. "And from your letter, it seems you do, too."

"In truth I do, and I will tell you all about it, but first let's enjoy an ice-cold bowl of Donegal oatmeal cream."

"My favorite homemade dessert!" exclaimed O'Byrne.

They ate at the kitchen table, and when they finished, O'Byrne walked to the parlor and rubbed his eyes with the heels of his hands.

"I've got all this chatter running between my ears," he said, "and I don't like it one bit."

"Tell me about it." Bridie smiled encouragingly. "Or would you rather simply rest for a few days?"

"I don't know that I *can* rest." He reclined on the parlor couch and closed his eyes. "I'm lost, Bridie. I can't remember when I got lost, but I'm lost as sure as I'm alive. I used to have a purpose in life, principles that mattered to me. Today I have no direction at all. I've killed men. I've stolen money, lots of money. I'm the reason Kathleen is dead."

Bridie tucked an afghan around his legs and told him to keep talking.

"Fighting for freedom, that was our aim." He propped himself on a pillow. "Now we steal for profit. We kill for revenge. I can't pretend any longer. I want to put the past behind me, but I don't know how I can."

Bridie rocked in her chair.

"Go to confession, Tossy. Ask God to forgive you. All the things you've done can be forgiven, and that's a cold fact. Talk to Father Donnallen here at Saint Patrick's. He's as old as the Dead Sea and just as salty, but he's a good man, a true man of the cloth. Father Donnallen will absolve you your sins."

"I suppose I could do that." O'Byrne could now add lying to his list of sins if he ever did get to confession.

"You can't mistake Father Donnallen, for he still wears the fiddleback vestments. He looks like a cleric in a sandwich board." She laughed and rocked. "Father took a bullet in the North, dead center chest, and he swears the thick weave of the fiddleback saved his life. Now about Kathleen's murder, we've been over this before."

"I know we have."

"You have to stop blaming yourself, Tossy," Bridie said, somewhat sternly. "The Brits killed her. They killed many of us, not just Kathleen, and you couldn't have stopped them anyway. You weren't even home."

O'Byrne shook his head so vigorously he nearly got dizzy.

"When they released me from Long Kesh, I wanted out of the brigade. I wanted out of the North entirely if truth be told. But I didn't leave, I stayed. And because I stayed, a hit squad came to kill me. But they killed Kathleen instead. I should be in the coffin, not Kathleen," O'Byrne shouted. "It should be me."

"Relax yourself now, Tossy."

"If I had listened to my senses and got out, Kathleen and I would be living in peace today. But no, I stayed, and because I stayed, Kathleen is dead."

"It's not your fault she's dead."

"The hell it's not." He tossed off the afghan and got to his feet. "It's my fault!"

Bridie stood next to O'Byrne.

"I'm going to make us a cup of hot tea. Slow down, boy. I'll be right back." Bridie went to the kitchen and returned carrying a tray with cookies and tea. She picked up a cookie and nibbled on it. "The time has come for you to move on from Ireland, Tossy. Belfast isn't Brigadoon. It won't disappear if you leave."

"I know that, Bridie."

"Sometimes I wonder if you really do," she said.

"There is nothing left for me here," he said. "Kathleen is gone."

"That's true, that's true," Bridie agreed.

"And then there's the stealing," O'Byrne said. "We're always stealing. I don't want to be part of it any longer. I want out."

Bridie pointed an arthritic finger at O'Byrne.

"You're finally making sense," she said. "Go away from here and start a new life for yourself."

"Where would I go?" O'Byrne went back to the couch and closed his eyes. "I have no money. I have no family, besides you. If I did leave, how would I make a living once I got there, wherever *there* is?"

"That's why I wrote to see you," she said. "I'll soon be selling my property."

"You're selling the house?"

Bridie didn't answer.

"Why are you selling?" O'Byrne sat up. "What aren't you telling me?"

"Don't worry about me." She walked to her bedroom and came back holding a stack of papers. "You'll get your inheritance when the estate is settled. I hope you use the money to leave Ireland." She handed O'Byrne a pen and said, "Sign the documents."

"I don't want anything, Bridie. Keep it for yourself."

"Please sign the papers," she said to him. "You will break my heart if you don't."

Not wanting to break her heart, O'Byrne reluctantly signed the papers.

"Come closer." Bridie looped a brown cloth necklace with two patches over O'Byrne's head. "These are Carmelite scapulars. They will safeguard you from harm and evil. I've sewn Saint Bridget's Cross to it for added protection. Now you'll be safe."

Part Two

CHARLESTOWN, MASSACHUSETTS

CHAPTER FIVE

I.

I clicked on the Red Sox game and it was clear from the announcer's voice that things were not going well. The A's were leading by nine runs, and it was only the second inning. Boston's ace had already thrown forty pitches, most of them wide of the plate, and the few balls that found the strike zone were roped for homers and doubles. The camera panned to the bullpen, where an aging reliever stirred in slow motion, offering little hope to stop the Oakland assault. The A's cleanup hitter dug into the batter's box, leveled a practice swing, and waited for a pitch. He got a fat one and launched a comet over the Green Monster, adding to a meteor shower of baseballs over Fenway Park.

I couldn't stomach another cloying rendition of *Sweet Caroline* in the eighth, if the game got that far before curfew, so I clicked off the TV and tossed the remote on the hassock. I decided I'd rather bore myself gawking at sell-by dates on soup cans than torment myself watching a ball club squat on the lawn. I grabbed the keys and went to the parish food pantry to do some prep work for the next distribution.

As I walked along Bunker Hill Street, the salty scents of tidal Boston washed away the angst of the game. My knee felt good, the best it had in years, and a resulting vigor enlivened my step. The sodium streetlights twinkled to life like city stars. On the western horizon the sunset spread like purple gas, and on the Tobin Bridge an endless stream of headlights congealed into a single beam.

Sundown in Charlestown.

I unlocked the pantry door and toed a granite wedge against the jamb to keep it ajar for the ocean air. After sorting and shelving five pallets of dry goods, a task that took two hours and change, I locked up the building and stepped out to the archway. I had no sooner pocketed the keys when I caught a whiff of tobacco in the air. The smell was fresh and strong and I looked around. At the fenced end of the archway I saw a bright orange dot, the tip of a cigarette, and the man smoking it spoke.

"Dermot Sparhawk?" he said.

"Yes?" Did I hear a brogue, maybe slurring? "Can I help you?"

The man came down the alley and stopped at the edge of the opening. He stood half in darkness, half in moonlight, and completely in fog. I noticed something glinting in his hand. It was a gun. Before I could react he shot me in the leg. Down to the pavement I went. He walked over to me with less urgency than the mop-up man in the Sox bullpen and shot the other leg. A spent shell pinged on the hardtop next to my ear. He pressed the warm barrel against my temple, letting me know that the next bullet was ticketed for my brain and that I was ticketed for the boneyard. With nothing to lose I slapped at his arm. A shot rang out and missed. I grabbed his hair and dragged him low, got hold of his gun hand and chomped on his thumb, sinking my grinders in deep.

He yowled and dropped the weapon. I groped for the granite wedge, found it, and slammed it on his head. I hit him again on the head. The second blow made a soggy sound on impact, as if it struck gray matter. I cocked my arm for a third clout, but he flopped onto his back. His mouth slackened and his eyes glazed. I looked at his face, blinked my eyes to refocus and looked again. I didn't recognize him. The pain began to set in and my head swooned. I flipped open my cell phone before I passed out and dialed 911. An operator answered and began her rote response, until I interrupted.

"I've been shot, Saint Jude Thaddeus Church, Charlestown, in the parking lot."

She continued to ask questions as if I were ordering a pizza, so I hung up. If I was going to bleed to death, I was going to do it in peace, and not with some nitwit babbling in my ear. My eyes closed, my eardrums pounded.

I heard a distant siren and the siren grew louder and louder until it blared. A car rolled to a stop ten feet away from me and a spotlight shined in my face. Two cops got out with their guns drawn and moved carefully into the alley. One of them leaned over the man who shot me and said, 'No ambulance needed for this guy.' The other one asked me if I was okay. I tried to nod yes. He pointed to the gun on the ground and asked if it was mine. Too weak to say anything, I tried to shake my head no.

The surroundings got hazy. Tinny sounds bounced off the archway and became distorted. Was I in an echo chamber? The cops talked about moose hunting in Maine and smoking cigars at a lakeside camp. Was I hallucinating?

An ambulance came into the lot and two medics got out. I think there were two, and one of them felt the gunman's throat and told the cops what they already knew, that he was dead. The other one applied compresses to my wounds. Things went from hazy to black. One of the medics said something about blood loss. They hoisted me onto a gurney and loaded me into an ambulance. I heard sirens again.

II.

The doctor who had tended my wounds the night before consulted with me when I awoke in the morning. He said that one of the bullets had hit my left leg, but had done little damage. The other one lodged in my right quadriceps. He told me that his medical team had removed the bullets, cleaned the wounds, and wrapped the gashes in pressure bandages. They administered intravenous antibiotic as a precaution against infection. They checked the pulses in my feet and were satisfied with the outcomes. They tested for artery damage, which could lead to an aneurism, and found nothing of concern. They gave me a transfusion to top off my blood level. He sounded like a mechanic recapping a tune-up.

When he asked me if I wanted morphine for the pain I said no, saying there was no reason for a recovering alcoholic to take an unneeded risk, although my AA sponsor, Mickey Pappas, might have referred to prescribed stuff as a freebie. The doctor then told me that I would need crutches until I could walk on my own. He grabbed his clipboard and left the room.

I fell asleep thinking of morphine.

Later that afternoon Superintendent Hanson and Captain Pruitt of the Boston Police Department visited me. I expected the police but not the brass.

"A superintendent and a captain," I said. "Was the commissioner tied up?"

"How are you feeling, Sparhawk?" Captain Pruitt asked with little empathy, as he wrapped his big black mitts around the bedrail and leaned over me. "You're feeling better than that poor bastard you turned into a chalk mark, I can tell you that much."

"Who was he?"

"That's why we're here," said Hanson, who wore his customary attire: a navy blue suit, a white broadcloth shirt with DMH monogrammed on the cuffs, and a purple tie dappled with Holy Cross crests. "We are hoping you can tell us who he was."

"I never saw him before," I answered.

"Are you sure about that?" Pruitt handed me a photo of the man who shot me. "Take a good look at him."

"I got a good look at him last night," I said. "I didn't know him. I'd tell you if I knew him."

"We think he's a Townie, Sparhawk," Hanson said. "But we haven't established his identity yet."

"He didn't have a wallet," Pruitt added. "His fingerprints weren't in CODIS. Did he say anything before you whacked him with that rock?"

"He said ouch." They didn't laugh. "He said 'Dermot Sparhawk,' that's all." I didn't mention the brogue or slurring or whatever it was I had heard in his voice.

"So he knew you." Pruitt surmised.

"He said my name." I cranked the bed to upright and something occurred to me. "If you don't know who he is, why do you think he's a Townie?"

Captain Pruitt looked at Superintendent Hanson, who nodded.

"Ballistics," Pruitt answered. "Last week a bank robber shot a Boston cop."

"I heard about it, in Hyde Park."

Pruitt continued. "The bullets we dug out of you matched a bullet we dug out of the cop. They were fired from the same weapon, the Walther PPS we recovered at the scene, *your* scene."

"The guy who shot me shot the cop?" This surprised me. Usually criminals dump their guns after a job, especially if the gun was used to shoot a cop.

"No," Pruitt said with authority, as if anticipating my conclusion. "We arrested a man for the cop shooting last week, a neighbor of yours named Jerome O'Shea. O'Shea is a longtime felon, as you must know. He's behind bars, awaiting trial. He was in jail when you got shot."

"Then O'Shea didn't have the gun when you arrested him."

"That's right," Pruitt said.

"Did you arrest the wrong guy for the cop shooting?" I asked. "Obviously, O'Shea couldn't have shot me if he was in jail. What's going on here?"

"I'll explain it later," Pruitt said.

"The man you killed had a $5,000 bill in his pocket," Hanson said. "I called the Treasury Department, because I wanted to know if the bill was authentic, and they sent a man over to examine it."

"What did he say?"

Hanson said, "He confirmed the bill was real, which I expected, because a vintage $5,000 bill had recently been stolen."

"From the Hyde Park bank?" I asked.

Hanson and Pruitt again looked at each other. Hanson nodded and Pruitt said, "Have you ever heard of the World's Fair of Money?"

"Nope, never heard of it."

"Each year the American Numismatic Association sponsors the event," Pruitt said.

Hanson added. "The Hynes hosted it this year. Two nights ago the fair was robbed. The thieves stole a $5,000 bill, the same bill we found on the man you killed."

"In self-defense," I said to Hanson, who has never been my biggest fan.

"They also stole four sheets of $100,000 bills. The Treasury Department lent the sheets to the ANA for the fair, and although the sheets are insured, they want them back."

"I don't see where I fit in."

"Are you joking or something?" Hanson shook his head. Not a single silver hair moved out of place. "One of the robbers shot you, Sparhawk. He waited outside your food pantry, called you by name, and shot you. Can you explain any of this?"

"I told you I didn't recognize the man." A thought came to me, a thought I didn't like. "You don't think I was involved in the Hynes robbery, do you?"

"We know you're not that stupid," Pruitt said.

"Thanks, Captain."

"Besides, we asked around," said Pruitt. "You were seen at an AA meeting in Everett at the time of the heist, witnessed by twenty or thirty people. Apparently, you chaired the meeting that night."

"So much for anonymity," I said.

Hanson said, "The Treasury folks are investigating the Hynes heist, so don't meddle in it. And one more thing, don't talk about the World's Fair of Money with anyone. We're keeping it out of the press for now."

III.

Two days later I was back on my feet and moving okay, albeit with a slight limp. I wouldn't be skipping rope anytime soon, but at least I could get around without crutches, and that was a good thing. After drinking a pot of coffee at my kitchen table, I headed out the front door for work. When I rounded Tufts Street, I saw a dark gray sedan with smoked windows and a small antenna parked in front of my office. A patrol car would be less conspicuous. Captain Pruitt got out. He raised his big face to the sun and closed his eyes. I stopped when I got next to him.

"Coffee, Captain?"

Pruitt nodded his head and we went inside. I put on the coffee and motioned for him to sit. He still hadn't said a word, so I spoke.

"I know I make great coffee, but I'm guessing you dropped by for another reason." I mixed two cups on the sweet side, plenty of cream and plenty of sugar. They were basically hot milkshakes. "What's up?"

"At the hospital you said you didn't know your assailant."

"I never saw him before that night," I said.

"And yet he knew your name."

"He said my name, but I didn't know him."

"Nobody seems to know him. We took fingerprints, DNA, dentals, and got nothing." Pruitt adjusted his large frame and the metal folding chair squeaked. "He had no tattoos, no scars, no wallet, no keys, no cell phone. His pockets were empty."

"Except for the $5,000 bill," I said.

"Yeah, except for that. We checked Interpol and found zilch."

"What's next?"

"We're running a composite sketch of him in tomorrow's newspapers." He drank some coffee, nodded, and drank some more. "We'll show it on TV, too."

"Not radio?" I waited for a chuckle that never came.

"The coroner reassembled his head and took a picture of it, but the picture was too gruesome for the public, nothing we could release to the press."

"Reality TV can't be too real," I said.

"So our sketch artist drew a composite using the photo as a model. We're releasing it tomorrow." He handed me a sheet of paper. "Here it is. Show it around the neighborhood, see if anyone knows him."

"Will do," I said and got up, but Pruitt remained seated. "Was there something else, Captain?"

"The shooter's blood alcohol content was point three two." He took another swig of the sweet stuff. "The guy was legless, Sparhawk. We're checking the bars and package stores in the area."

"At least he wasn't driving."

"Did anyone ever tell you you're not funny?"

"I'm serious." I actually *was* serious. "You said he had no keys, so he wasn't driving. Maybe he took a cab to Charlestown."

"Jeez, Sparhawk, we'd have never thought of that."

IV.

I walked home to eat lunch and noticed that Buck Louis's door was open. Buck, a paraplegic and former Boston College teammate of mine, lives in the downstairs apartment of my two-family house. The other tenant, Harraseeket Kid, is my cousin and a full-blooded Micmac Indian. He lives in the basement by choice. Kid likes the hum of the furnace in the winter and the whoosh of the sump pump in the summer.

I knocked on Buck's door.

"Come in," he yelled. I entered his apartment just as Buck rolled into the parlor. Sweat glistened on his face, which he wiped dry with a dishtowel. "I was doing dips on the arms of my wheelchair. You can really feel it in the triceps." He toweled the back of his neck. "Sorry I didn't get to the hospital."

"Your phone calls were plenty," I said.

"Do the cops know who shot you?" he asked.

"They're working on it." I paused. "The shooter knew my name. He said it before he shot me."

"He knew your name?" Buck rolled a few feet closer to me. "That means he targeted you."

"Yeah, he did."

"You said the police came to the hospital."

"A superintendent and a captain," I said.

"Why the higher-ups?"

"The shooter had a $5,000 bill on him." I told Buck about the World's Fair of Money heist at the Hynes. "The Treasury Department hasn't told the press yet."

"Probably too embarrassed," Buck said.

"The thieves also stole $12.8 million in $100,000 bills. The $5,000 bill must've been a souvenir of some kind."

"Like a kid getting a pennant at a ball game." He dried his forearms and hands. "So after the Hynes heist, one of the robbers shot you."

"It looks that way." I handed Buck the composite sketch. "This is the man who shot me. Ever see him before?"

Buck studied it. "Nope, but with that mick face he must be a Townie, maybe Southie."

"Funny you said mick, because I thought he had a brogue." I rubbed my wounded thighs with both hands. "According to Captain Pruitt the shooter was drunk. Maybe I mistook his slurring for a brogue."

"That'd be a first, a slurring brogue," Buck said. "I'm no detective, but if he knew your name, he must be a Townie."

"That makes sense," I said, except it didn't make sense. "If he were a Townie, I would have recognized him."

V.

It was my day off from the food pantry, and I planned to visit every barroom, package store, veterans post, and after-hours joint in Charlestown to show them the composite sketch of the man who shot me. I started on Terminal Street near the Mystic Piers at a gin mill called Melvin's Catch, which could have been called Melvin's Miss. It stood on a listing wharf propped up by rotting pilings.

I opened the sodden door, but only after I put my shoulder into it. The hinges squeaked and the musty air attacked my nostrils. When my eyes adjusted to the darkness I took in the room. The place was a dump, and the barman fit the surroundings, not too clean, not too bright. I showed him the sketch.

"Do you know this guy?" I asked.

"What he do?" he murmured, barely looking at the drawing.

"He shot me," I said.

"Never seen him before," he said, giving me a taste of my own neighborhood norm, the Charlestown code of silence.

On it went. Each visit to each bar proved to be the same, and the sameness began to erode my defenses. The smell of stale beer and spilt whiskey went from distasteful to delightful, and I found myself wanting more. The seedier side of life looked good again, too damn good, and at that moment a chilling thought came to me. I was one drink away from a straitjacket. I called my sponsor, Mickey Pappas, and told him what was going on. The Mick didn't like it. Drunks don't belong in barrooms he said to me. They shouldn't be in package stores, either.

I explained to him that I was trying to identify the man who'd shot me, and that I had to go to these places to ask questions. He said that if I went ahead with it, I should ask God for help. So I asked God for help and got the help I needed to stay sober. What I didn't get was an ID on the composite sketch.

That night I went to an AA meeting at the Teamsters building in Sullivan Square and sat in the front row next to Mickey. A man named Skinny Atlas spoke. Skinny helped me solve a case a few years ago, though he probably didn't realize it, and along the way I watched him get sober. After the meeting Mickey and I talked.

"Are you doing okay?" he asked. "Between the shooting and the gin joints, you must be jittery."

"I'm doing fine," I said.

"We got another sober day in the books." Mick slapped my shoulder. "Go home and get some rest."

§

At home that night I paged through the newspapers and saw the police composite sketch on the metro page of the *Boston Globe*, above the fold, as the ink slingers say. The caption read: 'Do you recognize this man?' It listed a phone number to call if you did. The caption said nothing about the Hynes robbery or the fact that the man in the sketch was dead. I wondered if it would do any good.

In the morning I went to the ten o'clock Mass, ate breakfast at the Grasshopper Cafe, bought the Sunday papers, and walked home. I read papers, filled in the crossword and Sudoku puzzles, and fell asleep on the couch. At four o'clock I woke up and called Jenny's for a pizza delivery.

Bored and getting cranky, I phoned Captain Pruitt, got his answering service, and hung up without leaving a message. I called Harraseeket Kid. Same thing, no answer. The Red Sox were playing the Tigers in an afternoon game at Fenway Park, and I turned on the radio to catch the score. One of Detroit's aces, they had more than one, had just finished striking out the side when my phone rang. It was Captain Pruitt. I turned off the radio and answered it.

"Thanks for calling back so quickly," I said.

"What's going on?" he grumbled. "Is there a problem?"

"Nothing's going on, that's the problem. Did anyone call about the sketch?"

"A few crackpots, nothing worth pursuing," Pruitt said.

"I didn't see it in the Sunday papers." The newspapers sat next to me on the couch. "Are you running it again tomorrow?"

"No," Pruitt said. "A second run wouldn't do any good. The callers were a bunch of lunatics."

We spoke a little longer and hung up.

Sitting around and doing nothing was beginning to wear on me. I needed to make something happen, anything to get things rolling, so I called the *Boston Herald*. I listened to a phone recording and selected option two, which forwarded me to advertising sales. To my surprise a human being answered. She said hello a second time, snapping me out of my stunned state. I told her that I wanted to place an ad in tomorrow's paper.

"It's too late for tomorrow," she said. "How about Tuesday?"

I told her that Tuesday would be fine.

"Which section?" she asked, in a business-like manner.

"The back page, I want everyone to see it." I answered.

"They'll see it there. Let me check something first. I'm putting you on hold." She came back about twenty seconds later. "Yes indeed, we can do that. We can run it on the bottom of the sports page, the best spot in the paper."

We agreed on the size and I told her what I wanted it to say.

"The heading should read $2000 cash reward for information on the police composite sketch." I thought for a second. "I want the sketch in the ad, too."

"We can't run the sketch again, not unless the police give us permission."

"Damn." I wanted the sketch in the ad. "The police gave me a full-size copy of the sketch. What if I scanned in *my* copy and emailed it to you? That way I'm the source of the sketch, not the police."

"That's an interesting angle." She hesitated. "Sure, I think that will cover us. Do you need anything else?"

"Put my phone number in the ad, too." I gave her the number, and we finished the transaction.

As soon as I hung up, my stomach stirred as if I had done something wrong. What was bothering me? Neither the cost of the ad nor the price of the reward would hurt me financially. I had plenty of money in the bank, thanks to a sizable finder's fee I'd received for the recovery of stolen art. I guess I was still not used to having money. I didn't have to sweat the monthly nut anymore, and I felt guilty about it.

VI.

The ad ran on Tuesday morning. By Tuesday evening I had fielded more than fifty calls, all claiming to know the man in the sketch. Most of them were scammers, probably the same scammers that called Captain Pruitt. Two of the callers struck me as legitimate. The first one insisted that we meet outside of Boston. She said this in a voicemail, and I called her back as soon as I got it. It took three calls before she finally answered.

"Are you serious about the two thousand dollars?" she asked. "I can use the money."

"I'll have the cash with me when we meet," I said.

"How come you care about the kid in the sketch?" she asked. "Why do you want to find him?"

"What's your name?"

"Never mind about names." The line went silent. I heard the striking of a match followed by an exhale. "I'm not sure I want to go through with this. It feels kind of creepy to me."

"I just want to talk to you," I said, trying to sound reassuring.

"Maybe I shouldn't have called."

"We can meet in a public place." I suggested. "Would you feel more comfortable if we met in a public place?"

"Oh, if we meet at all, we'll meet in a public place, don't worry about that." She sounded more poised now. "Are you going to hurt him? I won't get involved in something like that, because he wasn't a bad kid."

"All I want is information," I told her.

"He was really drunk." She took another drag and exhaled into the receiver. "I can tell you that much off the bat."

"I need to learn all I can about him," I said.

"You really have two thousand in cash?"

"All hundreds," I said.

"All hundreds, huh?" She puffed and coughed. "I'll meet you at Caffé Bella in Randolph, tonight at eight o'clock."

"I'll be there," I said.

"How will I know you?" she asked.

"I'll be the tall guy with a confused look on his face," I said. She didn't laugh. Nobody was laughing at my jokes these days. "I'll be wearing a maroon Boston College shirt with gold eagles on the sleeves."

VII.

At eight o'clock I pulled into Caffé Bella on Route 28 in Randolph and went inside, or at least I tried to go inside. The place was jammed and it was only a Tuesday night, not usually a big night for the restaurant trade. A tanned, platinum-haired bartender who could have posed for Victoria's Secret asked me if I wanted something to drink. I wasn't thirsty but I wasn't stupid, and I told her I'd have a Coke. She smiled and poured it and slid it to me on a cocktail napkin.

I was still drooling into my glass when another woman, who had no shot at Victoria's Secret, approached me holding a martini glass in her hand. Her wiry brown hair and pug nose went perfectly with the brown freckles that dotted her face. She had a buxom build, the body of a woman who enjoyed all of life's appetites.

"So you're the guy that ran the ad." She gulped some martini and tongued an olive into her mouth. "You said you were tall, but you didn't say you were a giant." She jerked her head. "This way, we can sit at the bar."

We sat on barstools away from the door. She raised her empty glass, and the Victoria's Secret bartender mixed her another one. My new friend said to me, "Did you bring the cash, because I'm not saying a word until I see the cash. It's not that I don't trust you, but I've been gypped before."

I took an envelope from my pocket. "I have it right here."

"You said two thousand."

"Was it two?" I took the $100 bills from the envelope. "I thought we said three, my mistake."

I counted out ten hundreds and put them back in my pocket and laid the remaining hundreds on the bar, all twenty of them. She plucked one at random and handed it to Victoria, who held it under a black light and signaled it valid with a tilt of her head.

"Your money's good," she said. "That's my friend Angel. She checked it for me."

"What's your name?" I asked.

"I already told you, no names."

"Okay, okay, no names."

I swallowed some Coke along with some pride and looked at the restaurant's trendy décor, its burgundy beams and wainscoting, its white stucco walls and ceiling. Two busboys cleared a path, and a waitress carrying a tray of food followed closely behind them. When she saw an opening, she shot through and delivered the food to her waiting customers. The whole thing played out like a power sweep. Angel, the intoxicating bartender, dropped the certified C-note back on the stack.

"Are you hungry?" I asked my informant. "How about dinner?"

"Does it come out of the two grand?" she asked.

"My treat, I insist." I smiled at her.

"In that case dinner sounds good." Without opening the menu, she said to the bartender, "I'll have the yellowfin tuna carpaccio and another martini." Her glass was still half full. "Make it with Bombay Sapphire this time, extra dry, two olives."

Angel said to me, "You should get the mozzarella salad as an appetizer. It's not on the menu, but I'll put it in for you."

I said yes to the mozzarella salad. I would have said yes to crawdads fried in motor oil if she recommended it. For the main course I ordered the hardwood grilled pizza with sausage and onions. I handed my canary the reward money and said, "Tell me about the man in the sketch. Where did you see him?"

"I won't say where I saw him, because I saw him where I work." She waited for me to protest. I gestured for her to continue and she did. "I won't drag work into this, because I need my job."

"Why don't you just tell me about him?"

She sipped her drink and contemplated where to begin. It took two more swigs before she found her bearings.

"He was Irish, off-the-boat Irish, and so were the other two men."

"What other men?" I asked.

"The men with him, they were Irish, too. I could tell from their accents, their brogues, whatever. I think they came from another part of Ireland. They sounded different than the guys we usually get, kind of gruffer."

My mind collated the data. She knew the bartender at Caffé Bella. She worked at a place frequented by Irish immigrants. Restaurant workers belong to a fraternity of sorts. They hang out together. Irish immigrants know where to find each other over here. They go to the same pubs. Caffé Bella was south of the city, so she probably worked at a bar or a restaurant in Dorchester or South Boston or possibly Hyde Park. I thought further. Irish joints are cropping up in Quincy Square, too. Hell, she could be working anywhere.

"What did the other two men look like?" I asked.

"One of them was big, not as big as you, but big." Her fresh drink arrived, and not a moment too soon. "He was bald-headed with dark hair on the sides. I thought he looked familiar at first, like maybe I saw him before, but I didn't. He was the leader." She picked up her glass and put a dent in the drink. "You could tell by the way they listened to him, he was the leader."

"And the other guy?"

"Oh, him." Her throat blushed. "He was a redhead. He had a red mustache and bright green eyes with brown flecks, handsome and a really nice guy." She drank a mouthful and turned away. Her head jerked back to me. "Are you looking for him, too?"

I'd hit a nerve and I didn't want to lose her. "I just want to know about the guy in the sketch."

"Why are you asking about him?"

Ah, what's the difference, tell her.

"He shot me," I said. "In self-defense I killed him."

"You killed him?" She put her glass on the bar and stammered. "He's dead? I can't believe you killed the kid."

"I had no choice." I turned to face her. "He was going to kill me."

She stared at me, her eyes bulging. "If he's dead, why do you care about him?"

"I have my reasons." I could see that she wanted more, so I gave her more. "He shot me twice and then he tried to blow my head off."

"Oh, my God." She drained the martini. The olives sat on the bottom of the glass, stranded. "What do you mean he tried to kill you?"

"He pressed a gun against my head." I finished my Coke. "I slapped his arm and the shot missed."

"How did you kill the kid if he had a gun?"

"I hit him with a rock," I said. "Two times I hit him. The blows fractured his skull and killed him. I called the police. An ambulance took me to MGH. I suppose they took him to the morgue."

"So the cops know about you." She seemed to be relieved by this fact. "When I saw the composite I almost called the police, but I didn't, because I didn't know anything about him, you know, the kid in the sketch."

Angel delivered the new martini and said, "You didn't tell me he was so good-looking, Delia."

"Shit, Angel, I told you not to say my name."

I chuckled. "Don't worry, Delia. I just want information."

"That's not the point," she said.

The food arrived and the conversation died down. The pizza tasted like it came straight from Rome, Italy. I didn't come up for air until I'd wiped out every crumb. I wasn't alone in my gluttonous attack. Delia dug in with equal ferocity, matching my eating rampage, bite for bite.

"Let me ask you something," Delia said, pushing away her clean plate and setting aside the tools of the trade, her knife and fork. "You placed that ad in the paper, and the ad said two thousand, so why pretend it said three?"

"I thought an extra grand might motivate you," I said.

"Motivate me?" She frowned. "What's that supposed to mean?"

"It means I'm willing to buy more information," I said. "For example, if you were to tell me where you work, I might feel compelled to give you the extra thousand."

"Sounds more like bribery than motivation."

"Think of it as a bonus payment."

"Give me a second to consider this so-called bonus payment." Her body seemed to relax, maybe from the martinis. Her jaw seemed to sag, maybe from chewing, and Delia started to spew. "I waitress at the Blarney Stone, six nights a week I'm there."

"In Fields Corner?"

"Yeah, Dorchester," she said, beginning to slur. "The redhead's name is Mac."

"Do you know his last name?" I asked, wanting more.

"He just said Mac."

"What about the other two guys?" I asked. "Any names?"

"They didn't tell me their names."

"Did they say where they were from or why they were here in Boston?"

"They ordered drinks and drank them," Delia said. "They didn't tell me anything, except what they wanted to drink."

The flow of info stopped just as quickly as it had started. I asked her a few more questions, drilling for additional ore, hoping the gusher hadn't run dry, but nothing new came to light. There didn't seem to be any point in hanging around, so I handed her the extra thousand and got off the stool.

"Thanks for your help," I said. "If you think of anything else I'd appreciate a call. Something might occur to you, you never know."

"No dessert?" she said.

"Excuse me?"

"It's not every day I get to eat at Caffé Bella and I want dessert."

"How thoughtless of me," I said, climbing back onto the stool. "Order dessert, Delia, whatever you want."

"What about you? I don't want to eat alone."

I told the bartender I'd have whatever Delia was having and a cup of coffee.

VIII.

At noon the following day I drove to a donut shop in South Boston, where Dorchester Avenue, Fifth Street, and A Street all run together. The reason for the trip, to meet the second caller I judged legitimate. He told me he'd be wearing a black Bruins cap, which wouldn't distinguish him much in Southie, but it was enough. I spotted him at the counter the moment I walked in.

He was sipping black coffee and reading the *Daily Racing Form* when I approached him. I stood right next to him, but he didn't look at me, even though I loomed in an obvious way. He flipped the page and kept reading. I cleared my throat like a lawnmower. He took a pencil from behind his ear and drew a faint star next to one of the horses and then he erased it. Now I was getting interested in his selection process, so I ordered a Coke and watched him. He underlined a horse named River of Dreams in the third race at Suffolk Downs, jockey Eddie Pollis, owners Preskenis and Collins. He kept underlining it until the pencil wore through the page. I thought of betting River of Dreams myself, but I had enough vices to deal with. I gave up and waited him out.

"You a cop?" he asked, looking up at me.

"I'm not a cop," I said. "I'm Santa Claus and I'm here to give you an early Christmas gift if you tell me about the man in the sketch. If you can tell me anything that's even remotely useful, I'll give you two grand. Sound fair?"

"Two grand always sounds fair to me," he said. "He wasn't a man, he was a kid, maybe eighteen, and he was stewed silly when he got into my cab." He doffed his Bruins cap, showing a comb-over of yellowish hair. The part started an inch above his ear, with the side hair brushed across the dome. It was the best argument yet for baldness. "I drive a cab in Fields Corner, been driving there since the seventies. I usually pick up customers at the supermarket and drive them home with their groceries."

"Tell me about the kid," I said, trying to guide him to the point of the meeting.

"There's not much to tell. He came out of the Blarney Stone, got into my cab, and said he wanted to go to Charlestown. So I said fine, I'll bring you to Charlestown. So I'm driving up Dot Ave and he tells me to pull over, he wants a jug of poteen. That's what he called it, poteen. Poteen is an Irish concoction made from—"

"I know, I know, hooch made from potatoes," I said, hoping to avoid a treatise on poteen. "Please continue."

"So I pull over and the kid goes into a package store and comes out with a pint of rye, no bag. He cracks it open and takes a belt. And then he asks me if I want a belt, and I said no thanks, I gotta drive."

I asked him which package store the kid went to, he told me, and I continued. "You said he was drunk when he got into your cab."

"The kid was blotto." The cabbie drank some coffee. "He had an Irish brogue. I could barely understand him, partly because of the brogue, partly because he was so drunk. But it was more than that. There was something about the kid. I don't know how to put it exactly, but he seemed off-kilter."

"What do you mean by off-kilter?" I asked. "Could you elaborate?"

He put down the cup and rubbed his jaw.

"The kid seemed scared. He was trying so hard to act tough, that he seemed scared. Does that make sense? Maybe it was the booze."

"Maybe he was drinking *because* he was scared," I said. "Maybe that's why he was hitting it so hard."

"I see that a lot in my job. A guy gets liquored up and all of a sudden he's as tough as Tyson." He laughed and shook his yellow head. "Then you see him the next day and he's back to normal, except for the black eye and scraped knuckles."

"Yeah, I know what you mean," I said, just to say something. I handed him the envelope of money. "Is there anything else you can tell me about him?"

"What do you mean?"

"Did anything unusual happen, anything out of the ordinary?"

"There was one thing." He opened the envelope and peeked inside. "Instead of taking the Expressway to Charlestown, he wanted me to take Boylston Street. I told him it was out of the way, that it'd run up the meter, but he didn't care. He wanted Boylston, so that's the way I went."

"Did he tell you to stop anywhere along the way?" I asked.

"He didn't tell me to stop." He put away the envelope. "But as soon as I turned onto Boylston he told me to slow down."

"Near the Hynes Convention Center?"

"How'd you know that?"

"Then what happened?"

"Then nothing. After we slowed down at the Hynes he told me to go to Charlestown." He put the Bruins cap back on his head. "So I merged onto Storrow Drive and drove over the Prison Point Bridge to Charlestown."

"Where did you let him off?" I asked.

"Hayes Square, in front of the church," he said.

"And what time was that, roughly?"

"About nine-thirty, give or take. I remember because the Sox were getting clobbered and I knew the game would be getting out late." The old railbird folded the racing form and tucked it under his arm. "I was trying to factor in the ballgame traffic, in case I got a fare to Kenmore Square later that night."

"Makes sense." I read the mailing label on the racing form. "How did he pay the fare?"

"What do you mean?"

It didn't seem like a hard question.

"Did he use cash, a credit card, how did he pay you?" I said.

"Why do you care how he paid? I mean, what difference does it make?"

He was holding back, so I tried a different angle.

"Thanks for your help," I said. "I'll ask the cab company how the kid paid the fare. What company do you work for again?"

"Hold it, don't do that." He face twitched. "Don't call my company."

I sat next to him and leaned on the countertop, so that my face was level with his.

"Do you think this is a game? Why do you think the police ran the sketch in the newspaper? They ran it because the kid is dead. I don't want to get you into hot water, but I want to know what happened that night."

"The kid is dead?" The cabby kneaded the bridge of his nose. "I didn't know he was dead. Look, I don't want to get in any trouble."

"How could you get in trouble?" I asked him.

"Shit, what the fuck did I get myself into?" His eyes looked away.

"What an idiot I am. I never should have called you."

"Tell me what's going on, Mr. Randell." I pointed to the mailing label. "I'm not leaving until I find out."

"I didn't figure you'd leave, didn't figure it for a second."

"Just tell me what happened and I'll be on my way."

He picked up his coffee cup and put it down, and then he shook his head as if he couldn't believe his own stupidity.

"I didn't log the fare." He looked around the coffee shop and then back at me. "I never called the dispatcher. Can we keep this between us? I could get fired for something like this, and who knows what the cops might do to me."

If he never reported the fare, the cab company would have no record of his trip to Charlestown, hence, nothing to tell the police if they were asked about it.

"It's between us," I said.

Everything the cabbie told me matched Delia's version of events. Funny thing, if he had simply told me that the kid had paid in cash, his secret would have been safe.

IX.

The next two days proved fruitless. During that time, three people called about the reward money, all saying they'd met the man in the sketch. When I asked them when they met him, two of the callers told me they met him after he was already dead. When I pointed this out to them, they both hung up. The third caller said that she spoke to him at a séance in Brockton, in an apartment building behind Marciano Stadium, making her the most credible witness of the bunch.

Another day passed with no calls. I was getting antsy, marking time, impatiently waiting for fate to deliver her prize. I needed information, anything to get me reignited, but nothing was coming in. How could I make something happen? I considered going to the séance in Brockton, recognized the sarcasm in the thought, and decided to go to an AA meeting instead. I knew of one that started in twenty minutes in East Boston, a group called McClellan's Felons, named for Bull McClellan, an Eastie cop who would empty the drunk tank and bring the sots to meetings. He took my father once. I got into my car and headed for the Callahan Tunnel.

I emerged in Maverick Square and navigated my way to Border Street, the location of the meeting. As I was driving by Project Bread and the Atlantic Works complex, my cell phone rang. I said a quick prayer that it was somebody calling about the composite sketch, even if that somebody turned out to be another chucklehead. I got my wish.

The caller, a soft-spoken woman with a tremor in her voice, asked about the ad in the paper. Before I could answer, she asked if she had called the right number, and then she asked about the reward money. Her voice went from trembling to frantic, as if panic had set it. I told her that she had called the right number and that the reward money was still on the table. She breathed a sigh of relief and said thank God, she wasn't too late.

I urged her to relax and assured her that she had called in plenty of time, and then I said, "Why don't you tell me about the kid in the sketch."

"Yes, I can do that. I think I can do that, I mean, I can tell you about him, a little bit anyway." She was all over the place. "I met him at a club in Davis Square."

She confessed that the meeting had been brief, no more than an exchange of hellos. I asked her when she met him and she told me. She had met him the night before he was drinking at the Blarney Stone. Her credibility inched forward. I asked her if she knew his name. She said that if he told her his name, she didn't remember it. She went on to say that she probably wouldn't have remembered him at all if not the newspaper sketch. She kept talking and seemed to be settling down. Her thoughts became more collected.

I listened to her as I drove along, grateful to be listening to anybody at this point. She said a few things I found interesting, so I agreed to meet with her. She wanted to meet tonight if that was possible, but she didn't want to impose. I told her that she wasn't imposing and that tonight would be fine.

"I'll meet you at the Rack Club in Chelsea," she said. "It's on Beacham Street in the meat-packing district. Do you know the area?"

I knew the area, all right. Beacham Street was dangerous enough in daylight, let alone in darkness, but at least the big trucks wouldn't be humping by at night.

"I know it," I said.

"Do you know King Arthur's Lounge?" she asked.

If Beacham Street was the toughest street in Chelsea, then King Arthur's Lounge was the toughest address on Beacham. Even Townies steered clear of the place.

"I know King Arthur's."

"The Rack Club is across the street," she said. "There's a parking lot in back. That's the best place to park, in back. You'll have the money with you I hope. Am I being too pushy? I've never done anything like this before."

"I'll have the money with me, and no, you're not being too pushy."

"I think I can help you with the sketch, but it has to be worth my while. I hope you understand." She cleared her throat. "Did I tell you I have a picture of him? I wasn't taking a picture of him specifically, but he's in the background with his friends. Will that help you?"

Will that help me? Was she kidding?

"The picture will definitely help," I said.

"You said cash, is that right?"

"Yes, cash," I said. "And don't worry. I'll make it worth your while. That's why I put the reward in the paper, to buy information."

She sighed again, sounding relieved.

"Ask the bartender for Shelley. That's me, Shelley. He'll point me out to you. I get off work at eleven-thirty. I should be there by midnight, ten past at the latest."

§

That evening I ate barbecued ribs at Tommy Floramo's (where the meat falls off the bone), attended an AA meeting at the Soldiers' Home, and drank too many cups of coffee at Dunkin' Donuts on Everett Avenue. At eleven-thirty I drove up Beacham Street, a bronco ride over potholes, hubcaps, and railroad tracks, and I parked in back of the Rack Club as instructed. The cars in the lot looked like losers in a demolition derby, and I had a feeling I'd be seeing more of the same inside.

I entered the club through the rear entrance at ten minutes to twelve. The bartender, an old geezer with a soft belly and a blooming face, was leaning against the bar watching a flat-screen TV, the only contemporary thing in the joint. He didn't turn to look when the door slammed behind me. Two hunched men sat on barstools drinking shots of something clear, and it was clear by the way they teetered on their stools it wasn't water. In one of the ratty booths, a dandy wooed a floozy, and she seemed to be enjoying the wooing, which probably didn't happen often to her. They sat together on the same side of the booth on the same Naugahyde bench, slurring sweet nothings into each other's cauliflower ears.

I said to the barman, "I'm looking for Shelley."

"Who?" he asked, with his eyes glued to the bar's flat-screen.

"Her name is Shelley. She said you'd know her."

"I didn't know they had names." He turned the channel. "I can't help you, unless you want a drink."

"I'll have a Coke, no ice."

"A Coke straight up? That's a first, even in here." He looked at me and sneezed on his sleeve. "Okay, pal, a Coca-Cola it is." He poured it into a collins glass from a soda fountain dispenser.

I sat in a booth and waited for Shelley. The two men at the bar ordered refills of tequila, sans the salt and lemon. They were as pickled as the worm in the bottle. The couple in the booth touched glasses and slobbered on each other, their passion budding with each rotgut swig. It was midnight and no sign of Cinderella. At twelve-thirty Shelley still hadn't arrived. At one o'clock the barman gave last call, and at one-thirty he told us to finish our drinks and leave the premises. I put my glass on the bar and went out the back door, saying to myself you can't win 'em all. Shelley must have got spooked.

On my way to the car, two white men stepped out from behind a cargo van and came toward me. One of them carried a bowie knife, the other one had a baseball bat. They were wiry men, fidgety and sniffling. Drug addicts no doubt. They crept closer to me, guardedly, like animals stalking prey. And I knew what they were going to say before they said it.

"Give us the money," the batsman demanded. "C'mon, let us have it."

I wanted to give them the money, I really did, but I couldn't. I'm a Townie.

"I can't do that," I said.

The two men came closer. This time the knifeman spoke.

"You're gonna get busted up bad, bones broken for nothing. Just give us the money and we all go home safe." He hesitated. "You might be big, but you ain't that big."

I scooped up a fistful of gravel and said, "I don't want to hurt you guys."

The batsman, no David Ortiz, plodded toward me and raised the bat. I threw the sandy mixture into his face, a beanball of dirt and pebbles. He dropped the bat and pawed at his eyes. I stepped up and booted him between the legs. He hopped off the ground, cupped his crotch, and pitched forward, shrieking.

The knifeman stood frozen, a man out of his element, but a man forced to make a tough decision within that element. I said to him, "Pick up your friend and go home. Get out of here and I won't call the cops."

He ignored my advice and came at me, waving the knife like an extra in *West Side Story*. I suppose he had no choice but to come at me. Two grand buys a lot of dope. He lunged like a fencer, thrusting the blade to within an inch of my gut. I jackknifed back, got hold of his knife hand, and forced the weapon away from my ribs. He tried to pull his arm away but I wouldn't let go. I jerked him toward me and head-butted his ear. The butt hit hard, hard enough that I saw stars. God knows what he saw. I drew back my head and blasted him again.

He reeled like a boxer in trouble, disoriented and looking for help. But in vacant lots on Beacham Street there is no help. There are no neutral corners or cut men to succor your wounds. You won't hear a bell to end the round, unless it's ringing inside your head. On Beacham Street, you're on your own.

I twisted his arm, but he bravely held on to the knife. Spreading my feet for leverage, I leaned in and torqued it once more. Something popped like a champagne cork. His arm rotated limply, flopping like a drumstick snapped from a turkey. I've never heard a wolf howl in the wild, but that's what I thought of when he wailed.

He fell to his knees and folded into a fetal curl. I kicked away the dagger, not that he'd be using it anytime soon. He wouldn't be using his arm for anything anytime soon, except to get painkillers. His partner, the batsman, crawled on all fours, searching for his breath, or perhaps his privates. Neither man seemed game to continue, so I walked to my car and drove home to Charlestown.

§

Up in my bedroom, with the shades drawn and the lights low, I thought about Shelley's phone call. I'd been too eager, and she sensed it, and she seized on it. She teased me until I was salivating and then hooked me like a guppy in a fishbowl. I'd been building momentum and I wanted to keep it going, and as a result, I ignored the warning signs and jumped into her trap. She did a nice job of it. I've seen this happen in football games, when a team uses a player's aggressiveness against him. They let him get away with a few things, and when he's ripe, the quarterback pump fakes, the player bites, and the receiver blows by him and catches the winning touchdown pass.

Game over.

I opened the Big Book of Alcoholics Anonymous. Step Ten suggests that we take a daily inventory of our actions, and when we were wrong, promptly admitted it. Was I wrong tonight? Did I go too far, drubbing those men the way I did? I contemplated the battle. I didn't put the boots to them after I subdued them. No gratuitous blows were struck. Once they were defeated I walked away. I concluded that I acted within the boundaries of street etiquette. Step Ten done, I got on my knees, thanked God for another day of sobriety, and went to bed.

CHAPTER SIX

I.

A massive salt dune edges the north side of Charlestown on Terminal Street, but unlike the dunes in Provincetown and Truro, this one didn't result from millions of years of natural events. It resulted from a few months of dump trucks piling salt there for snowplows to use in the winter. In the summer the mound is covered with a dark tarp, a blackhead on the face of our historic town, but I guess the salt has to go somewhere.

I was parked across the street from the briny bank, eating a meatball sub and drinking a Coke, when my cell phone rang. I flipped it open and a man spoke.

"Watch your back. There's a hit on you." He hung up.

His voice sounded familiar, but he never said my name. If the warning were legitimate, he would have said my name. Right? The phone rang again, and again it was a restricted number, but this time it was Cameron O'Hanlon, my cousin on the Irish side of the family. Cam was one of Boston's finest, and after we exchanged hellos, he asked me if I was busy tomorrow. I told him I wasn't.

"Good, because there's a memorial service at Holyhood Cemetery, and I'd like you to go with me."

"Did someone in the family die?"

"No, nothing like that. It's an annual event, something to do with Irish history, a tribute to a rebel fighter named John Boyle O'Reilly, whoever he was. Anyway, my sergeant is playing the pipes at the service and I told him I'd go. I haven't seen you in a while, and I figured I could treat you to a burger at Doyle's afterwards."

"You hooked me with Doyle's," I said.

Cam told me that the service started at ten o'clock and that Holyhood Cemetery was located in Brookline. He also said that the graveyard wasn't very big and that I'd have no trouble finding the site once I got there. I finished my sandwich and drove to the noontime meeting at Saint Jude Thaddeus. At the end of the meeting we stood for the Lord's Prayer, stacked the chairs, mopped the floors, and locked the door.

So far, no one had tried to kill me.

II.

The next morning I took Route 9 to Brookline and turned on to Heath Street for the burial grounds. A plaque at the entrance read Holyhood Cemetery, Consecrated 1857. I drove through the gates and rolled past the Kennedy family plot and countless statues of the Blessed Mother and the headstone of James Connolly, a triple jumper from South Boston who won the first gold medal in the modern Olympic Games.

I powered down the windows and cruised on an asphalt lane on a perfect summer morning. A lone acorn popped under my tire, prompting a group of mourners to look my way. I crested a hill and heard the faint whine of a bagpipe, the drone of the dead, and I followed it over a leafy knoll to the site of the John Boyle O'Reilly Memorial.

My cousin Cameron O'Hanlon was standing next to a kilted piper, who seemed to be catching his breath between toots. I joined them on the greensward. The gathering was small, maybe fifty or sixty people, mostly older, mostly of Irish descent: men with ruddy complexions, women with rosary beads.

A priest with an Irish timbre invoked a Gaelic blessing. A wind gust bent the shrubs surrounding us. The altar server, a freckle-faced boy wearing a white surplice, lit an incense thurible that emitted a funereal scent. A chipmunk bustled out of the bending shrubs and burrowed into a decaying stump. I must have arrived late, because the priest closed his breviary and brought the service to an end. The piper blew a choppy rendition of *Danny Boy*, and when he finished, Cam introduced us.

"Dermot, this is Sergeant Fran Dillon."

"You played great," I said to Fran, a tall man with kind blue eyes.

In typical Boston-Irish fashion, Dillon sidestepped the praise. "Henderson bagpipes, even a greenhorn can sound okay with them." He fitted the pipes into a hard case and went on his way.

"Doyle's for lunch?" Cam asked.

"Sounds good to me," I said.

As I walked through the thick grass the back of my neck tingled, maybe from the eeriness of a graveyard, and then goosebumps prickled on my arms. I searched the grounds, but all I saw were old folks walking back to their cars. Then I heard a crack. A bullet ricocheted off a grave marker and a chip of granite struck my forehead. Stars flashed behind my eyes.

"Get down!" Cam yelled.

He knocked me flat as a second shot rang out. We crabbed to a gravestone and took cover. Cam came up, gun drawn, but he didn't fire. He sprinted to the hedged perimeter and then a hundred yards beyond to a stone wall that enclosed the cemetery. I did my best to keep up with him, but my legs still ached from the surgery and slowed me down. I eventually caught up to him. We saw nothing of the gunman.

"Your head is bleeding," he said.

"A piece of granite hit me," I said.

"I have to call this in, Dermot. Stick around."

"Right" I touched my forehead and looked at my bloody palm. "I guess the burger at Doyle's is out."

III.

Four hours later I was standing on my front steps with Captain Pruitt, who was not too pleased with me. "What happened to your face?"

"I was born this way."

"Wise ass, I'm talking about the cut on your head," Pruitt scoffed. "Tell me what's going on. First you get shot at the food pantry, and now someone shoots at you in a cemetery. What are you into?"

"Maybe he wasn't shooting at me," I said, not mentioning the phone warning. "Somebody fired a gun, that's all."

"Don't get cute with me. He aimed at you and he fired at you. It's a good thing Cam O'Hanlon knocked you down or you'd be dead." Pruitt stared at me, his intense brown eyes studying my face. "Look, Sparhawk, you're not bad a guy, and I'd hate like hell to see you get killed, but I can't help you if you don't tell me what's going on."

"I don't know what's going on, and that's the truth." Why didn't I want his help? "If I find out anything, I'll call you. Right now there's nothing to say."

Pruitt grumbled and cussed and said that I was holding out on him, and that I was a prima donna, and that I was trying to be a hero. He finally gave up and went back to his unmarked car and drove away. Another car pulled up as soon as Pruitt left. My cousin Cam O'Hanlon, no longer in uniform, got out carrying a shopping bag.

"I was waiting for Pruitt to leave," he said. "Let's go inside."

We went up to my apartment and sat in the parlor. I asked Cam if he wanted something to drink. He said no and put the shopping bag on the coffee table.

"A Kevlar vest," Cam said. "Someone is trying to kill you, and I'm not going to let that happen. Do you have any idea who it is?"

"I wish I did," I said.

"I saw your ad in the *Herald*." Cam sat on the couch and crossed his ankles. "Did anyone answer it?"

I was surprised that Captain Pruitt hadn't shoved the ad in my face as part of his upbraiding. Maybe he was saving it for later.

"A few people called, mostly cranks. Two of the callers sounded promising, so I met with them." I thought about Delia, the Blarney Stone waitress. I thought about "combover", the cabbie who didn't log the Charlestown fare. The last thing they needed was to get dragged in for questioning. "They didn't tell me much."

"You're something, you know that? A maniac is out there trying to kill you, and you want to do it all by yourself."

"Cam, I'm just trying to–"

"Don't bullshit me, Dermot." He walked to the door. "Wear the vest and don't tell anyone where you got it."

IV.

The graveyard gunfire and the telephone warning had to be connected. Maybe everything was connected: the pantry shooting, the money-fair heist, the cemetery, the warning. Or maybe I was trying to connect random events, forcing things together that didn't belong together, but that didn't seem likely. Something was going on, and I was in the middle of it. There had to be a common thread.

I wanted to talk to my Micmac kin, Glooscap and Harraseeket Kid. I wanted to hear what they thought of all this, so I drove to their auto body shop in Andrew Square and parked at the Quonset garage at the end of the lot. Harraseeket Kid was standing over a workbench reading a computer monitor when I walked in. His shiny black hair was wound into a ponytail, his bronze skin taut and flawless.

I cleared my throat.

"I know you're there, Dermot. You can't sneak up on a Micmac." He said this as he stared at the screen. "Everything is online these days. If you need a bumper, you buy it online. It used to be you looked it up in a parts manual and called in the order. Now it's two clicks and the bumper is paid for and ready to be shipped."

"Is that good or bad?" I asked.

Kid turned and looked at me. "Did a low-flying airplane clip your noggin?"

I started to explain and he cut me off.

"I heard what happened," Kid said. "Somebody shot at you and a piece of granite ricocheted off your head. Cam told me about it. He's worried about you."

"I know he is."

"I told Cam he had nothing to worry about." Kid clicked off the monitor and a smile creased his reddish face. "I told him I'd be cleaning and loading my rifles tonight when I got back to Charlestown."

"I'm sure that put his mind at ease." I slapped Kid on the shoulder. "I'd like to talk to you and Glooscap."

"He's in his office, let's go."

We went to Glooscap's office and found him sitting behind his old wooden desk, lighting a bulldog pipe. His face could have been a model for the profile on a buffalo nickel: strong nose, solid jaw, high cheekbones, heavy brow, and pewter-colored hair. He blew out the match with a plume of cloudy smoke and told us to sit down.

"I need your help," I said, smelling the burning tobacco.

"Go on, Dermot," Glooscap said. "We are listening."

I talked about the pantry shooting and the newspaper ad. I told them about the cocktail waitress and the cabbie. I filled them in on the World's Fair of Money and the $5,000 bill and the $100,000 bills. I finished by telling them about the warning and the gunfire at the cemetery. I didn't bother telling them about Shelley. It didn't seem relevant.

"You just gave us an immense amount of information." Glooscap took the pipe from his teeth and examined the bowl. "According to the waitress and the cabdriver, the youngster who shot you at the food pantry was Irish."

"That is correct."

"The other shooter, the one at the graveyard, got away clean," Glooscap said. "It is logical to assume that the two shootings are linked and may have ties to Ireland."

Kid said, "The Irish thing worries me, Dermot. If they want you dead, you're dead, end of discussion. The guy who called to warn you, was he Irish?"

"Not Irish, he was Boston all the way, neighborhood Boston, not a yuppie." I leaned back in the chair. "He sounded familiar."

Kid said, "Let's go back to what Glooscap just said. What if the waitress, what was her name again?"

"Delia."

"What if Delia and the cabdriver got together and concocted their stories? What if they were looking to score a few grand and conspired to snow you?"

"It's possible." I smiled. That's what I loved about Kid. He always looked for the angles. "But I don't think so."

"Why not?" Kid leaned forward, ready to fight for his case.

"I must have answered fifty calls on that ad, and almost all of them were bullshit. It's funny how easy it is to spot a bullshitter after a while. You don't even have to try it's so easy. " I thought about all the phone calls and something occurred to me. "I learned an important lesson these past few days."

Glooscap asked, "What lesson did you learn?"

"I learned that cops know when someone is lying to them," I said. "All you need is two ears, two eyes, and half a brain."

"That's why cops work in pairs," Kid said. "The two half-brains add up to one."

"Show some respect, Kid," Glooscap said, tapping his pipe in the ashtray. "Our law enforcement personnel keep peace in this city."

Kid rolled his eyes and asked me, "What about the cemetery shooting? Did anyone see anything?"

"No one has come forward yet," I said.

"It's a good thing Cam was there to save your ass, or we'd be planning your funeral right now," Kid said.

"I know that."

Glooscap asked, "What do you plan to do, Dermot?"

"I don't know." An image of Cam knocking me down flashed in my mind. "Kid is right. I'm alive because of Cam O'Hanlon."

"So what are you going to do?" Kid persisted.

"Maybe I should hide out until I come up with a plan."

"Hide out?" Kid snorted. "Micmacs don't hide out."

I knew what Kid meant. I didn't like the idea either.

"What if they come at me hard, Kid? I'll be putting everyone around me in danger." I stood and paced the room. "What happens to Buck if they storm the house? He's in a wheelchair."

Kid said, "Buck is a damn good shot. He took care of business with that shotgun when he had to. And I have rifles in the basement."

Preparing for a Charlestown gunfight didn't seem like the best strategy, but it had to be part of the strategy. If they, whoever they were, attacked the house, we had to be ready for them. When I suggested I might hide out, I was suggesting it for Buck's sake. My instinct is to attack, and a man should follow his instincts.

"Here's what I propose," I said. "We defend the house twenty-four seven, never leaving Buck alone. At the same time, I'll find out who's behind this."

Glooscap said, "I will help guard the house. We can divide the day into three eight-hour shifts, so we are fresh and alert." He puffed the pipe, getting the bowl fiery orange. "Come to think of it, we can divide it into four six-hour shifts. A tribal friend named Vic Lennox wants to stay busy now that he is retired."

Kid chuckled. "Vic is perfect. He is one angry son of a bitch."

"What do you mean?" I asked.

"He bit off a man's nipple in a bar fight in Allston." Kid sat back as if savoring the moment. "Some asshole gave Vic trouble, and Vic chomped on the guy's chest, bit him like a wolf in the grasslands. No one will get near Buck with Vic on duty."

"Probably should wear a chest protector if you fight him," I said. Another crazy Micmac from Antigonish, God save us. "We have a plan."

§

I left Glooscap's office and walked through the garage with Kid at my side. He stopped near a car lift and said, "You need a gun."

"I'd probably shoot myself in the foot."

"I'm not joking." Kid folded his arms across his chest. "You need protection."

A train leaving Andrew Station squealed and decompressed its air brakes. The piercing sound froze our conversation, putting us in limbo. The hissing ceased and the train lurched forward with a clunk of steel wheels on steel rails.

I said, "I have nothing against guns, but I made it this far in life without one. I think I can make it the rest of the way without one, too."

"I'm telling you, Dermot, the world out there is a shit hole, full of lowlifes and thugs. Use your head, get a gun."

"I'll think about it," I said.

We said goodbye and I left the garage. As I was walking to my car, I thought I saw something moving near the Quonset garage. I stopped and looked. Tall weeds and cat-o-nine-tails swayed in the wind and obstructed the sunlight, changing the reflections on the casement windows. Maybe that's what caught my attention.

I was wrong.

A man walked toward me from the weeds, his smile broadening as he approached me. Did I know him? He had red whiskers and bright eyes, and he picked up speed as he got closer. My antennae went up for a second time, but they went up too late. He pulled out a gun and shot me. The bullet knocked the breath out of my body. He shot me again. I could barely breathe. Kid charged past me and tackled the man to the ground. Gasping for air, I jumped on the pile. Kid and I wrestled the man, rolling in the dirt like wild animals. The gun discharged. The man stopped fighting.

"Holy shit!" Kid screamed. "What's with your breathing?"

"I got shot in the chest." I gasped for oxygen. "I'm wearing a vest."

The impact of the bullets, I couldn't get air. Kid tore open my shirt as I lay flat on the ground. He stripped free the Velcro straps and peeled the vest off my torso.

Kid said, "No blood, the vest absorbed the bullets. The bruising already started. Your ribs are probably cracked."

My breathing began to normalize. After a few minutes Kid helped me to my feet and pointed at the attacker and said, "He's not doing so hot."

"No, he's not." I squeezed the words out.

Except for the blood oozing out of a hole in his throat, the gunman lay stock-still. More blood seeped from his ears and nostrils. I studied his face, I didn't know him. I bent over, or at least tried to. My ribs throbbed as I checked for a wallet. His pockets were empty. A cell phone rang. I frisked him again and found nothing. It kept ringing. I rolled him on his side, corrupting the crime scene, and spotted the phone underneath him. I picked it up to answer it. Before I could say anything, a man with a brogue as thick as Mulligan stew said, "Don't say a word, just listen. The hit is off, Mac. Forget about Sparhawk and come home." He hung up.

"Who was that?" Kid asked.

"An Irishman calling off a hit on me," I said.

"*Now* will you get a gun?"

Glooscap came out of the shop and asked if we got hit. We assured him we were fine. He said, "The police will be here shortly."

I took a picture of the dead man with my cell phone, and I tucked his cell phone into my pocket. Five minutes later a cruiser sped into the lot with its siren booming. Another one drove in behind it, followed by an unmarked car. Two uniformed cops cordoned off the area with yellow tape. A forensics team arrived and unpacked their van.

An older detective with gray hair and tired eyes looked at me. I was shirtless and bruising and aching like a bastard. He said, "You need medical attention. I'll phone for an ambulance. Let me see your license." I handed it to him. He went back to his car and got on the radio. When he returned he pointed at Kid and said, "Get in the back of my car. We need to talk downtown."

The detective grabbed one of the uniformed cops and walked him over to me. He told me that the officer would follow me to the hospital and drive me to headquarters after the doctors gave the okay. And that's the way it went. An ambulance took me to the hospital and a doctor examined me. She told me that my ribs were bruised but not broken, and that my welts were raw but not infected. After she cleared me, the cop drove me to headquarters.

V.

The police grilled me for three hours, and despite their verbal barrage, I didn't give them much of value. I didn't tell them that Cam had given me the Kevlar vest, and oddly enough they didn't seem to care where I got it. I didn't mention the dead man's cell phone or the Irishman's phone call. They finished the interrogation and let me out.

When I got home I saw that Buck's apartment door was open. He must have heard me in the stairwell, because he yelled for me to come in. Harraseeket Kid was relaxing in a recliner with a rifle on his lap. Buck was in his wheelchair next to him, unarmed. I sat on the couch and looked at Kid.

"How did it go at headquarters?" I asked.

"No problem," he said.

I rubbed my throbbing temples with the heels of my hands and said, "Someone wants to kill me."

"You should have been a detective," Kid quipped.

"And you two could get killed as collateral damage," I said.

"Nobody's going to kill us." Kid held up his rifle. "We can protect ourselves. We have an army of men at our disposal: Glooscap, Vic Lennox, you, me, Buck. I'm arming Buck with a shotgun, a pump-action twelve-gauge, which I'll be loading pronto. I'm buying him more ammo, too."

I wish I were still wearing my Kevlar vest.

"I talked to Glooscap on the way over here," I said, hoping to change topics and quell Kid's bluster. "We're relocating for a week."

"Relocating?" Kid snapped.

"I'll be getting a hotel room. You two will be staying with Glooscap in Dorchester." I turned to Buck and said, "Glooscap owns a huge house in Clam Point. It's a safe place."

Buck nodded. Kid shook his head in dispute.

"I say we stand our ground right here in Charlestown. We're gonna look like a bunch of pussies if we up and run." Kid waited for me to respond, but I didn't, and he kept talking. "How do we catch these guys if we run away?"

"We're relocating, not running away," I said. "To answer your question, I don't know how we're going to catch them, because I don't know who they are. I don't want anyone getting killed, including me. Moving is a safety measure, not a surrender."

"I don't like it," Kid said. "You've been shot to shit."

"I know that."

"And I want to blast back." Kid held up the rifle again. "I don't believe in foxholes, Dermot. I want to fight these bastards head-on."

"We'll get our chance to fight, but let's get our footing first." I looked at Kid and said, "Foxholes aren't a bad thing when you don't know who's shooting at you."

Buck added, "Dermot discussed the plan with your father, Kid. Glooscap is a smart man."

"Glooscap is a smart man," Kid mocked. "Gimme a friggin' break."

We talked more about it and got everything out in the open. Kid finally relented and agreed to the idea. Buck rolled forward.

"Where did you say in Dorchester?"

"Mill Street in the Clam Point section," I said. "We move tomorrow."

CHAPTER SEVEN

I.

The next evening I went to the Blarney Stone to talk to Delia. She walked by my table without noticing me, so I waited. She jotted down an order from a couple at the next table and then she came to me.

"What'll ya have?" she asked, staring at her jotter.

"A warm Coke," I said.

She looked up. "What are you doing here? I told you I don't want to involve my work."

"It's too late for that, Delia." I stood up. "What time do you get off?"

"You got nerve, you know that?" She knew I wasn't going to budge. "My shift ends in ten minutes. Why?"

"We need to talk."

"What if I don't want to talk?" She pouted.

"We have to talk," I said. "I'd rather not make a scene in here."

"Damn you!" She shoved the pencil in her breast pocket. "You're an asshole, you know that?"

"I do what I have to do."

"Meet me out front in ten minutes," she said. "I don't want you lurking around in here getting me in trouble."

"Outside in ten," I said.

I sat on the hood of my car and waited. Fifteen minutes later Delia came out of the bar and lit a Chesterfield non-filter with a match.

"I was hoping you'd be gone."

"Not a chance," I said.

The tobacco's effect showed in her posture. Her shoulders relaxed and her face calmed. She dragged again and exhaled a chimney's worth of exhaust into the air.

"What's so important you had to harass me at work?" she asked.

"I want to show you a picture." I brought up a photo on my cell phone. "The last time we talked you mentioned a man named Mac. Is this him?"

I showed her the image. Delia gasped when she saw it.

"That's Mac," she said in a shrill voice. "What happened to him?"

"Mac is dead." I told her.

"Dead?"

"He shot me, but I was wearing a bulletproof vest." I lifted my shirt and showed her the purpling welts. "We wrestled, his gun went off, and the bullet killed him."

"I can't believe this." She took a big drag. "Who the hell are you?"

"I didn't want to kill him," I said.

"If you didn't want to kill him, why is he dead?" She threw the cigarette at me and ran back to the Blarney Stone. When she got to the door, she turned and said, "Stay away from me or I'll call the cops."

II.

That night I stayed at the Boston Harbor Hotel at Rowes Wharf, a ritzy place that I never would have considered before the reward money. The facilities were tops and the staff was courteous, but I felt like an intruder, a voyeur peering into a world where I didn't belong. The feeling of being an outsider could probably be traced back to my growing up in the projects. A football scholarship and a college degree can't blot out a childhood of poverty.

Up in my room I took off my shirt and looked at myself in the beveled mirror. The two bruises were darkening on my chest, one below my heart, one on the side of my stomach. Earlier today the bruises were raw and red. Soon they'd be mushy and purple. Thank God for the Kevlar vest or I'd be dead.

I undressed and took a long, hot shower and slept well that night. In the morning I put on the courtesy bathrobe with a snappy logo on the breast and ordered room service. Fifteen minutes later an efficient Hispanic woman delivered a pot of coffee and a hot breakfast. I was drowsing in my bed with a full belly and enjoying the rising sun when my cell phone rang. The caller ID told me it was Superintendent Hanson. I prepared for his brusqueness.

"Hello, Superintendent."

"This is important, Sparhawk, so listen closely."

"Top of the morning to you, too," I said.

"I got a call from the commissioner, who got a call from the mayor, who probably got a call from some muckety-muck in Washington. They want you at headquarters today at four o'clock. Some big shot wants to talk to you."

Hanson didn't need to qualify the importance of his phone call by mentioning the commissioner and mayor and muckety-mucks. A call from a police superintendent is by definition important.

"What's it about?" I asked.

"Just be here at four."

He hung up.

§

At three-fifteen I went down to the lobby and told the desk clerk that I needed my car. A parking attendant retrieved it, I tipped him twenty, and twenty minutes later I arrived at police headquarters, where I ran into Captain Pruitt. He was standing outside the building smoking a Winchester cigar.

"Did Hanson summon you here?" he asked.

"Yup. Any idea what it's about?"

"Some honcho from D.C. wants to talk to you." Pruitt took a puff. "Anyone take a shot at you today?"

"Not yet," I said.

Pruitt chuckled and walked toward the parking lot. I stepped into police headquarters and an officer named Partridge, who sometimes served as Hanson's attaché, walked up to me.

"Follow me, Mr. Sparhawk." As we walked down a tiled corridor, Partridge said, "How are the legs?"

"Excuse me?"

"My partner and I answered the call the night you got shot," he said. "You were bleeding pretty badly."

"The legs are fine," I said. "Thanks for the help."

"All part of the job."

Partridge led me into a conference room, said good luck and left. Moments later Hanson came in, accompanied by a big man with a flawlessly shaven head, which shined as if it had been simonized. He had a reddish complexion and a prominent nose. The big man stared at me a little longer than he should have and said, "Are you part Indian?"

"Half Micmac," I answered.

"I'm half Lakota-Cherokee. My name is Kenny Bowen." He extended a sizable mitt and we shook hands. He looked at Hanson and said, "Thank you, Superintendent. That will be all."

Hanson wasn't used to being dismissed, and it showed in his awkward exit from the room. I smiled broadly as he slunk out, hoping he'd look my way, but he didn't. An opportunity lost. Bowen sat in a chair and invited me to join him across the table.

"I'm a private insurance investigator," he said. "I specialize in the recovery of big-ticket items. The companies I work for do not care how I get the stolen goods back, as long as I get them back. If I'm successful, which I usually am, I get twenty percent of the market value."

"Twenty percent sounds lucrative," I said.

"It is very lucrative." He crossed his brawny arms across his thick chest and leaned back. "A well-known insurance company has hired me to recover the four sheets of $100,000 bills that were stolen from the World's Fair of Money, a total of 128 bills."

"Hanson told me about the Hynes heist," I said.

"You killed a man who was holding a $5,000 bill, a bill stolen from the money fair. Do you have anything to say about that?" Bowen asked.

"Where's my twenty percent?"

"Right." Kenny Bowen slapped his big mitt on the table. "I didn't think of that."

"I killed him in self-defense," I said. "You can ask Hanson."

"I already asked him," Bowen said. "You killed another man, too."

"Also in self-defense, and only after he shot me twice in the chest," I said, sounding defensive.

"I'd have done the same in your position." He shifted in his seat. "In my line of work I look for patterns that lead to recovery, and the only pattern I have is you."

"I don't know anything."

"You don't know anything?" Bowen scoffed. "You killed a man who had a $5,000 bill from the money fair. You killed another man who might have been involved in the same heist. Nobody in law enforcement can identify either of these men."

"I'm going to save you some time, Kenny," I said. "I can't identify them, either."

He inhaled deeply and let a windy stream of air out his nostrils. He tugged his tie and pulled cufflinks. "I want to work with you, Dermot, the two of us together." He extended arms outward in a gesture of openness. "I'll give you half of my take, half the reward money if we recover the loot. We each get ten percent."

"That's serious money," I said. "What's your angle?"

"No angle." He rubbed his gleaming head. "You're the only person who knows anything about the robbery, besides the police, and they don't know much."

"I told you, I don't know anything."

"Yes, you do." He rolled his meaty neck. "I'm a businessman, Dermot. I look at the big picture, and the big picture is this: I need your help and I'm willing to pay for it. My offer has nothing to do with generosity or altruism. It has to do with money. I'd rather get ten percent of something, than twenty percent of nothing."

"You're looking at ten percent of nothing, because I can't help you." I got up from the table. "Besides, I work better alone."

"That's your answer?" Kenny said. "You work better alone?"

"That's my answer." I started for the door.

"I'm not a man who gives up easily," he said, squeezing the bridge of his nose with a thumb and forefinger. "I'm not going away, Dermot. You're the only lead I've got."

"Then I guess I'll be seeing you around."

"You can count on it." Kenny stood up. "You're staying at the Boston Harbor Hotel, is that correct?"

"How did you know that?"

"See how easy it was to track you down? And I'm not trying to kill you."

III.

Back in the hotel room I called Buck Louis at Glooscap's house and asked him about Sleddog the giant malamute, another displaced Townie.

"Sleddog loves trains," Buck said. "The house is up against the tracks, and he howls every time a train goes by. He is doing just fine, but I can tell that's not why you called. What's going on?"

"I need information on a guy named Kenny Bowen," I said.

"I'm logging on as we speak," Buck said.

"Bowen is about my age. He says he's half Indian, as in Native American. He works in the insurance field as a private investigator. Bowen seems aboveboard, but I want to make sure. Is that enough to get you started?"

"More than enough," Buck said. "Give me an hour."

I hung up.

I turned on ESPN Classic and watched a championship fight from 1962, between Emile Griffith and Benny "Kid" Paret. It was their third meeting, according to legendary boxing announcer Don Dunphy. At stake, the world welterweight title. The bell rang and the action began, with both fighters feeling each other out. The momentum went back and forth in the early rounds, neither man taking control of the match, a contest with plenty of action but not much excitement. Then in the twelfth round the intensity picked up. Griffith battered Paret into the corner, nailing him with power punches to the jaw and head. Paret got hung up in the ropes and Griffith loosed the missiles. The ref stopped the fight and the grainy footage changed to color. The analysts in the studio said that there was no return bout, because Benny Paret died that night at Roosevelt Hospital in Manhattan.

Buck called back and told me what he had learned.

"Kenneth Bowen graduated from Dartmouth College, summa cum laude, with a double major in economics and political science. He was an All-American shot putter on the track team and won the Ivy League title in both his junior and senior years. He then competed in the Olympics, representing the United Sates, but didn't medal. After the Olympics he spent three years at Oxford. Bowen is a Rhodes Scholar."

"Impressive resume," I said.

"From Oxford he went to Washington as an insurance lobbyist, where he lobbied for five years. Then he started a firm called The Bowen Group, whose chief client is the federal government." Buck paused. "This guy is plugged in, Dermot. I found pictures of him with senators. He attended a presidential ball."

"Great stuff, Buck. Anything else?"

"I don't know if this is important or not, but Bowen received a full scholarship to Dartmouth."

"Athletic? Academic?"

"The Occom Scholars Program for Indians," Buck said. "If an applicant is at least one-eighth Native American and smart enough to get into the school, said applicant goes for free. Bowen qualified."

"This guy's a modern-day Jim Thorpe."

IV.

I took a nap and awoke at nine o'clock. The night skies were gray with clouds, but even in darkness you could feel a front coming in. I got out of bed and stretched my arms to the ceiling. My spine went snap-crackle-pop, my head cleared, and my stomach growled for food. I called the front desk and they recommended the hotel restaurant, the Rowes Wharf Sea Grille, saying it had a four-star rating. I booked a reservation, showered, and went down to eat.

The dining room was almost empty at this later hour. The hostess seated me at a choice window table and handed me a menu. A waitress came and I ordered swordfish with asparagus and mashed potatoes. After the main course, I asked for coffee. The waitress was refilling my coffee cup just as the rain started to fall. It was a light rain, not much more than a Scotch mist. I listened to the droplets spatter the glass.

I initialed the bill and went out to Rowes Wharf to walk off the meal. The whitecaps were becoming choppier as the winds grew stronger, and the drizzle intensified to a heavy downpour. The deluge deadened the sounds of the city, and for some strange reason I felt secure, untouchable. I strolled on the boardwalk, anonymous in the squall, hidden amid the raindrops pelting the pavement. I came to the Northern Avenue Bridge, now a pedestrian bridge, and crossed it to the Seaport District as torrents of water drenched my clothes.

I was halfway across when a man came toward me at a fast pace, and it was apparent from his stride that he was focused and serious. I slowed down, and when I did, he unzipped his soaked windbreaker. Something was wrong. I ran for the railing to jump off the bridge, but I ran too late. He took out a gun and fired twice.

I was still on my feet.

He ran past me, bumping my shoulder. Another man who had been standing behind me fell to the pavement. Two bullet holes were bored into his head. The back of his skull was blown off. Shards of bone and chunks of brain stuck to the grating, glued by blood, and blood dripped between the grilles to Fort Point Channel below. A revolver rested in the dead man's hand, the hammer cocked. The man who shot him turned around and came back toward me.

I ran like hell, ducking and zigzagging so I'd be tougher to hit. The man caught up to me. I might as well have been running in the Dorchester mud flats wearing flippers. He sprinted in front of me and waved his hands. He said something I couldn't understand and then he said Kenny Bowen's name. He said that he was on my side, that he was hired to protect me. He raced ahead again and laid his gun on the ground. If this greyhound wanted to shoot me, he would have done so by now. I stopped running and panted for air. The man walked up to me.

"My name is Rat T. Kennedy," he said, showing no signs of exertion. "Kenny Bowen sent me to watch over you." He pointed back to the lifeless lump on the bridge. "That man was contracted to kill you. I pegged him in the hotel lobby earlier today."

"You pegged him in the lobby?" I was still catching my breath. "How did he find me there?"

"I don't know, but you better check out fast," said Rat T., a fit man with a red crew cut. "Another thing, you'd better get out of here before the police come."

"Why? I didn't do anything wrong."

"Explaining another dead body?" He picked up his gun and holstered it. "That's the last thing you need, Sparhawk."

He had a point. I could picture the interrogation, sandwiched between Hanson and Pruitt, with Partridge in the wings.

"Maybe you're right about that," I admitted.

I took Rat T's suggestion and got out of there, but I didn't like it. I was postponing the inevitable. Cops always get to the truth, even if they have to make it up.

§

I went back to the hotel, packed my stuff, checked out, and headed south for Glooscap's house in Dorchester. It was a five-mile jaunt that seemed like a Magellan journey, each mile a marathon, each exit a new time zone. With my nerves on tenterhooks and my mind on corpses, I slogged ahead on the Expressway, hydroplaning through sheets of water, and pulling up at Glooscap's without remembering driving there. Harraseeket Kid opened the front door.

"What happened to you?" he asked.

"Someone tried to kill me," I said. "I was staying at a hotel and a hit man found me there. How did he know I was there?"

"Come in out of the rain."

"I forgot the vest, figured I was dead."

"Come in, damn it." Kid swung the door wide. "You'll die of pneumonia and do the killer's job for him."

"I thought I was going to die, Kid." I stood in the rain. "A guy fired twice and killed the man behind me."

"You aren't making sense." Kid grabbed my shirt and pulled me inside. We went to the back room, where he threw me a towel. "Tell me what happened."

I told him.

"Any people around?" he asked.

"It was pouring out."

"Tell me more about Kenny Bowen," Kid said.

I told him about the meeting with Bowen at police headquarters. I told him about the background information that Buck dug up on him.

"Bowen needs you alive to find the money," Kid said.

"I guess you're right about that." I had to agree with him. "He hired a man to watch over me."

"Bowen supposedly saved your life tonight, Dermot."

"Supposedly saved my life?" I would have laughed if I had the strength. "What are you getting at, Kid? What do you mean by supposedly?"

"What if Bowen staged the shooting to get you on his side?"

"The back of a man's head was splattered all over the bridge," I said. "That would be hard to stage."

"Hard, but not impossible. How close were you to the dead body?" Kid asked. "How well did you see it? Remember, it was pouring out."

"I saw it clearly, at least I think I saw it clearly." I thought back to the bridge and my mind raced. "I don't know, I'm not sure."

V.

I slept until noon on a pullout couch in the three-season porch at the back of the house. A commuter train roared past and rattled the windows. Sleddog howled and moaned from the basement. In the kitchen I loaded the coffeemaker and started it brewing. Drops of coffee plunked in the pot and after a while the coffeemaker hissed and stopped dripping. I drank a cup and the caffeine cleared my head.

I turned on the radio, listened to the news, and heard nothing about a shooting in Boston. I saw the Herald on the counter and read the city section. Again, nothing about a shooting. Maybe Harraseeket Kid was on to something. Maybe Kenny Bowen had stage-managed the killing on the bridge.

But my thinking had cleared up after a sound sleep. In computer lingo, my mind had defragged. The scattered pieces of memory had reassembled into a lucid account of the shooting, and the imagery of it was nasty. Skull fragments, brain chunks, blood spillage. I pictured the lifeless eyes, eyes that could only belong to a dead man.

The killing was no hoax. Rat T. Kennedy blew the back of the man's head off. So why was there nothing on the news? Why nothing in the paper? Boston loves a juicy murder story, especially a murder outside a federal courthouse.

CHAPTER EIGHT

I.

That evening I parked in front of the Knights of Columbus and walked to Jackie Tracy's house on Chappie Street. I went up the stairs to his back porch, out of the view of cars and pedestrians and would-be assassins. The doorbell was gummed up with old paint so I knocked. Jackie opened the door and blinked when he saw my face. Jackie Tracy blink?

"Dermot?"

"Hey, Jackie."

He welcomed me in, but it was a halfhearted welcome, the type you'd get from a man who owed you money. He led me into the parlor. The Red Sox were on the flat screen playing the Orioles in Baltimore, with Boston wearing their road grays. Jackie waved to a chair and told me to have a seat. He sat in a recliner, drank some beer from a tall can, and said, "Look at that slob on the mound tonight. He's fat and lazy and doesn't give a shit about the game. Not an ounce of muscle on him."

"He must have a strong neck to hold up all those chins," I said.

"All those chins!" Jackie roared. "You have your old man's sense of humor, you know that?"

"Thanks, Jackie. What I don't have is a gun."

"A gun? What do you want with a gun?" He rested the beer can on his knee. "You're a good kid, Dermot. Don't go screwing with guns. You'll get yourself nothing but trouble."

"I already got nothing but trouble," I said. "People are trying to kill me, and they all had guns."

"Who's trying to kill you?" Jackie asked.

"I don't know who, and I don't know why, but they're bent on taking me out." I grabbed the remote and clicked the mute button. "I need a gun for protection, Jackie."

"Forget about guns." His eyes darted. "Leave town for a while, go away somewhere. Whatever it is will blow over."

"Blow over?" I said.

Jackie's body stiffened. He became cautious, looking at his watch, rubbing his forehead. No eye contact, no Townie warmth. He wanted me out of there, but why? What was going on? I studied him, the set of his jaw, the fear in his eyes, and it came to me. Jackie knew who was after me. I grabbed the remote and clicked off the game.

"A man called me the other day," I said. "He was a Boston guy, could have been a Townie. I think he was worried about me, because he gave me a warning. He said there was a hit on me."

Jackie stared out the window.

I continued, "He must have been a friend, because only a friend would warn me of danger."

"You have lots of friends," he mumbled.

"This particular friend was plugged in. He knew things that no one else would know. He knew there was a hit on me. Tell me, Jackie, how many people would know there was a hit on me?"

"How should I know?" he said without conviction. "Maybe it was a joke. Maybe the guy was having a little fun at your expense."

"The next day a man took a shot at me in Holyhood Cemetery. In the middle of the day he fired a gun at me. No, Jackie, it was no joke."

"Maybe someone from the projects called you," he said. "You know everybody in the projects. Some of those guys know things."

"This guy had inside information." I tried to make eye contact, but Jackie averted my gaze. "I appreciated what he did, by the way. Because the way I see it, he was looking out for me."

"Then he was a good guy."

"And then I got a second call."

"A second call?" Jackie turned and looked at me. "You got a second call?"

"I got two calls, Jackie. The second one came from an Irishman with a heavy brogue. He called to *cancel* a hit on me."

"You're making no sense." Jackie said, his poker face now gone. "Why would he call *you* to cancel a hit on *you?*"

"He didn't call me intentionally. He called a guy named Mac. Mac shot me at my uncle's garage. I was wearing a Kevlar vest."

"Thank God for that." He sounded genuine.

"Mac and I fought, his gun went off, and now he's dead. I bet Mac was the shooter at Holyhood Cemetery, too. If the cops can find a bullet at Holyhood, they'll compare it to the one they got from Mac's throat." I now had Jackie's full attention. "Mac was dead on the ground when his phone rang. I answered it. The man on the other end, the guy with the brogue I was telling you about, said, 'The hit is off, Mac. Forget about Sparhawk and come home.'"

"That's what he said?"

"That's how I knew the guy's name was Mac. Here's another thing. Mac had no identification, just like the shooter at the food pantry."

"Do the police know his name was Mac?" Jackie asked.

"Only you know and I know."

"We have to talk, Dermot," Jackie said. "And this talk we're about to have never took place."

I nodded.

"You have to let go of this thing. The men you're up against will stop at nothing."

"I'm going after them," I said.

"You don't want to do that."

"I need a gun, Jackie."

"A gun won't do you any good, because you're going up against an army, the Irish Republican Army. And they won't stop 'til they kill you."

"The Irish Republican Army?" I could hear my voice stammering. "What did I do to them?"

Jackie sighed and grunted. He looked up to the ceiling and shook his elephantine head. He lowered his eyes, looked out the window, and said, "A few years ago an Irishman went to your office, a little guy with a birthmark on his face. He asked you about some museum paintings."

"I remember him." I could still picture the runt's face. "He was a pushy little bastard. I didn't like him."

"Well that pushy bastard, as you just called him, is Liam McGrew, a high-ranking IRA soldier. The only reason he didn't whack you back then was another big shot called him off." Jackie leaned forward. "The kid you killed at the food pantry was Liam's grandson Alroy McGrew."

"Shit."

"You said it." Jackie picked up the remote, looked at it, and put it back down. "Liam is dying back there in Belfast and he wants you dead."

It didn't seem possible. "Liam ordered his grandson to kill me because I tossed him out of my office?"

"It wasn't Liam's idea to have Alroy take a run at you." Jackie drained his beer. "Alroy overheard Liam ranting about how he wanted to get even with you. The kid decided to do the job himself, probably to impress his grandfather."

"This is crazy."

"I need another beer." Jackie left the room and came back with a frosty.

"What about this guy Mac?" I asked.

"Mac was another IRA soldier." He reclined on the Lazy-Z-Boy and took a swig. "Two IRA guys are dead because of you."

"What did I get myself into?" I looked at Jackie's beer can, ice cold, freshly cracked open. "What about the guy on the Northern Avenue Bridge? Was he IRA, too."

"What guy on the bridge?" He brought the recliner forward. "Who are you talking about?"

I told Jackie what happened on the bridge. I told him about the man who saved my life, though I didn't mention Rat T. Kennedy by name. I didn't tell him about Kenny Bowen, either.

Jackie asked, "Who was the guy that saved you? What was his name?"

"Never mind about him." I leaned forward and opened my palms. "Now do you see why I need a gun?"

He reclined again and let out a belch.

"Leave town, Dermot. Liam McGrew is a very sick man, practically dead. He'll be history in a few months."

"A few months is a long time when someone is trying to kill you," I said. "Will you give me a gun or not?"

Jackie looked at the black flat-screen. "I'm sorry, Dermot, no gun."

Something didn't make sense. "Why did you tell me about Liam McGrew?"

Jackie stared out the window and didn't answer.

"Come on, Jackie, why did you tell me about Liam?"

"It has to do with Mac," Jackie said. "I sold a gun to Mac, but I didn't know he was buying it to kill you. If I knew that, I wouldn't have sold it to him, and that's the truth. There are levels of loyalty and sometimes the lines get blurred, but I would *never* set up a Townie to get killed, not unless he deserved it, and you don't deserve it. No more questions, Dermot. I can't say anything else."

I listened to Jackie, but my mind was elsewhere. It was sorting the information on Liam McGrew. A sketchy picture of the money-fair heist formed in my head, and minutes later the picture became clear. I knew what was going on, not all of it, but enough to get to the bottom of this mess. All I had to do now was triangulate and decipher. Simple, like a blind man solving a Rubik's Cube in the dark.

II.

The next morning I was sitting in Glooscap's kitchen reading the newspaper when Buck Louis and Harraseeket Kid came in. I had asked them to meet with me to discuss what I'd learned from Jackie Tracy.

"I'd like to bounce an idea off you guys," I said.

Kid said, "Let's hear it."

Buck rolled forward. "I love this stuff."

I thought about where to start.

"The kid who shot me at the pantry came from Belfast. His name was Alroy McGrew. The gunman at the garage also came from Belfast. His name was Mac. Alroy and Mac are members of the Irish Republican Army."

Kid asked, "The guy you killed at the garage was IRA?"

I told them the story about Alroy's grandfather, Liam McGrew. I recounted Liam's visit to my office a few years ago, and how I threw him out. Buck and Kid remembered Liam. Having established that, I moved ahead.

"Do you remember Halloran?" I asked.

"Sure, Halloran, the rich guy from Weston," Buck said.

"The smug bastard you straightened out." Kid added. "Of course we remember him."

"I believe that Halloran and Liam McGrew conspired to rob the World's Fair of Money. Big-time crimes call for big-time planning. You need money to bribe people, you need political clout to manipulate things. Halloran has both."

Kid countered. "But Halloran doesn't need money. He'd go to jail if he got caught. Why would a billionaire like Halloran take a risk like that?"

"Because it's not about the money for Halloran," I said. "It's about the power, the thrill. Crime gives Halloran a weird sense of fulfillment."

Kid asked, "Are you saying that Halloran was the brains behind the museum heist twenty years ago and the money-fair heist last week?"

"That's what I'm saying," I said. "We know that Halloran had a part in the museum heist. Remember the painting he bought?"

Kid nodded. "The painting turned out to be a forgery."

I thought back to the museum case.

"The thieves didn't know they were selling Halloran a forgery," I said. "They thought the painting was real."

Buck said, "Nobody would have thought it was a fake. The painting was stolen from a museum."

Kid asked, "So, why would Halloran hire Liam again? If Liam conned him once, why would he hire him again?"

"Because Halloran now knows that Liam didn't con him. He now knows what really happened the night of the museum heist. Halloran also knows the thieves didn't deliberately sell him a forged painting. He knows because I told him."

Buck rolled back a foot. "Sounds like you're guessing."

"It's a guess based on facts," I said.

Kid said, "But it's still a guess."

It might have been a guess, but all the pieces fit together.

"Alroy McGrew was Liam's grandson. Alroy had a $5,000 bill from the money fair. Liam is IRA. Two years ago Liam came to my office and asked about the museum heist, not directly, but that's what he was asking about. Halloran purchased a painting stolen from the museum from Liam McGrew."

Buck, sounding incredulous, said, "And from that small coincidence you've concluded that Halloran and Liam pulled off the money-fair heist, too?"

"Alroy McGrew was in on the money-fair theft. Nobody is disputing that," I said. "These two robberies were extraordinary, and although they happened twenty years apart, I am convinced that Halloran engineered both of them. And then he hired Liam McGrew to do the dirty work, execute the robberies."

We remained silent for a time, and in the silence my own scheme formulated.

"Kid, can you attach a snowplow to the wrecker?" I asked.

"It's the middle of summer," he said.

"I know, but can you hook one up?"

"Yeah, but why?"

"If we can spook Halloran into the open, if we can scare him into making a run for it with the money, we can nail him."

"How?" Kid asked, now sounding interested.

"We can block his driveway with the wrecker and plow," I said.

Kid shook his head. "No, I mean how can we spook him?"

"Leave that to me," I said. "If we can block him from bolting, that's all I need."

Buck rolled back and forth. "It sounds crazy."

Kid said, "We'll ram the son of a bitch head-on."

"We have to act fast. Get the wrecker ready, Kid." I thought about what else I wanted for the job. "Can we get a camera mounted on the plow?"

Buck said, "You'll incriminate yourself filming it."

"Nothing will end up in court." I assured them. "We'll use it against Halloran."

Kid said, "I know a guy in Southie who can mount a camera on anything. He has all kinds of surveillance equipment."

"Call him," I said. "Tell him we'll make it worth his while. I'll call Kenny Bowen. We're going to need him for this to work."

I called Kenny Bowen and said that I wanted to see him. We agreed on a time and a place. I went out to my car and drove to Cambridge.

III.

Kenny told me to meet him at twelve noon in the recesses of Harvard Stadium, where he trained with former Ivy League trackmen in a makeshift gym. I parked on North Harvard Street, facing the Charles River, and entered the ivied grounds through an open gate. Two young women wearing crimson shorts jogged on the track that circled the football field. They chatted as they trotted, showing no signs of fatigue. I walked under the U-shaped stands and heard a thumping noise in the distance. I followed the sound to a metal door that led underneath the concrete stands and went in.

Crouching into a deep squat with a barbell across his shoulders was Kenny Bowen. He exploded up, his legs driving, his back stable, his neck bulled. The bumper plates thumped with ferocity when he hit the top of the movement. He racked the bar and toweled his shorn head. Kenny was so absorbed in the exercise that he didn't hear me come in. I cleared my throat.

He turned and said, "Ready for a workout?"

"Not today." I looked at the drab surroundings. "Nice setup you got here. It makes you feel like, ah—"

"Like a man?"

"That fits." A single light bulb lit the spartan room, adding to its dungeon charm. "The place is perfect."

"I'll give you a key," he said. "What's on your mind?"

"Who is Rat T. Kennedy?"

He laughed and shook his shining head.

"Rat T. and I met at the Millrose Games when we were in college. He ran the mile for Northeastern." Kenny threw the towel to the corner. "Is that why you wanted to see me, to ask about Rat T. Kennedy?"

"A miler." I laughed. "He chased me down in a second." I picked up a fifty pound dumbbell and curled it with my right arm. "What happened to the body on the bridge? How come there was nothing in the news?"

"The FBI handled the cadaver," he said. "The FBI is handing all of it. The press, the investigation, forensics, they have it covered."

"I guess that explains it." I dropped the dumbbell and picked it up with my left hand and curled it a few times, talking as I pumped. "I need your help."

"I've been waiting for you to say that." Kenny's Cherokee nose reminded me of Glooscap's honker. "What do you need?"

"I know how to get the money back," I said. "And I know who's trying to kill me. I need your help on both."

"That's what I've been waiting to hear." He nodded, seemingly pleased. "My offer still stands. You get half the reward money on everything we recoup."

The reward money sounded good, but staying alive sounded better. I determined that Kenny Bowen would give me the best chance at staying alive, and at that moment I decided to trust him. My gut told me he was okay.

"I'll tell you what happened," I said. "And then I'll tell you what I intend to do about it."

I went through everything I knew, and then I told Kenny my plan. He seemed impressed with the info, but less impressed with the plan.

"Tell me your plan again," Kenny said. "I think I missed something."

"I am going to Halloran's house and ask him to give me the sheets of money."

"That's it?" Kenny's head dropped. "That's your plan?"

"Yup, that's my plan."

"What if Halloran says no?" Kenny said, and then waved his hand. "Let me put it another way. When Halloran says no, what is Plan B?"

"If he says no, I'll take the money away from him." I crossed my arms, shrugged, and cracked my neck and shoulders. It felt good to lift a few weights. It felt foreign, too. "That's where you come in."

"I'm ready," Kenny said, now sounding eager. "What do I do?"

"Can you get a search warrant for Halloran's house?" I asked.

"Based on what?"

"Based on a lie," I said. "If I swear that I saw the sheets of money in Halloran's house, can you get a search warrant?"

"You'll be charged with perjury, obstruction, and who knows what else." The eagerness left Kenny's face. "You could end up in prison."

"Do you want to get the money back or not?" I stepped up to him. "Halloran is nothing more than a crook, a wealthy crook, a serious crook, but a crook. He'll stop at nothing to keep those sheets. He will cheat, bribe, intimidate, whatever it takes."

"You make him sound like a mobster."

"He is a like a mobster, a coward too, and I want to take him down," I said. "Halloran is connected to the top. That's why I need you, because you operate on the same level as Halloran."

"I'm not sure how to take that."

I moved closer to him, getting in his space. "If you want the money back, if you *really* want it back, we have to get tough with this clown. We have to bust heads. So I'll ask again, can you get a search warrant if I swear out an affidavit?"

"Give me a minute to think, will you? You're coming at me fast." Kenny picked up a fifty-pound dumbbell and did one-armed presses. On the last rep he dropped the weight to the floor and blew out air. "The probable cause is weak. And even if we got a warrant, Halloran could get it quashed."

I sat on a weight bench. "Can we coerce a judge?"

"What?"

"Halloran must have enemies," I said. "You don't get to where he got without burning a few people along the way."

"Let's suppose he has enemies," Kenny said. "What does that have to do with coercing a judge?"

"The heist is a federal case," I said. "The Treasury Department is involved."

"It is a federal case." Kenny agreed. "Treasury is my client."

"Who would prosecute this type of case?" I asked.

"The US Attorney's Office in Boston," Kenny answered.

"You must know people in the US Attorney's Office."

"I do." Kenny sat next to me on the bench. "I'm familiar with Maddy Savitz."

"The US Attorney in Boston?" I said.

"The US Attorney for the District of Massachusetts." Kenny got off the bench and squatted low, leaning his back against the wall. "I don't know Maddy personally, but I can reach out to her through a connection."

"Can you set up a meeting with her?" I asked.

"Why?" Kenny looked up from where he sat.

"So we can ask her if there's a federal judge who will *say* he's issuing a search warrant. The judge doesn't have to actually issue one, just start the process."

Kenny got up from his haunches and walked around the room with his hands on his hips, probably wondering why he ever asked to partner with me that day in police headquarters. He stopped in front of me. "Let me see if I have this straight. You want me to set up a meeting with the US Attorney so we can ask her to file papers for a bogus search warrant against Halloran?"

"The worst she can say is no," I said.

"You don't get it, Dermot. You don't know how it works."

"I know exactly how it works." I got off the bench and stood next to him. "If Maddy Savitz and Halloran are enemies, she will go after him. Whether for a federal crime or simple revenge, she'll go after him."

"To use your logic," Kenny countered, "if Maddy Savitz is aligned with Halloran, he gets warned and we get nothing."

He had a point.

"Do some checking around," I said. "Find out if Maddy and Halloran are friends."

"It won't be easy to find out," he said. "Nothing ever is in politics."

"Find out what you can and we'll go from there," I said.

"I don't know." Kenny rolled his neck, except he wasn't rolling his neck, he was shaking his head. "We'll never get a search warrant, not a chance."

Was he listening to what I said?

"I don't care about *getting* a search warrant," I said. "I just want Halloran to *think* we're getting one."

§

I sat on a bench in Peter Looney Park and watched the kids shooting baskets as their coaches offered pointers. Dip the knees, keep the head up, follow through. They were the same pointers I heard growing up. One of the kids got the hang of it and sank five jumpers in a row. My cell phone rang. It was Kenny Bowen.

"You are not going to believe this, Dermot. Maddy Savitz wants to meet with you tonight at six o'clock."

"Will you be there?" I asked.

"She wants to meet with you alone at her office," he said.

"You have some serious pull, Kenny."

"It's all about Halloran," Kenny said. "Just the mention of his name got you the meeting. Now it's up to you. In the meantime I'll be at the O'Neill Building talking to my clients in Treasury. Maybe we can team up with Maddy on this one."

I had two hours to prepare for a meeting with US Attorney Maddy Savitz. I knew nothing about her, not what she looked like, not why she agreed to see me. It was time to get to work.

I drove to Glooscap's house and found Buck Louis studying in the three-season porch that faced the tracks. A commuter train tore south, highballing for Quincy, Braintree, and beyond. The conductor blew the whistle at the Victory Road overpass and Sleddog answered with a howl. I knocked on the door and Buck looked up, his brown eyes focused, his dark brow crunched in concentration.

"Dermot," he said, laying down his pen.

"I need your help, Buck."

§

The US Attorney's Office is located on the ninth floor of the Moakley Courthouse, a newer building that sits on a choice lot facing Boston Harbor. I got through security without a snag and saw Maddy Savitz waiting on the other side of the lobby. She wasn't hard to spot, with her long chestnut hair reaching halfway down her back. Her enormous brown eyes followed me across the foyer as I moved toward her. She wore a dove gray skirt and a French blue blouse that was open at the neck, all topped off with a string of white pearls. And then I saw the saddest sight I had seen all week, a wedding ring on her finger. Oh, well.

"Mister Sparhawk?" she said.

"Call me Dermot."

"And you can call me Maddy. Let's take the elevator to my office." She led the way. "I usually walk the nine flights, but I heard you'd been shot in the leg."

"Both legs," I said, in a play for sympathy. I regretted it as soon as I said it.

"I also heard about your college football injury." Maddy pressed the up button and looked at her watch. "Is it true that you are still hobbled by it, the football knee?"

"My playing days are long over, brief as they were."

She had looks, smarts, charm, and the ability to win over a person inside of a second. She'd be unstoppable if she ran for public office, a shoo-in as the pundits say. And it was evident that the research Maddy had done on me dwarfed the research Buck and I had done on her. That's why she's a US Attorney, she leaves nothing to chance. The elevator doors opened with a ping.

We went into her office, a commodious space with direct water views. On one wall was a framed picture of Maddy at the Holocaust Memorial in Boston. She was pointing to an etched number on one of the glass towers, a somber look on her face. On a different wall hung a happier photo, Maddy smiling with Boston Bruins star Patrice Bergeron. They were holding the Stanley Cup and slapping a high five. Maddy closed the door and invited me to have a seat. She rolled a chair out from behind her desk and sat next to me, no barriers between us.

"I know the basics of the heist at the Hynes," she said. "Make your case and I'll make my decision."

"Just like that?"

"We work fast in this office," she replied.

"I guess you do." So I got right to it. "A man named Halloran orchestrated the Hynes robbery. He hired a team to pull it off, but he masterminded it. I can't prove any of this, of course, but I know he did it."

"You sound confident."

"I've dealt with Halloran in the past," I said. "His modus operandi at the Hynes was the same as another big crime he arranged years ago."

"You also sound obsessive," she noted. "Are you motivated by revenge, perhaps? Does payback play a role in your fervor to bring down Halloran?"

"Yes, it does," I said. "I hate him."

"You hate him?" She laughed. "Well, at least you're honest. Back to the robbery, the person who engineered the job had ample resources. We know this because a private security firm named Ironclad left the door open for the thieves to walk in. They were bought off to look the other way. The owner of Ironclad is nowhere to be found."

"Privatization at its finest," I said, "the highest bidder wins, in this case Halloran."

"The price for the fix had to be exorbitant," she said.

"Thus the man behind the curtain had to be chock-full of money," I said. "Halloran robbed the place and I want to get him."

"I have gleaned that much already." She half smiled. "I don't think I'd want you after me."

"I can take Halloran down with your help."

Maddy got out of her chair and walked to a small refrigerator in the corner of the office, grabbed two bottles of water, and handed me one.

"It's not that simple," she said. "I can't act on a hunch."

I got up and walked to the windows and watched a tugboat chugging through the inner harbor, riding low with a tank full of diesel.

"I need a bird dog, Maddy, someone who will scare Halloran from his roost. Once he's in the open, I can take him down."

"How do you propose to scare him from his roost?" she asked.

"With a search warrant," I said.

"You need evidence to get a search warrant." She joined me at the window and looked out. "A gut feeling doesn't cut it."

"I'm talking about a bogus warrant." I looked at her against the harbor backdrop. She was even more beautiful up close. "As I understand it, law enforcement agencies will sometimes execute a bogus warrant to check for internal leaks."

"Leaks are always a concern," Maddy agreed.

"Think of me as a plumber."

"What you're suggesting happens on occasion, staging bogus warrants to safeguard against leaks."

"Can you make it happen on this occasion?" I asked, not quite begging. "Can you put a sting into play to nail Halloran?"

"It's possible," she said. "Nothing you discover can be used in court, so I'm not sure why I should go along with it. Do you understand what I'm saying?"

"You're saying 'What's in it for me?'"

"It's politics, Dermot."

"For one thing, you'll find out if you have any leaky pipes." I thought about something Kenny said earlier, that as soon as Maddy heard Halloran's name she agreed to see me. "For another thing, you get a free shot at Halloran with my fist."

She smiled when I said that.

"I'll think about it," she said.

At least she didn't say no.

IV.

The next morning I drove to Halloran's estate in Weston, the toniest of Boston's tony suburbs. As I cruised along Boston Post Road, passing some of the most desirable properties in the Commonwealth, I plotted my approach to bring down Halloran. For the plan to work I had to jolt him out of his comfort zone, shake him like a soda can and hope he popped. And then there was Karl Kloosmann, his bodyguard, who could kill a man as easily as stepping on an ant. I had to get Kloosmann on the defensive, too, but that wouldn't be hard, since he was an imbecile.

I pulled into a semicircular driveway that looked like the Indianapolis Speedway cut in half and parked under a carport at the front entryway. I rang the bell and waited. To my surprise, Karl Kloosmann answered the door. His massive trapezius muscles bunched on his neck and crept up to his ears, the Incredible Hulk of Weston. I wondered if the dense tissue slowed the blood flow to his brain.

"What the fuck are you doing here?" he said.

"Promoted to houseboy, Karl?"

He wore banana yellow pants and a lime green polo shirt. The getup contrasted with his stevedore forearms and tree-trunk torso.

"What do you want?" he asked.

"Tell Halloran I need to talk to him."

"You don't give orders."

"Tell him it's about the $100,000 bills." I stepped past Kloosmann into the shady foyer. "Move your ass, Karl. I don't have all day."

"We'll settle this later."

Kloosmann went deep into the house. Five minutes later he returned and told me to follow him. We walked down a corridor that could be described as a marble airstrip and entered a room with floor-to-ceiling windows. Halloran sat in an oversized leather chair with his legs crossed, a member of the landed gentry in all his glory.

"Thanks for seeing me, Halloran." I sat on a couch without being asked. "I'm here to do you a favor."

"And what, pray tell, is that, Mr. Sparhawk?" He ran a delicate hand through his styled white hair.

"I came to collect the $100,000 bills you stole from the World's Fair of Money."

"You are off base as usual, but I suppose I should expect that from a project boy." He sighed. "I didn't steal anything. Why don't you run along home before something untoward happens to you."

"You yourself didn't steal anything, because you don't have the balls for that, but you set up the heist." I stretched my arms overhead and made myself at home. "You hired Liam McGrew's crew to do the job for you, the same crew you hired to rob the museum twenty years ago."

"You're full of shit, Sparhawk," Kloosmann butted in. "Totally full of it."

"You convinced me, Karl. I'm full of it." I turned to Halloran. "I killed Alroy McGrew, Liam's grandson. Alroy had a $5,000 bill on him from the heist. I killed a second IRA man named Mac, full name to be determined. Mac was in on the heist, too."

"Humor me, Mr. Sparhawk," Halloran said. "How do you plan to prove that I had anything to do with this alleged heist?"

"I don't plan to prove anything," I said. "I plan to lie. I'm going to the US Attorney's Office after I'm finished with you, and I'm going to tell her that I saw the sheets of money in your house. I'll swear to it on an affidavit."

"No one'll believe you," Kloosmann said. "You're nobody."

"And you're a gofer, Karl, a trained seal," I said. "The only reason you eat is you lick Halloran's ass."

"Gofer?" Kloosmann's face exploded red. He leaped in the air and snapped a karate kick to within an eyelash of my nose. He chopped at imaginary things in the air, shrieking and grunting as his hands flailed away, and then he landed in front of me like a ninja warrior and said, "When this is over, I'm gonna break your back."

"Can you hear my teeth chattering?"

Kloosmann was stupider than I thought. He wasn't quite retarded, but someday he could be if he smartened up. I said to his boss, "What do you say, Halloran? Save yourself a headache. Hand over the money and keep your freedom."

He pursed his lips as if pondering my offer and stared at me.

"Get out," he said.

"You're making a mistake," I said. "The federal marshals will be ringing your bell in the morning, search warrant in hand."

"We'll see about that," he said. "Karl, please show Mr. Sparhawk to the door. We are finished here."

V.

I called Kenny Bowen and told him to set the plan in motion at the Treasury Department. I called Maddy Savitz and told her that Halloran was ripe to be rousted from his roost. I called Harraseeket Kid and asked him if the wrecker was ready. Kid assured me it was all set, and we agreed to meet at his garage in an hour.

When I got there, Kid had the wrecker up on the lift, studying the chassis with the aid of a droplight. He adjusted something and said, "She's ready to go. All I have to do is attach the plow."

"Nice work, Kid."

"The camera is set, too. Let me show you." We went to the parking lot. "My buddy welded a short length of rebar to the top of the plow."

"You painted the plow black?"

"Matte black, so you can't see it at night. We're going tonight, right?" Kid went back to the camera talk. "He welded a piece of flat-iron to the rebar. Then he attached the camera with steel clamps, nice and secure, ready to film the whole thing."

"Will the camera take the thump if we collide?" I asked.

"*If* we collide? What's this 'if' stuff? I'm gonna whack the shit out of Halloran, knock him out of his Gucci shoes. And don't worry about the camera. The camera will take a thump." Kid grabbed the rebar and shook it. "She's rock solid, strong as granite ledge. Another thing, Vic Lennox is the cameraman. He knows how to work the remote."

A third man?

"The front seat will be crowded." I could see that Kid wanted Vic with us. "It's not a bad idea to have another man along, just in case."

"What time do we ambush Halloran?"

"I'll meet you here at nine o'clock," I said.

"I'll hitch the plow."

VI.

At noontime Kenny Bowen called me while I was eating a hotdog at Castle Island. I wiped the mustard from my mouth and answered the phone. Kenny vacillated as he spoke.

"I don't know, Dermot. I can't be sure, but I think our little ploy could work."

"You're not exactly brimming with confidence."

"Too many moving parts to be confident," he said. "The success of the trap comes down to the Treasury Department and the US Attorney's Office. If there's a leak in either agency, it could work."

"What if one of the department heads is on the take? He or she could warn Halloran about the phony search warrant."

"See what I mean about moving parts?"

"Yeah."

"This is the most interesting case of my career," Kenny said. "We need a combination of honesty and dishonesty *within* multiple departments for it to work."

"And if there is no leak the plan flops."

"That's right." Kenny laughed. "Can you believe it? I'm actually hoping the departments are corrupt."

Of course Kenny was hoping for that. He wanted to get the reward.

"If you had to give odds, would you go fifty-fifty?" I asked.

"More like sixty-forty," he said, "against."

I repeated what Kenny told me to make sure I had it straight.

"For the plan to work there has to be a leak in either the Treasury Department or the US Attorney's Office, and the leak has to be at a lower level, because a lower-level worker won't know the warrant is a trap."

"Or a leak in the magistrate judge's office, the issuer of the search warrant," Kenny said. "We kept the magistrate judge in the dark about our ploy against Halloran. We get three cracks at this thing: a leak in Treasury, a leak in the US Attorney's Office, or a leak in the magistrate's office."

"Three cracks," I said. "So *if* there's a mole, and *if* Halloran gets tipped off by the mole, and *if* Halloran tries to make a run for it, I'll be waiting for him. You're right about the moving parts."

CHAPTER NINE

I.

From Castle Island I drove to the L Street Bathhouse for an AA meeting. The topics ranged from gratitude to acceptance to powerlessness. The last speaker summarized the meeting, saying that she gratefully accepted the fact that she was powerless over alcohol. We said the Lord's Prayer and filed out of the building.

I got in my car and drove toward Morrissey Boulevard, having no destination in mind. With time to kill before my rendezvous with Harraseeket Kid and Vic Lennox, I kept driving and ended up at a penny arcade on Nantasket Beach. I dropped twenty dollars on Skee-ball and left the prize tickets for whoever found them.

I walked to Nantasket Beach and took in the ambience—in other words, I watched the girls walk by in bikinis. After an hour of sun and spray, I left the beach for South Boston. I pulled into Kid's garage and couldn't believe what I saw. Vic Lennox was swinging a hatchet in a chopping motion, apparently for practice. Harraseeket Kid was pushing a snub-nose revolver into his waistband, but only after he gave the cylinder a spin.

"We're ready." Kid untucked his shirt over the gun.

"I just want to block Halloran's car," I said. "I don't want to cleave him open or gun him down."

"Okay, let's go," Kid said, ignoring me.

"Hey, I don't want anyone getting hurt tonight," I said. "I just want to block him. Do you understand?"

"Sure, we understand." Kid got in the driver's side and slammed the door. "We don't want to get hurt, either."

I looked again at Vic Lennox. He was decked out in faded denim from head to toe. He could have been auditioning for a part in *The Trial of Billy Jack.*

Vic sheathed the hatchet. "Let's go, men!"

The three of us squeezed into the front seat, nobody bothering with seat belts. Kid gunned the engine and hauled out of the lot, leaving a wake of gravel dust behind us.

We ramped onto the Mass Pike and drove for Halloran's house in palatial Weston. After driving twenty minutes west, we exited the pike and drove into Weston. The homes got bigger and the lots got vaster as we drew closer to Halloran's address. The road was dark when we got there. There were no streetlights or stores or nearby residences, a bonus for us, since we wanted to remain unseen. Kid backed onto the soft shoulder across from Halloran's long driveway and killed the engine and headlights. All was quiet. We waited in the truck and watched the hours pass. It was now three in the morning.

"Halloran didn't take the bait," Kid said. "We're sitting out here like a bunch of fools while he's inside sleeping."

"It's early." Vic responded. "Halloran is smart, he's biding his time."

"Halloran is smart." I agreed with Vic. "We'll stay until dawn."

"What if nothing happens?" Kid asked.

"Something will happen," I said. "Halloran can't risk staying put with the stolen money. He has to make a move."

"He doesn't have to do a damn thing," Kid argued. "The guy's a billionaire. He could burn the money, and it wouldn't make any difference to him."

"You're wrong, Kid. It *would* make a difference to him, because it's not about the money. It's about the thrill of stealing it. If he burns the money, he loses." Was my guesswork on Halloran correct? I didn't know for sure, but it was all I had. "Halloran needs to know he got away with the heist. If he gets away with it, he wins, he gets his fix. I'll take it a step further. I'd bet he likes that we're challenging him. It's another hurdle for him to conquer. His victory will be that much sweeter if he wins."

"Except we're not going to let him win," Kid said, sounding more on board with the plan. "Because we're going to stop him."

"Yup, we're going to stop him," I said.

At four o'clock a light went on inside the house, and another one went on outside the garage. Vic Lennox grabbed his field glasses.

"The garage door just opened," he said.

Kid started the diesel, which rumbled in a low growl.

"Take these." Vic handed us Popsicle sticks. "Bite down on them so you don't crack your teeth when we collide."

"I just want to block the car," I said.

"I'll block it, all right." Kid whispered. "Everyone quiet."

A vehicle rolled out of the garage and came down the curving driveway. Vic Lennox leaned forward with his glasses. "It's a Lincoln Navigator."

Kid pulled a lever that raised the snowplow. "I want it eight inches off the ground, so the SUV takes the brunt of it."

"Just block it." I repeated. "Block the driveway, that's all."

"Sure, I'll block it." Kid stepped on the emergency brake and shifted into drive. "I don't want them to see the brake lights."

"The camera is filming," Vic said. "Buckle up, boys. It's Popsicle time."

The SUV moved slowly down the driveway and was about ten feet from the street. We bit onto the Popsicle sticks. Kid released the emergency brake and floored the gas pedal. The wrecker roared forward, leaving rubber on the soft shoulder, and shot across the road and up Halloran's driveway. Kid hit the halogens, floodlighting the property like a ballpark. The driver shielded his eyes and Kid rammed the SUV head on. Never in my life had I heard such noise, a cacophonous crunching of metal.

"Bull's-eye!" Kid screamed. "Dead center!"

I jumped out of the wrecker as shattering glass tinkled onto the tar, and I ran to the SUV as I spit out pieces of Popsicle stick. Karl Kloosmann, the driver, was bloody and groggy, but that didn't stop him from pulling out a gun. He opened the door and looked up, his eyes were blinking and unfocused. He raised the gun. I slammed the door on his wrist and the gun dropped to the ground. I slammed it again and this time it thumped his head. He fell to the driveway and reached for the gun. I tried to punt his head, missed, and caught him in the throat. And then Vic came from behind me and smashed Kloosmann's hand with the flat side of the hatchet. Kloosmann choked for air like a wheezing asthmatic and collapsed onto his back. I picked up the gun and threw it into the darkness.

Harraseeket Kid dragged Halloran out of the back seat and stuck the revolver in his face and yelled, "Where's the fuckin' money!"

"I don't know what—"

"I'd tell him if I were you, Halloran," I said. "He'll blow a hole in your head."

Kid cocked the hammer as tears rolled down Halloran's cheeks.

"Tell us," I said. "Where's the money?"

"The hatchback." Halloran sobbed. "The money's in the hatchback."

I popped the hatchback and saw a cardboard tube. I opened the end of it and removed the sheets of $100,000 bills. I unrolled the sheets and walked to the front of the SUV and held them in front of Halloran. I grabbed his hair and jerked up his head.

"Vic, get some footage of Halloran's face with the money," I said.

Vic worked the remote like a drone pilot. "I got plenty, let's get out of here."

"Come on, Dermot, move your ass." Kid was already in the wrecker.

Kid was shifting into gear when I hopped into the truck. Vic continued to film the wreckage of our assault. We sped out of Halloran's neighborhood, ramped onto the Mass Pike, and headed for South Boston. We went through the Weston toll plaza and through Newton Corner and past Boston University. When we reached Fenway Park we looked at each other and burst into laughter. Ten minutes later we pulled into the garage.

Kid parked in the main bay and turned off the engine. I yanked down the overhead door. We gathered in the middle of the garage, nobody speaking a word. The rising sun fought through the grimy windows and spilled daylight onto the oily floor. Still no one spoke. Kid walked to Glooscap's office. Vic and I followed him inside.

Kid looked at me and said, "Why are you smiling?"

"I liked slamming that punk."

We had another good laugh, until Kid cut it short.

"Now what?" he asked.

"Now I go to Halloran's house and threaten him," I said.

"You threatened him just now," Kid said. "He was whimpering like a puppy."

"The next threat could land him in a federal prison." I held up the cardboard tube. "I'll sic the Treasury Department on him if he doesn't do what I say."

We talked a little more and laughed a lot more. I found the violence of the ramming exhilarating, like hitting a quarterback.

"Get some sleep," Vic said, pointing to the couch in Glooscap's office. "You'll need your strength for later. Kid and I will stand guard. Ain't nobody getting past us."

I crumpled onto the couch and fell asleep.

II.

I rang Halloran's doorbell at five o'clock that afternoon and an ailing Karl Kloosmann answered it. A bulky cast encased his arm from fingertip the elbow. Wires and elastics caged his mouth. Unable to speak, he nodded to the hallway, and I followed him to the big sitting room, where Halloran sat with his legs crossed. His expression showed nothing. No rancor, no anger, nothing. I sat on the sofa across from him.

"Any whiplash?"

"How dare you come to my house after last night?" Halloran's face reddened, matching the scrapes on his cheeks. "Karl's larynx is irreparably ruptured. His jaw is badly broken, and so is his arm and hand. You're lucky you didn't kill him."

"I'd say he's lucky I didn't kill him."

Kloosmann croaked something indiscernible, paused, wrote a few words on a piece of paper and passed it to Halloran with his unplastered hand.

"Karl wants you to know that the car door broke his jaw, not your foot."

"Noted." I tossed a DVD to Halloran, who showed surprisingly quick reflexes when he caught it. "Footage from last night's crash, it shows you with three sheets of $100,000 bills, but there's a problem."

"What problem?"

"You only had three sheets," I said. "The thieves stole four sheets."

Halloran and Kloosmann looked at each other. Kloosmann, who would never make it as a card player, blinked. Halloran's mouth dropped. The mention of the fourth sheet surprised them. The lads from Belfast had buffaloed Halloran.

"You got taken, Halloran, hoodwinked by the boys in the old brigade." I lay back on the sofa. "You received only three of the four sheets."

"You are wrong." Halloran regained his composure. "You're making no sense."

"I pieced most of it together, but I'll need your help to fill in the rest."

Kloosmann grunted. Halloran raised his hand as if to say he'd handle it.

"I assume you're engaging in levity, because I wouldn't help you if there were a gun pointed at my head."

"In a manner of speaking, a gun is pointed at your head," I said. "You're in a box, Halloran, and you are going to tell me everything I need to know."

"I don't think so."

Halloran nodded to Kloosmann, who aimed a pistol at my head. Kloosmann loved his job as an enforcer. I had gotten lucky last night, catching his head in the car door.

"Well, Sparhawk." Halloran smiled. "I could have Karl put a bullet in your head this very second."

"You could, but there is something you should know first," I said.

"And what is that?"

"The DVD I just gave you, I also gave a copy to my lawyer. If anything happens to me, he'll bring it to the US Attorney's Office downtown, and that US Attorney doesn't like you very much."

"I couldn't care less," he said, and he meant it.

"My lawyer will also give a copy to the press." I could see that Halloran wasn't fazed, so I tried another tactic. "And if you're extremely lucky, you'll live long enough for the Feds to arrest you, or for the newspapers to disgrace you."

"What do you mean if I live long enough?" he asked.

"My friends from last night, the crazies in the truck, they're Micmac Indians and they're family. They come from all over the Canadian Maritimes. You can't track them down and you can't buy them off."

"So?"

"So if *any* harm comes to me, they will kill you." I faced Halloran. "Let me repeat what I said. If any harm comes to me, they will kill you."

"I understood you the first time."

"I don't think you fully understood me." I rested my feet on the coffee table. "If *anyone* harms me, you get a tomahawk to the head. For example, if the IRA comes at me, you pay with blood."

"I can't control the IRA," he said.

"At least you admit to knowing them."

"That's not what I meant." His face went red. "Don't put words in my mouth."

"The IRA is a problem for me," I said. "They've tried to kill me three times."

"Too bad they didn't succeed." He uncrossed his thin legs. "I can't do anything about the IRA."

"You have to keep me alive, Halloran," I said. "The only way to keep me alive is to tell me what you know about the Irish Republican Army."

"I don't think so." He recoiled slightly.

"They duped you again, didn't they?"

"They did no such thing."

"They stole four sheets of money and gave you three. You don't owe them a thing. You can save your ass by helping me save mine. Come on, Halloran, use your goddamn head. Tell me about Liam McGrew."

"I never heard of him." Halloran tapped his fingertips together. "I'm not saying another word."

"You're making a mistake."

"I've said all I'm going to say on the matter." Halloran gestured to the hallway. "Leave my house immediately."

I couldn't blame him for dummying up. Who in his right mind would finger the Irish Republican Army?

"Rest up, Karl. I'll see myself to the door." I pointed at his neck brace. "You look good in a turtleneck."

III.

It was eight in the evening, and the daylight was fading as fast as the Red Sox' pennant chances. Tonight they were in Seattle to play the Mariners in the first game of a nine-game road trip. After Seattle it was on to Oakland and Anaheim. I called Kenny Bowen to tell him about the sheets of money.

Kenny asked, "Did Halloran bite on the fake warrant?"

"He bit like a snapper," I said. "He tried to make a run for it and we stopped him."

"Did you get the money?" he asked.

"Yes and no," I said. "I don't think you'll be too disappointed."

"Yes and no? Too disappointed?" Kenny sounded exasperated. "Did you get the sheets or not?"

"I'll fill you in when I see you."

"A lot of people went out on a limb for you on this," Kenny said. "Maddy Savitz, the Treasury Department, me, other people you don't even know about, we backed you."

"I said I'll fill you in when I see you." Now I was the one who sounded exasperated.

He agreed to my stipulation, but insisted on meeting tonight. I told him that tonight was fine, that I wanted to give him the money as soon as possible. He liked that I had the money. I just didn't have all of it, and that's what I needed to talk to him about.

Kenny said, "Meet me in an hour at Greenberg's Nightspot, the corner of Columbus Ave and Camden Street.

"See you in an hour."

I drove to the lower end of Roxbury and parked on Columbus Avenue, not far from Northeastern University. With $9.6 million in the tube under my arm, I warily got out of the car and walked to Greenberg's, looking over my shoulder every half-stride. Talk about inviting a mugging.

I entered the club through a set of swinging doors, which led to another set of swinging doors, which opened to a big carpeted room lit by soft purple bulbs. The walls were paneled in butterscotch satinwood. The prints on the walls were oversized and art nouveau. The overall atmosphere was hushed and cool.

In the middle of the room sat a black Steinway grand with a glowing lacquer finish. Playing the piano was a black man who looked to be in his early fifties. He wore a black tuxedo, a white tux shirt, and a black bowtie. A glossy brass plaque read: Pianist, Zack Sanders. Zack finished an animated tune and announced to the room that it came from the Great American Songbook. He then played a bluesy number.

A woman with dark hair and dark eyes walked up to me and asked if I'd like to be seated. I told her that I was waiting for a friend.

"Is your friend Kenny Bowen?" she asked.

"That's him," I said, ready to converse with her on any subject she desired.

"Follow me."

She was easy to follow, with her hips swaying and shoulders rolling. She led me to a small round table and walked away. Fifteen minutes later Kenny Bowen joined me. I handed him the tube.

"Three sheets of $100,000 bills," I said. "Halloran didn't have the fourth sheet. I don't think he ever had it."

"Great work, Dermot." He opened the end of the tube and partially removed the sheets. "I never thought I'd see these again."

"One is missing," I said to him. "Liam McGrew must have kept the fourth sheet for himself. Maybe it was part of the deal."

And then I thought about Halloran's reaction when I mentioned the fourth sheet. It wasn't part of the deal. Liam swiped it. A waitress came to the table. To my great sorrow it wasn't the woman who seated me. Kenny and I both ordered coffee.

When she left, I said, "I'm going to Belfast."

Kenny sat forward and waited for me to look at him.

"Forget Belfast," he said. "Forget about the fourth sheet. I have a friend in Scotland Yard and more friends in Irish intelligence. I'll handle the fourth sheet."

"I'm going to Belfast, Kenny."

"You did a tremendous job," he said. "Go home and relax."

"I haven't been home in a week," I said. "Assassins are looking for me and they aren't going to stop. I'm going to Belfast to settle this thing."

"They'll kill you over there. Use your common sense."

"I'm fresh out of common sense." I took a drink of coffee and returned the cup to the saucer. "You're a resourceful guy, Kenny. I gave you Alroy McGrew. You must have come up with the other names by now, the names of the men trying to kill me."

Kenny tamped the bills back into the tube and tapped it on the table.

"The man you killed in Southie was named William McAfee. McAfee was an IRA operative, smart enough to stay out of the limelight, hence no criminal record."

"How did you track him down?" I asked.

"I forwarded the picture you gave me to a colleague in Irish intelligence." He stopped tapping.

"What else?"

"Does the name Thomas O'Byrne mean anything to you?"

"Should it?" I asked.

"He's the big bald Irishman you told me about. O'Byrne is back in Belfast now." Kenny paused. "He did time in Long Kesh Prison, a hunger striker, too."

"A true believer."

"O'Byrne got out in May of '84," Kenny said. "In August of '84, a British hit squad killed his wife. They were gunning for O'Byrne but killed her by mistake."

"I'm sure that endeared O'Byrne to the Orangemen." I thought about the Hynes robbery. "O'Byrne probably took the fourth sheet back to Belfast with him."

Kenny handed me a photo. "This is Thomas O'Byrne."

"Is it recent?" I asked.

"Recent enough," he said.

"What about the third man?"

"Ah, the mysterious third man that Rat T. Kennedy thwarted," he said. "I can't find a thing on him. My Irish contacts couldn't track him down."

"Will you keep on it?"

"Of course I'll keep on it, but I need more time." He slapped my shoulder, signaling a change of topics. "You have a great deal of money coming to you."

"I'll worry about the money later," I said. "Halloran and I have one thing in common. It's not about the money."

"What do you mean?"

"It's not important." I thought about the trip in front of me. "On to Belfast."

"I can't talk you out of it?" he said.

"I'll be on a plane tomorrow if I can book one that fast," I answered.

"I'll keep after the third man," Kenny said to me. "When I find out more, I'll call you. I have a feeling he's important."

§

I withdrew three hundred dollars from an ATM on Gallivan Boulevard and drove to the Blarney Stone. I went inside and saw Delia serving a table of customers. I waited until she finished and said, "Hello, Delia."

"You again." She wiped her tray with a bar towel. "What do you want now?"

"One last favor and you'll never see me again."

"Promise?"

"Promise." I showed her the photo of Thomas O'Byrne. "Is this the big Irishman you saw in here that night?"

"Let me see it." She stared at it for a good five seconds. "He looks younger in this picture, but yeah, that's him."

I gave her the cash and went back to Glooscap's house for a good night's sleep before my flight.

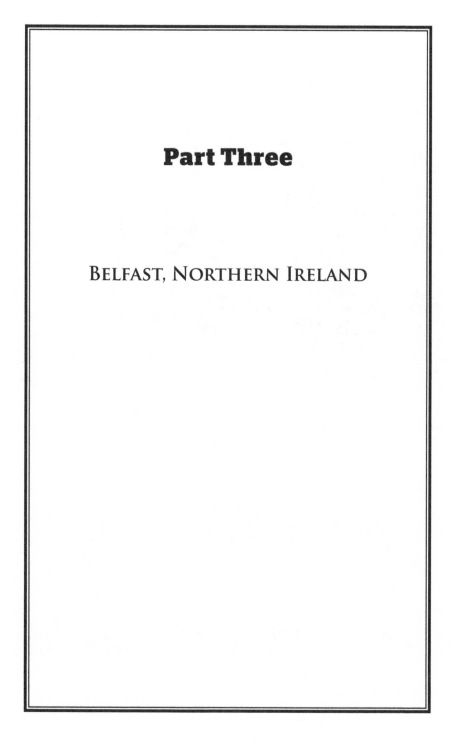

Part Three

BELFAST, NORTHERN IRELAND

CHAPTER TEN

I.

O'Byrne sipped his afternoon Guinness from a tall glass in Slattery's Pub. The room was empty except for a small gathering of retired railroad workers who sat at a table. Public reunions must be nice for the law-abiding, a simple pleasure an IRA soldier would never enjoy. He took another swig, and at that moment the biggest man O'Byrne had ever seen walked into the pub. He made K look like a pigmy. It wasn't just his height and width; it was his bone structure, his corded wrists and huge hands and tree-trunk neck. The railroad men stopped talking when the behemoth strode by. He sat on a barstool next to O'Byrne, and the railroaders commenced chatting.

The big guy ordered tonic water with a lemon twist. Slattery served him with a long arm, as if he were feeding an exotic animal, not wanting to get too close lest he get bit. O'Byrne finished his beer and tapped the glass on the bar top. Slattery refilled it with creamy stout, stopping twice along the way to let the head subside. Slattery knew how to pour stout. O'Byrne turned to the big fella.

"You're on the minerals, I see." He pointed at the tonic. "Do you want me to Irish it up for you?"

"No thanks."

"You're not drinking?" O'Byrne asked, perplexed.

"Not today," the man answered. "Just tonic water."

"The accent, you're a Yank." O'Byrne studied the man's face. *Tonic watah? A Bostonian.* "You're in Belfast now, did nobody tell you? You've strayed far from the safety of your homeland."

"That's right, O'Byrne. I strayed."

"And, by Jesus, you know my name." O'Byrne swirled the beer in his glass, creating a miniature whirlpool. "Go feck a cow, Yank. Get out of here while you still can walk without crutches."

"Not until I'm finished," he said.

"Oh, you're finished all right." O'Byrne waved the big man closer. "C'mere lad, I have to tell you a question."

"And what question is that?"

"Are you looking to get yourself killed?" asked O'Byrne.

"I'm looking to stay alive," the man answered.

"Then you should go into hiding for a spell, let things blow over. There's no shame in that." O'Byrne said this in calm tone, a father offering advice to a son. "As we say here in Ireland, a good run is better than a bad stand."

"Everybody keeps telling me to go into hiding until things blow over." The colossus paused. "Nothing is going to blow over. Three men have tried to kill me so far, and I have a feeling more are on the way."

"Three, you say?"

"Alroy McGrew, William McAfee, and a third man I don't know."

"I haven't a notion what you're talking about, not a blessed clue."

"Yes, you do." The big man faced O'Byrne squarely. "You know exactly what I'm talking about. You were in Boston with Alroy and McAfee."

O'Byrne tapped his glass on the bar. There was no sense denying it, the big man was Dermot Sparhawk. How to get rid of him?

"Have ye any loose change in your purse, Dermot?" O'Byrne stared at him. "Because I suggest you get on the Dublin bus and ride it to the terminus. Then purchase yourself a plane ticket and go home alive."

"I have no change," Sparhawk said. "I deal in folding money, $100,000 bills."

"Ah, you damned fool. And I suppose you think that your coming to Belfast shows great courage." O'Byrne leaned on his elbows. "And maybe it does at that. Every dog is bold in his own yard."

"I'm not courageous and I'm not bold," Sparhawk said. "I'm fighting to stay alive, and I think you want me alive, too."

"I want you alive, you say?" O'Byrne drank a swallow of beer. "What gave you the daft idea that I want you alive?"

"Your phone call to Boston," Sparhawk said. "You called William McAfee to cancel a hit on me. I answered that call, you know."

"You're mad."

"McAfee was already dead when his phone rang."

"What are you saying?" O'Byrne sounded genuinely puzzled.

"McAfee's cell phone rang after I killed him." Sparhawk explained. "I'm the one who answered his phone."

"You answered it?"

"You said, and I quote, 'Don't say a word, just listen. The hit is off, Mac. Forget about Sparhawk and come home.'"

"Jesus, Mary, and Joseph," O'Byrne muttered to himself, and then added with a bite, "Go away from me."

"And because you canceled the hit on me, I assume you want me alive."

"You're acting the maggot. Making leaps, you are." O'Byrne eyed Slattery to make sure he wasn't within earshot. "It wasn't me on the phone. You have it all wrong, I tell you, all wrong."

"It was you, O'Byrne. As soon as I heard your voice today, with that brogue as thick as Mulligan stew, I knew it was you." Sparhawk arched his back and cracked his neck. "You came to Boston with Alroy McGrew and William McAfee. The three of you robbed the World's Fair of Money. The three of you drank at the Blarney Stone, paying for rounds with hundred-dollar bills."

"You know nothing, nothing. Get away from me!" O'Byrne flung his free hand in the air in a get-lost gesture. "You *think* you heard me on the phone? You *think* I went to Boston. That doesn't prove a thing."

"Maybe not, but this does." Sparhawk pulled out a cell phone and pressed C2 on the contacts list. "This belonged to William McAfee."

"Did it now?" A phone rang in O'Byrne's pocket. "Ach, damn!"

"Answer it, O'Byrne. It's not long distance."

"All right, I take your point. Put that thing away." O'Byrne gulped another mouthful of drink and slowly lowered the glass to the bar. He signaled for another stout and told Slattery to bring him a double Jameson with it. O'Byrne finished both drinks before he spoke again. It seemed that a long time had passed. "Alroy, I can understand. But how did you beat Mac? Mac was a tough mug, especially with a gun."

"I was wearing a vest when he shot me."

"A vest, you say." O'Byrne hoisted the shot glass to his lips and noticed it was empty. "Mac had a tender heart for a hired gun. He could never shoot a man in the face."

"I'm glad for that," Sparhawk said.

"No doubt you are."

They sat at the bar, neither man saying a word, and the seconds turned into minutes and the minutes slipped away. The railroad workers finished their drinks, bade each other farewell, and went out the door. Slattery worked at the far end of the bar taking inventory, clipboard in hand, counting the bottles in one of the liquor cabinets. O'Byrne turned to Sparhawk.

"It seems we both have some thinking to do, don't we now?" O'Byrne scoffed. "A great deal of thinking at that."

"I'm staying at the Maryville House," Sparhawk said. "I'd rather work with you than against you, but either way I'm seeing this through to the end. You know where to find me."

"Is it all of ye or just yourself?"

"What do mean?"

"Are you alone?" O'Byrne asked.

"It's just meself," Sparhawk said with a feigned brogue.

"This won't end well for you, I'm sorry to say." O'Byrne gripped his beer glass. "You don't seem like a bad sort, but you're out of your depth here in Belfast."

"Why should Belfast be any different?"

"Indeed." O'Byrne watched Sparhawk leave Slattery's Pub. When the door closed, O'Byrne murmured to no one in particular, "Who have you sent my way, MacNisse, my savior or my slayer?"

"What was that, O'Byrne?" asked Slattery.

"Huh? Oh, 'twas nothing."

"Where did that monster drift in from, *Gulliver's Travels?*"

"Ah, he was just a blow-in from the States wanting to know about the black taxi tours, that's all."

§

An hour later O'Byrne found himself kneeling in Clonard Monastery, praying to his intercessor, Saint Angus MacNisse of Connor. If MacNisse could alter the course of a wild river to save a Kells monastery, certainly he could alter the course of human blood to save a man's soul. He whispered to MacNisse as if they were confidants.

"Sparhawk knows of my call to cancel the hit. The irony of it, Sparhawk answering that call. What if Liam learns of this? What then? I'm a dead man, MacNisse. Liam will kill me as sure as I kneel here at your feet. Sparhawk holds my life in his hands."

II.

I phoned Kenny Bowen from my room at the Maryville House, but he didn't answer. Maybe he was pumping iron under Harvard Stadium, or maybe he was screening his calls. I reclined on the bed and fell asleep.

At seven o'clock I awoke and checked my cell phone. Still nothing from Kenny Bowen. I decided to go out for the evening, so I took a taxi into Belfast and got off at Donegal Square. Following the hotel clerk's recommendation, I ate at an open-air shanty on Arthur Street, ordering fish and chips with salt and vinegar and a side of slaw. The clerk's advice was spot-on, as they say here.

After walking off the meal, I caught an AA meeting in a church basement in Victoria Square. The last speaker, a scratch golfer, said he scored par or better on every hole except the nineteenth, where he bogeyed on Bushmills. We ended the meeting with an Our Father and everyone joined in. It seemed that AA in Northern Ireland was a nonsectarian affair, a truce among drunks.

The night was cool and the air was breezy, so I bought a sweatshirt with no logo. No sense setting myself up as a target. Of course, Liam McGrew had already painted a bull's-eye on my back. I walked to the banks of the River Lagan and watched the torrents swirl near the shoreline. At Waterfront Hall the Hollies were performing. I bought a ticket from a scalper and went in and listened to a few songs. After they played "Look Through Any Window," I left the concert and cabbed back to the Maryville House.

It was nearly ten o'clock and the sky was still blue. I thought of Yogi Berra's line about the poor sun conditions in left field at Yankee Stadium: It gets late early out there. In Belfast it stays early late. Day eventually turned to dusk and dusk turned to darkness and I nodded off in my room. At midnight Kenny Bowen called. He asked me how the day went, and I told him about my meeting with O'Byrne, omitting one piece of trivial information, that for some reason I liked the son of a bitch.

"You two met," Kenny said. "That's excellent. I'm impressed."

"O'Byrne was having an afternoon pint at Slattery's Pub, just like you said."

"You found him at Slattery's then."

"I didn't expect him to be there, but I walked in and there he was." I kicked off my shoes. "I told O'Byrne I was staying here at the Maryville House."

"Was that smart?"

"Maybe, maybe not, I'll find out soon enough," I said.

"Did you talk to him about the sheet of money?"

"I mentioned it indirectly, but I didn't want to rush him," I said. "He's too damn smart."

"I like your approach, giving O'Byrne time to think it over," Kenny said. "As for the third assassin, I can't find a thing on him. My connections in Ireland can't put a name to the face. They found no matches on fingerprints or dentals."

It didn't surprise me when Kenny said that his Irish connections couldn't identify the third man, because the third man hadn't struck me as Irish.

"The third man wasn't like Alroy and McAfee," I said. "He was different."

"Can you elaborate?"

"I don't think he was Irish." I pictured the man's face, even though there were two bullet holes drilled into it. I pictured his attire, which didn't match Alroy's and McAfee's. "The way he dressed, he could have been an American."

"I don't think so," Kenny said. "The FBI found nothing on him, and believe me, they checked. I made sure of it."

"It was just an impression."

"I called a friend in Scotland Yard who is well connected in Northern Ireland, mostly in Belfast and Portadown. Maybe he can identify him."

"I hope so," I said.

"How about you? What's your plan?"

"I'm going to wait for O'Byrne to make the next move." I said. "I don't like waiting. I'd rather make something happen. But over here, dealing with the IRA, I believe it is better to wait."

"I don't like that O'Byrne knows where you're staying," Kenny said. "It puts you in danger."

"I wasn't any safer in Boston, remember?" I thought it over. "O'Byrne is with the IRA. He can find me anyway."

"What if O'Byrne starts to worry about Liam McGrew?"

"What do you mean, starts?" I said. "He's already worried about him."

"But what if O'Byrne gets nervous about the call he made to McAfee, the call canceling the hit on you. He might panic and tell Liam you're in Belfast."

"He might," I said, "but I don't think he will. As far as O'Byrne is concerned, I'm the only one who knows about the call."

"That's my point," Kenny said. "O'Byrne might kill you to keep it that way. If you're dead, Liam can't possibly find out about the call. Do you understand what I'm saying? O'Byrne is safer with you dead."

"O'Byrne won't do that."

"How can you be sure?"

"He called to stop the hit on me, Kenny. He was trying to save my life." Why did I feel so sure that O'Byrne wouldn't harm me? I thought more about it and concluded that my certainty was based on nothing more than intuition. "This will sound stupid, but I'll say it anyway. I met him face-to-face. I don't think he will hurt me."

We continued to talk about O'Byrne's phone call, and Kenny said, "I'd like you to give me O'Byrne's number."

"Why do you want it?" I asked.

"To tell him I know about the call to McAfee," he said. "If O'Byrne realizes that another person knows about the call, he gains nothing by killing you."

"It could backfire."

"I'll tell O'Byrne that if any harm comes to you, I'll tell Liam Mc-Grew about the call. Now please give me his number."

I thought it over.

"I can't do that," I said. "I need O'Byrne to trust me."

"Trust?" Kenny laughed. "He's an IRA gunman, a ruthless killer."

"The answer is still no," I said. "If I get out of Belfast alive, I'll get out because O'Byrne trusts me."

"You're nuts." A moment of silence lingered on the line. "I'll call you tomorrow. I just hope you're alive to answer."

"Aye, me too."

"Aye?"

I turned down the covers and went to sleep.

III.

Liam McGrew had been discharged from the hospital and was convalescing at his flat in Shaftesbury Square. Since Alroy's death, Liam had been in and out of the ward, dealing with a dicey pulmonary condition. When O'Byrne heard that Liam had been released, he called him right away. Thankful for the call, Liam invited O'Byrne to dinner, and O'Byrne said yes. He got to Liam's at six o'clock.

They sat around Liam's Formica table as yesterday's roast beef reheated in the oven. O'Byrne chuckled to himself. Leave it to Liam, tempering hospitality with frugality, inviting a friend to supper and serving leftovers. He must be part Ulster Scot.

Liam cleared his throat. "'Twas gracious of you to come by tonight."

"Must feel good to be home, eh, Liam?"

"Aye, it feels grand." He sat up with effort. "Not that I minded the hospital food. People are forever complaining about hospital food, and for the life of me I haven't a clue why. The food was simply splendid."

"'Tis good to know."

"It's good to know if you end up in a hospital." He inhaled through his mouth. "Make us a cup of scaldy, will you?"

"Sure." O'Byrne boiled the water and poured the tea and raised his cup. "To happier days ahead."

"Hmm, happier." Liam gurgled.

"What's on your mind, Liam?" O'Byrne said.

"You're right, I've got something on my mind." Liam rested his chin on his fist like Rodin's *The Thinker*. "I've always been a careful man, as you well know, and I've surrounded myself with men I can trust. Trust, that's what I value most in a friendship. Loyalty, too. Trust and loyalty."

"Those are fine qualities, to be sure," O'Byrne agreed.

"But trust and loyalty are in rare supply these days." He turned the oxygen knob. "Traitor! I won't abide a traitor no matter how long I've known him. A bloody turncoat can destroy an army of soldiers in a twinkling."

"What's all this talk of traitors and turncoats?"

"Ach, I'm blowing off steam. How do the Americans say it? I'm venting, yes, I'm venting. You know what I'm talking about, don't you, O'Byrne? You're familiar with the Yanks and how they speak."

"We were only in Boston a short time, Liam."

"Still, you pick up on their sayings, their idioms."

"I suppose so."

"Americans are everywhere nowadays, even here in Belfast." Liam took a breath. "Mostly tourists, no doubt. Why, I heard that a Yank wandered into Slattery's Pub just the other day. A big strapping lad and he went right to you. Do you remember him?"

"I remember him. And as you said, he was a tourist." O'Byrne sipped his tea, stalling to regain his composure. "I suppose he came to me because I was the only patron in Slattery's at the time, except for a few railroad hands sitting at a table."

"A tourist in Slattery's?" Liam made a face. "I find the prospect of a tourist in Slattery's highly unlikely, don't you?"

"Apparently the lad lost his way and ended up at the pub, that's all."

"And yet he stayed and talked to you for quite a long time."

"We chatted," O'Byrne said. "And then he left."

"From where did this lost soul hail?" Liam asked. "Did he come from Boston by chance?"

"He never told me."

"Did he tell you his name?" Liam's tone grew deeper, more accusatory. "Usually when two lads meet they introduce themselves."

"If he told me his name, I don't remember it. Probably something Irish, though. He was here on holiday, visiting family." O'Byrne fought to relax. "We talked for a while, that's true, but it was just small talk."

"What do you mean by small talk?"

"You know what I mean." O'Byrne now felt at ease for some reason. "We talked of famine and farmlands and bog fires and ancestry, nothing important. You know the touristy types, Liam. They have the depth of a summer puddle."

"Slattery told me that the talk was intense, low whisperings and hands covering mouths, everything secretive." Liam sucked for air. "Slattery said that you doubled up on Jameson's."

"Slattery is a feckin' eejit." O'Byrne snapped back. "I should slap the shit out of him for running his gob."

"Slap the shit out of him? Whoa, boy!" Liam burst into laughter. "Slattery is a feckin' eejit, isn't he?"

"Aye," O'Byrne said. "Speaking of Americans, what's going on in Boston?"

"What's that you said?"

"What's going on in Boston?" O'Byrne set aside the teacup. "Alroy gets killed and then McAfee. I'm curious about Boston."

"Hmm, Boston." Liam sipped his tea. "The Boston situation is fiddly, O'Byrne, very fiddly indeed. I have chosen to move it up the chain of command."

"I don't follow," O'Byrne said.

"I handed the Boston problem over to the Army Council. The council will decide how to handle it."

"To use an American idiom, will the council be keeping you in the loop?"

"Of course they'll be keeping me in the loop." Liam's red blotch darkened. "Remember Alroy, my grandson, killed in Boston? Of course they'll be keeping me in the lousy feckin' loop!"

O'Byrne nodded as if he understood.

"Has the Army Council made a move yet?" O'Byrne asked.

"Why do you ask?"

"I heard something that I found troublesome." O'Byrne tinkered with his teacup. "I heard that a third man took a run at Sparhawk in Boston."

"What did you say?"

"And this third man was killed for his efforts," O'Byrne said, "killed by Sparhawk himself."

"What third man?" Liam's eyes bulged. "Who told you this?"

"Jackie Tracy told me." O'Byrne finished his tea. "He told me about a third attempt on Sparhawk's life, a third failed attempt."

"Jackie is mistaken," Liam bellowed. "He's wrong."

"That's what he told me." O'Byrne thought about it. Maybe Liam was out of the loop after all. Maybe the Army Council had brushed him aside and ordered the hit without telling him. "Jackie is reliable."

"In this case he's pretty goddamn unreliable." Liam caught his breath. "The Army Council would have told me if they went after Sparhawk."

"Maybe they didn't go after him," O'Byrne said, just to see where it would lead.

"I don't follow your logic," Liam said. "If the council didn't go after him, and I didn't go after him, who *did* go after him?"

"Maybe it was a coincidence."

"A coincidence, you say?"

"Maybe Sparhawk was in the wrong place at the wrong time. Maybe it was bad luck, a case of happenstance," O'Byrne said.

"Yes, happenstance," Liam said, grasping at O'Byrne's explanation. "Pure chance, as you say."

"That could explain it, Liam."

"Indeed, that explains it."

Despite Liam's fervor to avenge Alroy's murder, Liam seemed too feeble to pull it off. O'Byrne thought about the Army Council, who were anything but feeble. The Army Council had the resources and the reach. *They* had probably hired the third man. Yes, indeed, O'Byrne concluded, it was the Army Council. Besides, Liam would have simply told O'Byrne if he had hired the third man. Sparhawk had killed Liam's grandson.

IV.

The morning sun brightened my room at the Maryville House. I showered, shaved, dressed in my best, and went to one of the inn's tearooms for coffee and pastries, which they call tray bakes. I opened the *Belfast Telegraph* and read an opinion piece by a columnist named Eamonn McCann, who championed labor unions, and I thought of the Teamsters in Charlestown. I finished the paper and finished my coffee. I had time on my hands and an obligation to fulfill, and today was my chance to fulfill it.

When my mother lived in Belfast, years before she immigrated to Boston, she had an aunt who treated her dearly, her Aunt Bridget O'Hanlon. Bridget lived in the Republic of Ireland, in the County of

Louth, in the town of Dundalk. My mother, who died from the drink when I was seven years old, talked of Bridget every day, more so when she was in the spirits. I'd always wanted to meet Bridget, and today I had time to do just that.

I rented a car and drove south for County Louth. An hour later I crossed the border into the Republic of Ireland and kept driving to Dundalk. It was like driving from Boston to Worcester, without the tolls, traffic, and hostility. I located Bridget's house in Seatown Ward, parked the car, and walked to the front door. After taking a deep breath I knocked. An elderly woman opened the door. Her cheeks were sallow, and her skin was loose and dry. She looked up and said, "I hope to God you're a friend and not a foe, the size of you."

"I'm a friend," I said, "though we've never met."

"That much is true. I'd have remembered a leviathan like you."

"That's a whale of a compliment," I said. She didn't laugh. "My name is Dermot Sparhawk, which probably means nothing to you. My mother was Mary O'Hanlon. I am hoping that you are her Aunt Bridget."

She folded her hands across her chest and sighed.

"Sweet Mary O'Hanlon, my favorite niece." She opened the door and told me to come in. "And you are Declan, Declan O'Hanlon you said."

"My name is Dermot Sparhawk."

"Come into the parlor, Declan, and make yourself at home. You were but a child when your mother died, and yet you've grown into a handsome, burly lad. Come into the kitchen and let me get a look at you. Sure, you must be starving."

"I'm fine," I said. "You don't have to–"

"You must taste my Donegal oatmeal cream, for it is the best in the land. I use only the finest pinhead oats in Ireland." She opened the refrigerator and removed a large glass container and spooned a serving into a bowl. "Sit and eat. I'll be back in a snap."

Bridget walked out of the kitchen and returned ten minutes later. In the meantime, I had wiped out the dessert, which was excellent.

"Where did we leave off?" she asked.

"We were talking about the finest pinhead oats in Ireland." I sensed that she was nervous about something, probably me. "You must be wondering why I dropped by like this. I was in Belfast, and I had time on my hands, and I–"

Someone rapped the door knocker and Bridget went to answer it. A man came in. He wore a drab olive suit and a perfectly knotted necktie with red and white diagonal stripes. His white shirt was pressed to the crisp and the cuffs were monogrammed in Irish script. They came into the kitchen and Bridget introduced him to me. His name was Martin McGovern.

Bridget said, "Declan, I'll be right back. I have to get something in my room."

Martin McGovern extended his hand and said, "It is nice to meet you, Declan."

"My name isn't–"

"Bridget is a bit overwhelmed by your visit." Martin patted my shoulder in a friendly way. "She needs to rest now. Let's go into the parlor where we can sit and talk for a time. We need to discuss a few things."

Discuss a few things? I followed him into the parlor. Martin unbuttoned his suit jacket and sat in a chair. I sat, too. I got the impression that he was waiting for me to speak, so I did.

"I showed up unannounced and it looks as though I made a mistake," I said. "I didn't mean to upset her."

"You did nothing wrong."

"And yet she called you."

"Bridget is quite emotional at this time," Martin said. "She is not at all well, I regret to say. Bridget asked me to tell you that she is dying of cancer."

"I didn't know that," I said, feeling foolish. "I'm sorry to hear the bad news."

"The doctors give her a week to live, maybe two." He took off his glasses and dabbed his eyes with a hankie. "She wants to die at home."

Martin set his glasses on an end table. "I have known Bridget for many years. We belong to the same parish. I serve as a deacon. She is a Eucharistic minister. We are dear friends." He put his glasses back on. "Bridget loved your mother, and she believes that your visit is a gift from God."

"A gift from God?" I said.

"She got to meet you before she died."

I thought about my mother and what Aunt Bridget meant to her.

"When my mother was a girl in Belfast, Bridget was good to her," I said. "As you now know, Bridget O'Hanlon was my mother's aunt."

"You referred to your mother in the past tense."

"She died when I was seven," I said. "I came into some money a while ago, quite a large amount actually, and I wanted to give some to Bridget."

Martin smiled and crossed his legs.

I continued. "That's why I visited today, to see if I could help her financially. I also wanted to meet her. She was so kind to my mother." I made eye contact with Martin. "I'm glad she has a good man looking out for her."

"We look out for each other." Martin deflected the compliment with a flip of his hand. "The money won't help her much at this stage. As the saying goes, you can't take it with you."

"No, you can't."

We silently sat in the parlor, and the silence started to get awkward. I took the cue and stood up.

"I should be getting along, Martin. I've imposed long enough." I looked at Bridget's room, hoping to see her one more time. "I'd like to say goodbye to Bridget, but I probably shouldn't bother her again."

"She is very tired."

"Please tell her I said goodbye." I went to the door with Martin. I stopped and faced him. "I'd like to pay for Bridget's funeral, the whole affair. I want to pay for it."

"Why?" Martin asked, stepping back.

"For my mother," I said. "She would have liked that we paid for it."
I gave Martin my number, which he typed into his cell phone. "Please
call me when the time comes."

"This is generous of you." He tucked the phone into his jacket
pocket. "And because of your generosity, Tossy will inherit that much
more."

"Who's Tossy?" I asked.

"Tossy is Bridget's godson," Martin said. "She left her belongings
to him. You remind me a bit of Tossy. He is a good man in an unre-
fined way."

"Thanks for the compliment, I think."

"It *is* a compliment. Too many smoothies make a mess of the world
these days." He stuck out his hand. "It was a pleasure to meet you, sir."

"Likewise, Martin." We shook hands.

I was just about to leave when Bridget came out of her bedroom.

"Hold on, Declan." She reached up and looped a brown cloth
necklace with two brown patches over my head and said, "These are
the Carmelite scapulars. I have sewn a gold Saint Brigit's Cross to it
as an added defense. Wear it for protection. The Lord will never let
you down."

"Thank you," I said, and tucked the necklace into my shirt.

The Carmelite scapulars, Catholic dog tags. If you are wearing
them when you die, you bypass purgatory and go straight to heaven. I
hoped this was true, but I also hoped I wouldn't find out anytime soon.

CHAPTER ELEVEN

I.

O'Byrne sat in the last pew of the Clonard Monastery with his body angled so he could see the doors. He thought about Liam McGrew and Dermot Sparhawk and the IRA Army Council. He thought about the third man, the assassin who failed to kill Sparhawk in Boston. Who was this third man and who hired him? O'Byrne had suspected that Liam had hired him, but now he wasn't so sure. Liam seemed genuinely surprised when O'Byrne told him about the third man. Maybe the Army Council contracted the hit. He thought about Dermot Sparhawk again.

O'Byrne had sent a message to Sparhawk, requesting a meeting with him here at the Clonard Monastery at this very time. Would Sparhawk show up? And what if he didn't? Would it suggest that he went back to Boston, or would it suggest that he was dead? O'Byrne's torment ended when one of the monastery doors opened and Sparhawk walked in. He sat next to O'Byrne in the same pew.

"This place has more chambers than a nautilus shell," Sparhawk quipped.

"It's a sacred haven, the Clonard, the only place I find peace these days."

"No one will bother you in here, that's for sure," Sparhawk said.

Though they spoke softly, their voices echoed in the hollows and alcoves. O'Byrne blessed himself and said, "Do you believe in God, Dermot? Because I believe in God, and I believe he'll forgive me my sins."

"I hope he forgives sins," Sparhawk said. "If not, I might as well get fitted for a red union suit right now."

"This is no place for levity," O'Byrne said. "This is a holy shrine."

"I meant no disrespect." Sparhawk blessed himself, which seemed to be a gesture of solidarity with O'Byrne. "I'm listening."

"I believe God judges us most harshly on sins of omission," O'Byrne continued. "When we fail to act when we are called to act. Do you agree?"

"I never gave it much thought."

Though Sparhawk seemed to be indifferent to the question, O'Byrne pursued the topic nonetheless.

"The Lord will forgive the sexual dalliance or the impulsive drinking spree or even an act of extreme violence," O'Byrne said. "But I don't think he'll forgive a sin of omission, turning your back on a friend when he needs your help. Am I right?"

"I'm not a theologian, O'Byrne." Sparhawk gazed at the stained-glass windows. "What a magnificent building."

"Aye, 'tis."

"Why did you call me here today?" Sparhawk asked.

"Liam suspects you're in Belfast." O'Byrne craned his head and gazed at the vaulted ceiling. "He all but said it the other day."

"That's not good news, but it's not surprising news, either."

"He suspects that I know you're in Belfast." He thumbed the rosary beads in his hands. "You put me in harm's way. I'm a dead man if he finds out we talked."

"I won't tell him."

"You won't tell him. My God, you haven't a clue." O'Byrne let loose a laugh that filled the side chapels. "Do you not understand, lad? You'll never get the chance to tell him. If he finds out you're here in

Belfast, by God, he will kill you. If he knew you were at the Maryville House, he'd burn it to the ground."

"Let's hope he doesn't find out."

O'Byrne leaned back in the pew and absorbed the beauty of the monastery. He listened to the sounds of the outside world and smelled the burning candles.

"Why did you come to Slattery's that day?" O'Byrne asked.

"Because I want to end this thing, right here in Belfast," Sparhawk said. "I can't live life looking over my shoulder. If I get killed, I'll get killed in Belfast."

"But did you why come to me?"

"You called off the hit on me," Sparhawk said. "You called it off because you want no more sins of omission staining your soul."

"I suppose you're right about that." O'Byrne laughed again, but not as loudly. "My *boyo* in heaven, Saint Angus MacNisse of Connor, has quite a sense of humor."

"Who's Saint Angus MacNisse?"

"Doesn't matter," O'Byrne said. "So a third man came at you in Boston. Tell me, what did he look like?"

Sparhawk closed his eyes and began to speak.

"He was an older man, probably in his sixties. He wore a dark suit with pinstripes. White shirt, red tie, silver cufflinks, cordovan wingtips—all of it was quality stuff. He had a trim build and thinning hair. His hands looked soft, not the hands of a workingman. He wasn't fat, but he wasn't solid, a man with a desk job. The only thing that distinguished him was a gun."

"Did he speak at all?" O'Byrne waited. "Did he have a brogue?"

"He never spoke to me, because he never got a chance to speak," Sparhawk said. "I didn't even see him until he was dead."

"How is that possible?"

"Another man, who was hired to look out for me, shot the third man twice in the head. Right there on the bridge he killed him."

"So he never spoke to you, this third man." O'Byrne palmed his scalp. "Usually the Irish give you a little something, like 'This bullet is from Liam McGrew,' or something like that. I don't know why we do that, but we do."

"I don't think he was Irish," Sparhawk said.

"Not Irish?" O'Byrne sounded surprised. "How can you be sure?"

"No real reason, just an impression."

"That's not very persuasive." O'Byrne folded his hands. The rosary beads were back in his pocket. "Did Alroy and McAfee strike you as Irish?"

"McAfee did, yes. I couldn't really see Alroy because it was dark. I thought I heard a brogue, but Alroy was so drunk it could have been a slur." Sparhawk waved his hand as if something came to him. "I wasn't surprised when I found out Alroy was Irish, but I would be surprised if the third man was Irish."

The two men kept talking. O'Byrne asked Sparhawk what he planned to do next, and Sparhawk told him he wasn't entirely sure. They rose from the pew in unison and genuflected in the aisle as one. At the holy water font, they dipped their fingers and blessed themselves. They left the monastery in staggered fashion, Sparhawk first, O'Byrne fifteen minutes later. One can never be too careful in Belfast.

II.

O'Byrne took a bus to the Teagueland Inn, a Belfast barrelhouse favored by the weary lads of Sinn Fein, located in the working-class enclave of Sailortown. He was sitting alone in the rear of the bus when he removed a revolver from his waistband. He released the cylinder and checked the bullets. The gun was fully loaded. He bent low and eyed the front sight. He fingered the trigger, clutched the grip, and with a flick of the wrist he snapped the cylinder shut and tucked the gun back in his waistband.

The Teagueland Inn was also favored by members of the Army Council, who gathered there to discuss matters that needed discussing. And if no matters came up that needed discussing, they'd stay the night anyway in case such matters arose. The bus pulled up in front, the last stop on the route, and O'Byrne got off.

The sun sank hard in the Ulster west, casting a dreary pall over the Clarendon docks. The waters rested calmly, barely lapping the pilings, barely indicating the war zone that had once raged here. O'Byrne went inside the inn and ordered whiskey at the bar, and he looked around the room. Sitting alone at a table near the kitchen was Salty McBrine, a longtime council member in good standing, a man O'Byrne could trust. He walked to Salty's table and cleared his throat. Salty looked up and seemed pleased.

"O'Byrne, it has been too bloody long. Pull up a chair and join me for a taste." Salty drank some ale. "What brings you to Sailortown on this gray evening?"

"I needed a change of scenery, I suppose." O'Byrne sat across from Salty and placed his whiskey on the table. "And some pleasant company."

"So it's pleasant company you're after."

"Aye." O'Byrne sipped. "Pleasant company and pleasant conversation are hard to come by these days."

"Indeed, indeed, both are scarce in the North," Salty said. "People think the Troubles are over, but they're not."

"No, they're not," O'Byrne agreed.

"So now, how are the lads at Slattery's faring?"

"Good, very good," O'Byrne said.

They talked and drank through three more rounds. Salty switched to the hard stuff, Bushmills Black Bush his choice, and he began to show the whiskey's effect. When O'Byrne detected a slur in Salty's speech, he made his move.

"Did you know that on this very day in 1922, Michael Collins himself was killed?" O'Byrne signaled the bartender for another round. "'Twas a bad day for the big fellow, a fatal day indeed. He was traveling from Dublin to Cork when they got him."

"Aye, you're right about that. That's where they ambushed him, Cork, possibly slain by his very own." Salty drank. "The Treaty caused fierce quarrels. Anti-treaty Irish stood accused of killing Collins, and maybe they did at that. We'll likely never know."

O'Byrne nodded to Salty. "Black '47, the potato famines, the repeal of the Corn Laws, the Brits exporting grain while a million Irish starved, it's a wonder any of us survived." He waved for another round. "Another million fled Ireland all together. America, Australia, Canada, they left for good, too."

"They did at that, they did at that, none to return to their ancestral home."

"They settled all over the world, the United States, especially," O'Byrne said. "New York, Philadelphia, Chicago, Boston."

"Don't forget about the Appalachian backcountry and the Carolina Piedmont, the Irish weren't all city folk, O'Byrne." Salty slugged down the whiskey. "I have relatives in New York, out in Brooklyn, in the Red Hook section, firemen and policemen. I went to Red Hook once. You'd think I was Saint Patrick himself the way they treated me."

"I have people in Boston."

"Have you been to Boston?" Salty asked. "It's a grand town, lots of Irish."

"Not to visit family, no."

"Well, I highly recommend it." Salty put his glass on the table. "Have you been to Boston on other matters?"

"I visited a couple of times in the past."

"But not to see family?"

"No, not family," O'Byrne said quietly.

"Did you go on holiday?"

"No, not holiday," O'Byrne said.

"You went to Boston, but not for family or holiday." Salty was now leaning forward in his seat. "Perhaps you went for matters pertaining to army business. Was it army business then, the Boston excursion?"

Salty was asking if it was army business, which meant that Salty knew nothing about the trip to Boston. Liam never told him about the job.

"I respect the chain of command," O'Byrne said. "Liam is my commander, the head of our cell. Do you understand my position?"

"It is a good thing to honor the chain of command." Salty looked over his shoulder and then back at O'Byrne. "Liam is your immediate commander, after all."

"I'm with him a long time now, Salty."

"And a loyal soldier you've been. You never shied away from sacrifice, as I well know, being your cellmate in the Maze."

"Hard times in the Maze back then," O'Byrne said. "Sleeping in shite, the stench, the maggots."

"The hunger strikes, the blankets, the billie beatings, the dirty protests."

"The hosings and torture."

"Thank God it's in the past," Salty said, the whiskey's effect vanishing from his eyes. "Tell me now, this business in Boston, what did it entail?"

Liam never told the Army Council about the World's Fair of Money. He never got the okay from the high command, and more importantly, he never paid tribute to the cause. This was bad, very bad indeed. And then there were the deaths. Alroy McGrew, William McAfee, and the third man, whoever he might be, all dead. Liam implied that the Army Council had hired the third man, but they couldn't have hired him, because Liam never told them about Boston. And what about Mr. H's payment of two million dollars? What about the sheet of $100,000 bills? Was Liam hoarding it for himself?

O'Byrne's loyalty to Liam waned in light of this information. What did he really owe Liam anyway? Still, Liam had rank. And Liam had fought for the cause. There had to be an explanation, surely there had to be.

Salty repeated, "O'Byrne, I asked you about Boston."

"It was nothing, just a trip."

"Just a trip? And when did this trip take place?"

"Not long ago, Liam can fill you in."

"Liam neglected to tell us of this American foray," Salty said, his eyes now alert. "I've never known Liam's crew to leave Belfast."

It seemed that the Army Council didn't know about the museum job from two decades ago, either. Where had that *money* gone? And the paintings, what about the paintings? A Rembrandt, a Vermeer, a Degas, worth hundreds of millions. Was Liam freelancing without the council's approval?

"He probably forgot to mention it." O'Byrne tapped his empty glass on the table. "Liam has been ill."

"Liam's been ill, you say. Then it was just an oversight on his part, not telling us about Boston. Is that what you're saying, O'Byrne?"

"Aye, that's what I'm saying." His job was done. O'Byrne got up from the table. "It was a good talk we had, Salty. I need to be getting home now."

"Are you still living on Divis Street?"

"I am indeed."

"I'll be stopping by for a cup of tea someday soon." Salty stood. "We have more to discuss."

"The kettle will be boiling."

O'Byrne shook Salty McBrine's hand and left the Teagueland Inn.

III.

I ate pot roast with mashed potatoes and green beans at a Shankill Road tavern, washing it down with pistachio cake and tea. After walking off the supper I returned to the Maryville House and drank coffee in the front lobby. In my room I stretched out on the bed, but I couldn't unwind. I turned on the TV, but the local cable didn't carry the Red Sox, sparing the people of Belfast one form of torture. I was wondering how many games the Sox were out of first place when my cell phone rang. Kenny Bowen was calling.

We exchanged hellos and it became apparent that Kenny had something to tell me, something he was building up to, probably something good. Excitement infused his voice, so I listened without interrupting. Interrupting would have ruined the dramatic flow. He eventually got to the point.

"I know the identity of the third man," he said, "but it makes no sense to me."

"Tell me about him."

"I'll tell you about him, but I can't see the third man's connection to either Liam McGrew or the IRA."

"What's his name, Kenny?" I asked.

"His name is Phillip Webb, a highly decorated British Army Intelligence officer who specialized in counter sabotage in Belfast and Derry. He spent a great deal of time in London, too."

"Phillip Webb was with the British Army?"

"That is correct," Kenny said.

I said to verify, "Phillip Webb was the gunman on the bridge, the man Rat T. Kennedy shot in the head."

"I confirmed his identity with Scotland Yard, but I still can't figure his link to the IRA, especially his willingness to kill for Liam McGrew."

"He must have had a reason," I said.

"How does a top British Army soldier fit with the IRA?" Kenny shuffled papers and apparently found what he wanted. "Listen to his credentials. Webb earned one of his many medals by foiling an IRA arms shipment off the coast of Londonderry, in the town of Tullyverry. He and his battalion killed four IRA rebels that day."

"Four of them?"

"Webb was a one-man wrecking crew as far as the IRA was concerned. You should see his list of arrests." Kenny shuffled more papers. "He loved collecting trophies and medals for acts of valor. He thrived on the recognition."

"What else does the report say?"

He shuffled papers again. It must have been quite the report.

"Phillip Charles Webb graduated first in his class at the Royal Military Academy Sandhurst, the British equivalent of West Point. Before Sandhurst he attended Eton, where he excelled as a student and an athlete."

"Why would a superstar like Webb come to Boston to shoot me?" I asked. "It doesn't fit the pattern."

"What pattern?"

"Alroy McGrew and William McAfee, both IRA soldiers, tried to kill me, which makes sense. And then Phillip Webb, a decorated British Army Intelligence officer, tried to kill me, which *doesn't* make sense. Webb doesn't fit with the other two men. He's not IRA. More than that, he's their enemy. So why would Webb do the IRA's bidding?"

"An excellent question."

"Yeah, but what's the answer?"

"Webb doesn't fit on the face of it, and yet he must fit in somehow. I'll keep digging to see what else I can find out. Hold the fort," Kenny said. "I have a call coming in from Scotland Yard. I'll get back to you." And he hung up.

I tried something that was a reach for me: I brainstormed. It wasn't exactly a synaptic tsunami. As I brainstormed along, I was raising more questions than I was arriving at answers. For example:

Why would a British Army Intelligence officer, a man who had stopped numerous IRA maneuvers in the past, agree to kill me for the IRA? What was it that motivated Webb? I couldn't come up with an answer, so I flipped my thinking around. What if the IRA had nothing to do with Webb? What if Webb acted on his own? I thought about that for a while and came up with another question. What if Webb's attempt on my life had something to do with the money fair? I mulled over that prospect, and I decided it didn't seem likely. He wouldn't get reward money if he killed me, so why would he do it? What was driving him?

I sifted the information, looking at it from ten different angles, and something clicked into place, a possible reason for Webb to fly to Boston to put me to sleep. He was taking orders from Liam Mc-Grew. It had to be Liam. This led to another question. Why would Webb be taking orders from Liam?

I weighed and reweighed the information. Liam McGrew and Phillip Webb, an IRA chieftain and a British Army Intelligence soldier, conspiring to kill me. I almost felt special, bringing warring factions together. But why would they team up? They had nothing in common, or did they? And if they had something in common, what the hell was it, and why did it involve me?

I kept on brainstorming and I arrived at a plausible if fantastical explanation, an explanation I never would have thought of if not for the shenanigans between the Boston office of the FBI and the Boston mob. Paid snitches.

What if Liam was an informer to the British Army? And what if Webb was his handler? I was making an assumption, and a crazy assumption at that, but I ran with it anyway. Act as if, they say in AA.

So I acted as if it were true. And if it were true, there had to be more to it. Why would Webb go the extra mile for Liam, more precisely, the extra three thousand miles? Why would he go to Boston to kill me? He wouldn't do it to avenge Alroy, no way. What was I missing?

I closed my eyes and let my mind drift, which was a more typical state for me than brainstorming. I had nearly drifted off to sleep when it hit me, the motive I was looking for. The heisted money. Cash conjoined Liam and Webb like Siamese twins. The robbery of the World's Fair of Money, the missing sheet of $100,000 bills—*that* was the bond that yoked them.

Thirty-two $100,000 bills, a total of $3.2 million, $1.6 million apiece if they split it. That was a lot of cash, an amount worth killing for. Duty to cause? Loyalty to country? Those ideals had nothing to do with Liam and Webb. If I was right, Liam betrayed Catholic Belfast and Webb betrayed England, in a slimy partnership built on greed.

IV.

I was asleep atop the covers when Kenny called back. I picked up the phone and he jumped right in.

"I just got off the phone with Scotland Yard," he said. "Phillip Webb was a double agent. Liam McGrew was his informant."

"It makes sense, doesn't it?"

"You're not surprised by this information?" Kenny sounded disappointed.

"I did a little speculating on my own while I was lying here, and the agent-rat alliance occurred to me."

"But why did Phillip Webb go to Boston to kill you? The grudge was between you and Liam, so why did Webb get involved in a petty squabble like that?"

"It's not petty if you're the one getting shot at, Kenny," I said.

"Come on, you know what I'm saying."

Something about Kenny's story didn't jibe.

"Why did Scotland Yard tell you about Webb and Liam?" I asked. "That's top-secret stuff, so why the loose lips in London?"

"One of the deputy commissioners is a close friend of mine," Kenny answered. "We were roommates at Oxford. He trusts me, so he told me about Webb and Liam."

Something else didn't jibe. "How is it that a Scotland Yard man in London knew about a British Army Intelligence officer in Belfast?"

"You have a curious mind, Dermot." Kenny paused. "My friend serves as liaison between London and Belfast. Thus, he is linked to the British Army in Northern Ireland, a dotted-line connection as they say."

"Back to loose lips, your friend took a pretty big risk telling you about Webb and Liam. I know he trusts you, but information like that leaks out, it could jeopardize their cover." Dummy me. "I get it. Scotland Yard cared only about Phillip Webb, and now he's dead. They don't give a damn about Liam McGrew."

"They didn't really give a damn about Webb, either. My friend was ambivalent about Webb. On one hand, he thought Webb was fairly productive, an agent who delivered on IRA movements. On the other hand, he thought Webb was an opportunist, a climber out for personal gain. My friend also thought that Webb was a thief, and that Webb and Liam had worked together on robberies abroad."

"And yet Webb was highly decorated."

"Which gave him the perfect cover, a man beyond reproach. My friend theorized that Liam fed Webb small-time stuff to make their partnership look legitimate. Liam would throw Webb a few crumbs, so to speak. In return, Webb would give Liam early warning when something was coming down in Belfast."

"And then they'd pulled off robberies on their own," I said. "They were in cahoots."

"But why would Webb go to Boston to kill you?" Kenny asked.

"To get himself a big payday," I said. "Liam probably offered Webb a share of the $100,000 bills. Webb gets a piece of the $100,000 bills for killing me. That was the deal." I gave it more thought. "Liam also needed Webb to launder the money, which gave Webb a bit of leverage."

"It sounds like three-dimensional chess."

"Webb is dead," I said, thinking as I was speaking. "Liam still needs to sell the fourth sheet of bills, unless he already unloaded it."

"*Unless* he unloaded it? You think he still has it?"

"Maybe."

There was a long pause on the line, and it lingered longer than it should have. Dummy me again.

"You don't owe me anything, Kenny."

"What are you taking about?"

"The $100,000 bills," I said.

"I still don't know what you're talking about."

"It's okay with me if you go straight to Liam McGrew," I said.

"What do you mean?"

"I understand the situation. You were hired to recover the stolen money. It's your job to get it back, and I don't want to get in the way of your job."

"Dermot, we're working on this together."

"Buy the sheet directly from Liam, with no middleman to muddle things up. It's easier that way."

"And leave you hanging in Belfast?" He sounded ticked off. "I don't do business that way."

"I understand the circumstances." I paused for a beat. "It's okay with me."

"But it's not okay with *me*," he said. "We're going to see this through to the end, the two of us, side by side, that was the agreement. I don't take shortcuts, and I won't backdoor you. I thought we had an understanding. What kind of a man do you think I am?"

"I'm trying to get you the money."

"The hell with the money," he said.

"I'm in Belfast to stop Liam from killing me. That's my priority, staying alive. Retrieving the money is secondary. From my side of it, even if I got my hands on the money, Liam still wants me dead. From your side of it, I could get killed and you still don't have the money. It's simple logic. It's okay with me if you go straight to the moneyman, Liam McGrew."

"I won't do that, Dermot."

"It's all right if you do. That's all I'm saying."

"That's *all* you're saying? Well, there's another saying, and an Irishman named Oscar Wilde said it. 'A true friend stabs you in the front, never the back.' If I were going to make a deal with Liam, which I'm not, I'd tell you upfront."

"I never said you wouldn't."

"Don't you get it? This is all of one, getting the money, saving your ass, the two are inseparable. Got it?"

"Yeah, I got it."

"Are we okay?"

"We're okay." If not for Kenny I'd be dead. Webb would have killed me on the Northern Avenue Bridge if Kenny hadn't hired Rat T. Kennedy to save my life. "Sometimes my mind goes–"

"Yeah, mine, too."

V.

O'Byrne was sipping tea in the kitchen when he heard a soft knock on the door. He opened it and saw Dermot Sparhawk standing in front of him. O'Byrne hustled Sparhawk inside and closed the door behind him.

"What are you doing, trying to get me killed?"

"We need to talk," Sparhawk said, pulling out a chair and sitting at the kitchen table. "It's important."

"Make yourself at home, why don't you," O'Byrne said with a flippant tone. "The nerve of you coming here."

"A cup of tea would be nice," Sparhawk countered.

"A cup of tea, you say?" O'Byrne stared at Sparhawk's face. "I suppose a touch of hospitality wouldn't hurt anybody."

O'Byrne made a cup of tea for Sparhawk and placed it in front of him. Sparhawk bowed his head and let the steam warm his face.

"I just got off the phone with a friend in Boston." Sparhawk raised his head from the cup and looked straight ahead, no expression on his face. "He's connected in high places, and he knows how to use those connections."

"You're lucky to be having friends in high places," O'Byrne said. "And I suppose your friend told you some things."

"He told me about a man named Phillip Webb." Sparhawk turned the cup halfway around in the saucer, one hundred and eighty degrees. "Do you know him?"

"Never heard of him."

"Webb was a British Army Intelligence officer," Sparhawk said, sniffing the dying steam. "Webb is the man who tried to kill me in Boston last week."

"Is that so?"

"This friend I was telling you about, the connected guy, he hired a man to watch over me. The man watching over me shot Webb before Webb shot me. He's dead."

"British Army Intelligence, you say?"

"That's what I said, British Army Intelligence."

"They're a nasty lot." O'Byrne thought about Kathleen's murder, killed by the Brits decades ago. In a perverse way, Kathleen's death could be attributed to collateral damage. The hit squad meant to kill O'Byrne, thus her killing could be deemed an act of war. It had taken O'Byrne decades to come to this conviction, Kathleen's death as an act of war. "Bless the saints you're alive, Dermot. Now why would a

British Amy Intelligence officer go after an American like you in Boston, Massachusetts?"

"I asked myself that very question," Sparhawk said.

"And did you come up with an answer?"

"My friend told me that Phillip Webb was a rogue agent. He also told me that Scotland Yard suspected Webb of double dealings. They'd been tracking him for some time now. Webb infiltrated the IRA as a double agent."

"Is that so?"

Sparhawk leaned his elbows on the pine table and said, "Webb worked with Liam. Liam was Webb's informer."

"Ah, your head's in the sand, up to your neck in it." Liam, a tout? It couldn't be true. But if it were true, everything O'Byrne stood for was a pile of shite. "You're wrong about Liam."

"I'm not wrong. Webb was working with Liam. Liam fed Webb details on IRA operations, and Webb would then undercut you guys."

"Never!"

"Liam and Webb also plotted crimes abroad." Sparhawk kept going. "That's why Webb went to Boston to kill me. Liam promised Webb a piece of the money-fair heist for the hit. Your boss is a traitor and a thief, O'Byrne."

"Liam might be many things, but he is not a traitor." O'Byrne walked to the kitchen counter and poured whiskey into a cup. "He is a true son of Ireland, a rebel soldier to his core. He would never betray the cause."

"He betrayed the cause," Sparhawk said. "And he profiteered on the side, using the cause for his own financial gain."

"Bullshit!"

"Think about the stolen paintings from two decades ago. Think about the $100,000 bills from last month. Did Liam turn in the money to the so-called Irish cause, or did he keep it for himself?"

O'Byrne then remembered his talk at the Teagueland Inn with Salty McBrine. It seemed that Salty knew nothing of the robberies in

Boston. Maybe Sparhawk was telling the truth. No, it couldn't be true. O'Byrne slammed his cup on the table.

"Liam is no traitor."

"Let's pretend that Liam turned in the money," Sparhawk said.

"He did, I tell you."

Why was O'Byrne insisting on something that he knew wasn't true? Was he so committed to Liam that the truth didn't matter?

"If he turned it in, why did Webb go to Boston to kill me?" Sparhawk asked. "If Liam turned in the money, Webb gets nothing for killing me, because there'd be nothing to get. So why did Webb go to Boston? Can you answer that question?"

"I don't know why he went."

"Phillip Webb was in the middle of a profiteering scheme with Liam McGrew." Sparhawk took the last of his tea. "I got dragged into it when I killed Alroy. That's when it got personal for Liam."

"You're wrong."

"If I'm wrong, why did McAfee come after me?"

"Ach, you're wrong!"

"That's what happens when a family member gets killed, things get personal," Sparhawk said. "Alroy was Liam's only kin, I'm told."

"That much is true." O'Byrne allowed. "Alroy was the last of the Belfast McGrews."

"And I was the guy that crushed his skull with a rock," Sparhawk said. "Liam wanted me dead, even if it meant using a British soldier to kill me."

"I don't believe that for a bloody second, not for a bloody feckin' second," O'Byrne was now yelling. "No way possible."

"Who else could it be but Liam?" Sparhawk asked. "Who else wanted me dead?"

"How am I supposed to know these things?" O'Byrne pointed his finger at Sparhawk. "Get out, Dermot. Go on now. Leave before something bad happens to you."

At the door Sparhawk turned and said, "I'm on your side, O'Byrne."

§

O'Byrne thought about the conversation with Sparhawk and a question came to him. Why did he get so defensive when Sparhawk accused Liam of wrongdoings that O'Byrne himself had suspected of Liam? It didn't make sense. Why was he fighting Sparhawk's thrust? He thought back to Sailortown. O'Byrne had grown suspicious of Liam after his talk with Salty at the Teagueland Inn. Sparhawk's charges reinforced what O'Byrne feared, that Liam was a thief who was out for himself, that the Irish cause was nothing but a secondary matter to him. O'Byrne had some serious thinking to do.

CHAPTER TWELVE

I.

O'Byrne walked into Slattery's back room with a pint of beer in his hand and saw Liam McGrew sitting in his chair, waiting for him. O'Byrne had asked Liam for a meeting, and Liam, tired of being housebound, agreed to meet him at Slattery's Pub. Liam stared at an open jug of whiskey as he spoke.

"Well, you called me here, O'Byrne." He gurgled. "What do you want?"

"We need to talk," O'Byrne said, with a deferential tone in his voice.

"I'm all ears, O'Byrne, big feckin' rabbit ears." He belched. "What do you have to say for yourself?"

O'Byrne studied Liam's darkening face, his flushed complexion and watery eyes. Liam had been drinking and a foul mood had hold of him.

Liam said, "Go on, I'm listening."

"The subject is a bit delicate."

"What am I dealing with here, a feckin' girl? Look at the puss on ya." Liam poured whiskey into his glass, spilling some on the table. "Spit it out, man!"

"I've heard some things, not that I believe them for a second."

"You've heard some things, boohoo." He mocked O'Byrne. "As if I feckin' care what you heard or what you believe."

"Liam–"

"And obviously you believed them or we wouldn't be here talking now, would we?" He whacked the table with his blackthorn walking stick. "Okay big ears, tell me what you heard? What do you want to ask me about? I'm listening."

O'Byrne finished his pint and filled the bottom of his glass with whiskey from the jug. "These things I've heard, they, ah–"

"Speak! Are you a man or a mouse?"

O'Byrne drank the whiskey in a single gulp and slammed the glass on the table.

"Who is Phillip Webb?" O'Byrne said, and then he repeated. "Who the feck is Phillip Webb?"

"I never heard of him." Liam's blotch blazed. "Phillip who?"

"Phillip Webb worked in British Army Intelligence in Belfast." O'Byrne poured more whiskey from the jug. "Phillip Webb was the third man."

"What third man, what are you talking about?"

"The third man in Boston," O'Byrne said. "After Alroy and McAfee failed to kill Sparhawk, Webb gave it a try. He too failed and he too met his demise."

"I can't say I'm sorry that a Brit met his demise."

O'Byrne waited for Liam to look at him.

"You're lying, Liam. You knew Phillip Webb."

Liam didn't get mad, didn't explode as O'Byrne had expected him to do, he didn't react at all. He simply sat back and nodded his head.

"I paid Phillip Webb for the hit on Sparhawk," Liam admitted. "I paid him out of my own pocket."

O'Byrne asked Liam how much he paid Webb, but Liam refused to answer, saying it was none of O'Byrne's business. The two men went quiet for a time, and then Liam's expression changed. His color returned to normal and he seemed to regroup. Liam thumped the table with authority and spoke in a low grumble.

"Did you ever think you're alive because of me?"

"Alive because of you?" O'Byrne snorted. "You'll have to explain that one to me, Liam."

"The raid at Tullyverry, do you remember it?"

"Aye, I remember it." O'Byrne was still seething. "How could I forget? I remember we lost four men that day."

"But you weren't one of them, were you?" Liam gripped the stick so tightly his knuckles went white. "I warned you, didn't I? I told you to keep clear of Tullyverry. Did that fact slip your mind? I warned you because the operation got compromised. Does any of this ring a bell inside that thick head of yours?"

"Four men dead, forgive me if I'm not giddy."

"I tried to get word to the whole squad, but I couldn't." Liam insisted.

"Right, you tried."

"Tullyverry was forty years ago, forty feckin' years ago. There were no cell phones back then, so how could I get word to the others? I am haunted by Tullyverry, O'Byrne. It has haunted me every night of my life." He tapped the stick on the floor. "I'll tell you something else, something I couldn't tell you before, because Webb was still alive. Phillip Webb tipped me off to Tullyverry. He got word to me at the eleventh hour, very late in the game. If I had found out earlier, I could have saved the whole crew, but as it turned out I could only save you and Mac."

"Liam, I wasn't questioning your–"

"Questioning, you say? Ach, we all question things. But tell me this and tell me no more, do you believe me?" Liam waved his hand. "Think about what I told you and think about this. In our business we get our hands filthy dirty, handling scum to get what we need. I have eaten shite for the cause, too much shite if you want to know, and I'm proud to have eaten it, and I'd eat it again."

"Liam, easy now."

"If I hadn't wallowed in shite with the likes of Phillip Webb, you'd be dead. You'd be feckin' dead!" Liam sat up. "I don't expect blind loyalty, nay, but I *do* expect the benefit of the doubt. You might be asking yourself, why? Why didn't Liam tell me about Phillip Webb? I didn't tell you because it was too damn dangerous. I was protecting you, O'Byrne, just as I've always protected you. I saved you at Tullyverry and I've saved you from other calamities you don't even know about. So think about *that* when you're sitting in judgment of me."

II.

I called O'Byrne at noontime but he didn't pick up. When his answering service kicked in, I hung up. A few minutes later he called me back.

"I was praying the Angelus at the Clonard Monastery when your call came in," O'Byrne said. "The church bells ringing, the candles burning, 'twas a holy moment indeed. Are you familiar with the Angelus?"

I told him that I was familiar with it and said, "The angel of the Lord declared unto Mary, and she conceived by the power of the Holy Spirit."

"Behold the handmaid of the Lord," O'Byrne said, keeping the prayer going. "Be it done unto me according to your word."

"And the word was made flesh and dwelt among us," I said. "We need to talk. Can we meet in Dundalk?"

"Dundalk, you say?"

"Do you know it?"

"Aye, I most certainly do know it. But why Dundalk?"

"Because it's not Belfast." Then I told him the real reason. "I visited family in Dundalk recently and I liked the town. We'll have more privacy down there."

"Aye, indeed, Dundalk is a second home to me," O'Byrne said. "It has a very special place in my heart, second only to the Clonard."

"Where's a good place to meet?" I asked.

"I know of the perfect spot," he answered. "On the banks of Castletown River there sits a cozy family tavern named Herrick's. I'll meet you there at six o'clock."

"I'll see you then."

§

I drove to Dundalk and found Herrick's Tavern right where O'Byrne said it would be, on the banks of the Castletown River. More precisely, it was adjacent to the Dundalk Bridge, or as the woman who gave me directions told me, the Big Bridge. I went inside. It had the homey atmosphere that O'Byrne had promised, including a blazing fireplace and copper sconces on every post. The barman smiled and waited for me to order. I asked him for tea with milk.

"Barry's or Bewley's?" he said, still smiling.

I told him I'd have Barry's, which he served in a clay teapot. I finished the first cup and was working on the second when O'Byrne came in. He pointed to a table in front of the fireplace and sat at it. I picked up my tea and joined him. We said hello and shook hands, and it was all measured and cautious.

"The smoked shoulder is the best in County Louth," he said. "It could be the best in the entire world. I highly recommend it to you."

"Okay," I said. "I'll give it a try."

We both ordered smoked shoulder. O'Byrne told the waitress he'd have a pint of Guinness, and I stuck with tea. We didn't talk much at first. We ate and drank. I finished the meal, which lived up to O'Byrne's billing, and I ordered a Coke to wash it down. O'Byrne pushed his plate away and theatrically rubbed his belly. The waitress handed us desert menus. I thought of Aunt Bridget, and I asked her if Herrick's carried Donegal oatmeal cream.

Before she answered, O'Byrne said, "My godmother makes the best Donegal oatmeal cream in all of Ireland."

"I'd have to taste it to be convinced," I said, "because my great-aunt makes the best I've ever had."

The waitress told us that Herrick's didn't serve Donegal oatmeal cream, and we went without desert. O'Byrne ordered another Guinness. When the waitress left the table, he said, "Now that the niceties are out of the way, tell me what's on your mind."

"I want to talk to you about Tullyverry," I said.

O'Byrne placed his pint on the table and stared at me. "How do you know about Tullyverry?"

"My friend in Boston told me about it. It was in Phillip Webb's report." I waited for a group of customers to walk by the table. "You lost four comrades at Tullyverry."

"I almost got killed myself." O'Byrne admitted. "If Liam hadn't gotten word to me when he did, I'd have been the fifth to die. The Brits were after our gun shipments. They captured two ships and sank another that night."

"The Brits *knew* about the gun shipments ahead of time," I said.

"That seems obvious, doesn't it?"

"An informer told them about it." I paused for effect. "The informer was Liam McGrew. Liam told Webb about the shipments."

"No feckin' way. He never told Webb anything like that." O'Byrne finished the remains of his Guinness and signaled for another one. "You have to let this go, Dermot, this obsession with Liam McGrew."

"Let it go?" I chafed. "He's trying to kill me."

"That's not what I meant," O'Byrne said.

"What *did* you mean?"

"You make him out to be a spy or some such thing. Liam has done some irregular things, I'll admit that much, but that doesn't make him a traitor," O'Byrne rubbed his forehead. "It's Phillip Webb. Webb was a Brit. You can't trust Webb."

"You can't trust Liam, either," I said. "I know all about Webb's activities, and I know all about his work with Liam. My friend read Webb's reports to me."

"The reports were probably faked to make Liam look bad," O'Byrne said. "The Brits would do that, you know. They would pit us against each other to create strife within the ranks."

O'Byrne was dug in. His loyalty to Liam would be tough to break. The only thing I could do was bombard him with facts and hope to shatter the bond between them.

"Liam was in league with Webb." I leaned across the table and grabbed O'Byrne's arm. "Liam told Webb about Tullyverry."

"You can't prove any of this, none of it at all."

"Liam is the lowest thing an Irishman can be," I said. "He is an informer to the British government."

"I don't believe that, not for a bloody second."

My cell phone rang. It was Kenny Bowen. I told O'Byrne I had to take the call.

III.

Sparhawk answered the phone, spoke briefly, but mostly listened. The call lasted a long time. His jaw tightened and his face blanched. Sparhawk folded the phone and put it in his pocket.

"I can't believe this," he said to himself. "Un-fuckin'-believable."

"What's wrong?" O'Byrne asked. "You're as white as a birch tree."

"That was my friend in Boston." Sparhawk stared up at the ceiling. "He's received more information."

"Did he now?" O'Byrne looked at Sparhawk's face, trying to get a read on it. "What information?"

"I don't know how to tell you this," Sparhawk said, still staring at the ceiling. "It's bad."

"Don't be a cheeky bastard, talk to me about it."

Sparhawk signaled the waitress and said, "Double Jameson straight up."

"You don't drink."

"I know I don't." His eyes turned to O'Byrne. "The drink is for you."

"What in blazes is going on, Dermot?"

Sparhawk drew a breath and said, "My friend just told me that a British Army hit squad murdered your wife."

"Is that all?" O'Byrne breathed a sigh of relief. He was bracing for something worse. "That's yesterday's news, decades old. I knew about it years ago."

"They murdered her."

"They killed her but they intended to kill me." O'Byrne leaned forward to explain. "Kathleen's death was an accident of war. I was the target."

"Kathleen was the target."

"No, Dermot." O'Byrne winced at the memory of it. "The Brits meant to kill me, but I wasn't home."

"The Brits knew you wouldn't be at home," Sparhawk said. "That's how they planned the murder."

"What do you mean, planned?"

"They knew Liam would draw you away from the house, leaving Kathleen alone and vulnerable. With you out of the way, they could kill Kathleen without a struggle."

"What are you saying?" O'Byrne looked straight at Sparhawk. "What the feck are you saying?"

"The Brits targeted Kathleen, not you."

"You're out of your feckin' mind." O'Byrne gulped down the double Jameson. "I was the target. Me!"

"Liam told them to kill her."

"Stop it, stop what you're saying."

"O'Byrne, I am really sorry but it's true. Liam ordered Webb to murder Kathleen." Sparhawk continued, undeterred. "Webb led the hit squad that night. He led it because Liam told him to lead it. Liam wanted to make sure everything went right."

"Everything went right?" O'Byrne face turned red with fury. "Everything went wrong that night. And you're wrong, too!"

"I wish I were wrong," Sparhawk said in a flat tone.

"You're as crazy as a loon." Veins throbbed in O'Byrne's neck. "Why would Liam kill Kathleen? What would he gain by killing her?"

"Your loyalty."

"My loyalty?" He reached for the whiskey but the glass was dry.

"According to Webb's report, Liam thought you were walking away from the cause." Sparhawk spoke calmly and clearly, as if addressing a jury. "Liam sensed you wanted out of Belfast."

"How could he possibly sense that?" O'Byrne said. "There's no way in hell he could know that."

"My friend obtained more of Webb's reports. Webb took notes like a recording secretary. He wrote everything down." Sparhawk walked to the fireplace and kept talking. "Liam thought you were leaving Belfast—that's what it said in Webb's report. He killed Kathleen to keep you here. Liam needed you for his criminal undertakings. Webb needed you, too. They were a team, you were the robber."

"Impossible," O'Byrne said.

"Liam knew that if the Brits killed Kathleen, he'd own you forever." Sparhawk came back to the table and sat like a prosecutor who finished presenting his case. "Kathleen's murder was no mistake. It was ordered by Liam, it was executed by Webb, and it was done to keep you from leaving Northern Ireland."

IV.

I drove back to the Maryville House thinking about the conversation with O'Byrne. The premise that Liam was behind Kathleen's murder would be tough for him to accept, especially since it came from me. O'Byrne had been with Liam his whole life, and I showed up a week ago. I couldn't drive a wedge between them that easily. I had no history here, no standing whatsoever, but at least I had given O'Byrne something to think about.

When I got back to the Maryville House, I called Kenny Bowen. "How badly do you want the fourth sheet of bills?"

"Are you trying to be funny?" Kenny said. "It's worth a fortune to me, to both of us. I want it as badly as the other three. Do you know where it is?"

"I know a man who will show me where it is, but he'll need some coaxing."

"Coaxing? What are you talking about?"

"I'm talking about a plan to get the money back," I said. "The plan is somewhat harebrained. It is convoluted, too."

"It can't be more convoluted than the fake search warrant," Kenny said.

"You got three sheets of money back because of that fake search warrant."

"Hey, no complaints," he said. "I'm so used to the standard approach that your unconventional ways throw me."

"And make you money," I added.

"Touché, monsieur," he said.

"Let's talk about my next doozy of a plan," I said. "I'll need money up front. Can I get my share of the reward, the ten percent?"

"Not until the job is completed," Kenny said. "Do you know how much money that is?"

I was no math whiz, but ten percent of thirty-two $100,000 bills came out to $320,000.

"If I put up the money, will I get reimbursed?"

"Do you have that much at your disposal?" he asked.

"I fell into some money a while ago." I told him. "A very large sum."

"What did you fall into, a diamond mine?"

"Answer the question, Kenny." I pushed. "I want to make this happen."

"Sure, sure, you'll get reimbursed, but you'll have to recover the sheet first. No sheet, no refund, understood?"

"I understand."

"*Can* you get it back?" he asked, sounding hopeful.

"It depends," I said.

"It depends on what?" he asked.

"It depends on how big a risk you're willing to take, because you'll have to be a bit nuts to do what I'm about to ask you to do."

"A bit nuts?" Kenny said. "And that's coming from you. If you think it's a bit nuts, it must be insane." He sighed. "Tell me what you need."

I told him.

§

Using contact C2 on McAfee's cell phone, I called O'Byrne, who answered without enthusiasm. He told me to get rid of Mac's phone before I got in trouble. I told him I needed to ask him a favor.

"I want you to set up a meeting with Liam McGrew," I said.

"I was right," O'Byrne said. "You're feckin' crazy. He'll shoot you in the head, you know."

"Tell Liam I want to talk about the World's Fair of Money." I thought for a second. "Tell Liam I'm afraid of him, and that I want to meet him inside the airport, so he can't get a gun past security. I'll meet him in the Café Bar."

"His cousin or in-law or comrade will probably be working in airport security and let Liam walk through armed."

"I'll take that chance," I said. "Set it up for tomorrow afternoon at five o'clock."

"Is there anything else you'd like?" O'Byrne asked, sounding cynical. "Do you want me to call the Queen of England and set up a meeting with her, too?"

"There is one more thing," I said, "and it is the most important part of the plan."

"What plan?"

I told him.

V.

O'Byrne called Liam to set up the meeting with Sparhawk, or at least try to. He worried that Liam might think it was a trap. O'Byrne thought about Sparhawk's take on Kathleen's murder. He wasn't sure if he believed it, but he didn't dismiss it out of hand, either.

Liam picked up the phone.

O'Byrne said, "It's me."

"Have you any more charges to hurl my way?" Liam grumbled. "Any other insults or rumors or half-truths?"

"I apologize for that, Liam," O'Byrne said. "I got confused."

"We're in a cutthroat business, O'Byrne, a profession reserved for the cold blooded." Liam affected his orator's voice. "Spying, bugging, double-dealing, we are called to engage in all forms of clandestine activity, and we are called to second-guess every person we encounter, even our closest allies."

"'Tis a tough life we live," O'Byrne said.

"Indeed, it is very tough." Liam breathed heavily. "I sense you have something to say to me."

"Sparhawk contacted me," O'Byrne said. "He wants to meet with you."

"Perfect!" Liam howled. "I'll blow his feckin' head off. Where are we to meet?"

Liam's reaction surprised O'Byrne. Liam never asked how Sparhawk made contact. Was it face-to-face, over the phone, by letter or by email? Liam didn't ask.

"He wants to meet you at Belfast International," O'Byrne said. "He'll be in the Café Bar at five o'clock tomorrow."

"The airport is crawling with law enforcement." Liam now sounded hesitant. "They have security everywhere."

"That's why Sparhawk wanted to meet you there, to feel safe."

"We'll see about safe," Liam said.

They hung up.

§

O'Byrne called Jackie Tracy in Charlestown to get an update on the Boston situation. Jackie answered the phone, and O'Byrne said, "How are things in Boston?"

"If you're asking about the Red Sox, things couldn't be worse, unless the Yankees win it all." Jackie laughed. "But you're probably more interested in dead bodies and hit men and ballistics and stolen sheets of money."

"Indeed, I am."

"The cops still haven't identified Alroy and McAfee," Jackie said. "They haven't identified the third man either, whoever he is."

"And the robbery?"

"Nothing in the newspapers, nothing new with the police," Jackie said. "I searched the Internet. Nothing there, either. You guys are home free as far as I can tell."

"Any problems with the gun Alroy used?" O'Byrne asked.

"No problems at all, the police are flummoxed." Jackie laughed again. "Everything is coming up heads for you guys, for me too."

"There is another matter I'd like to ask you about," O'Byrne said. "It has to do with Tullyverry."

"Tullyverry?" Jackie sounded bewildered. "That was more than thirty years ago. Why do you care about Tullyverry?"

"What happened that night in Tullyverry?" O'Byrne asked.

"I'm not sure I can help you," Jackie said. "Can you be more specific?"

"How close did the Brits come to catching you?"

"Catching me?" Now Jackie *really* sounded bewildered. "You lost me."

"The Brits seized two boats at Tullyverry that night and sank another," O'Byrne said. "How did you escape their dragnet? How did you get away?"

"I didn't have to get away," Jackie answered. "I wasn't even there."

"You weren't there?" Now O'Byrne was the one who sounded bewildered. "If you weren't in Tullyverry, where were you?"

"I was here in Boston watching the Red Sox blow the World Series against the Mets. It was game six and—"

O'Byrne interrupted. "What do you mean you weren't in Tullyverry?"

"Liam called me a week before the scheduled shipment and told me not to come. He said he smelled a rat or something like that. He didn't want me to risk going there."

"A week before, you say?" O'Byrne asked.

"Yeah, a week before. How come?"

VI.

I sat in the Café Bar and watched as smiling greeters embraced arriving passengers. Everyone was happy, joyous, and free, as we say in AA. The last thing they were worried about was getting whacked by the IRA. The café itself was an open affair, bordered by brass railings and elevated two feet above the terminal floor. The raised platform provided an excellent view of pedestrian traffic. I spotted Liam across the way.

He came toward me, his shillelagh clicking, his face snarling, his oxygen tank dragging like an anchor in muck. He took the handicap ramp into the café, and when he got close enough, he stared at me with ruthless eyes, two cesspools of cruelty. I hadn't seen Liam since the day I threw him out of my office in Charlestown. I wish I had *that* decision to do over. But you don't get a mulligan with the IRA. He sat at the table and wasted no time.

"You killed my grandson." He pulled the tank closer and twisted the knob. "Now I will kill you."

"You sent a boy to do a man's job." I leaned forward. "Alroy drank himself blind the night he shot me. The simpleton couldn't kill me from a foot away he was so drunk. I didn't want to kill him, but I had to. He left me no choice."

"You bastard!" Liam croaked.

"I wish you could have heard the blows." I smiled. "I crushed his skull with a big chunk of granite. The thuds made a sickening sound, especially the second one. And his screams were horrific."

"I'll kill you!"

Liam raised his stick and swiped at my head. I yanked it out of his hands and broke it over my knee. Liam looked at it. His face screwed into a pink coil of flesh.

"That blackthorn shillelagh belonged to my father."

"Now it belongs in the trash." I tossed the splinters aside. "Let's discuss the reason I ordered you here."

"You didn't order me here." Liam drew a breath, but not without difficulty. "Nobody orders me anywhere!"

"I have the $100,000 bills." I leaned forward again, getting closer to him. "I found your stash, Liam. You picked a stupid place to hide it, which was no surprise."

"Bullshit!" He wheezed.

"I'm returning the money to the United States Treasury." I tapped a cardboard tube on the table. "Treasury is sending a couple of agents to meet me today. I'll be exchanging this tube of money for an extremely handsome reward."

"You're full of shite, Sparhawk." His eyes darted back and forth, scanning the terminal. "What sheet of money? I don't know what you're talking about."

"This one." I uncapped the tube and removed the $100,000 bills. "Should I spread it on the table so you can inspect it?"

"Put it away, buffoon." Liam searched the surroundings, probably for agents. "Put it away I said!"

"You stole this from the World's Fair of Money." I held it up. "You also stole three other sheets, which you gave to Halloran. I took Halloran's away, too."

"Liar." He choked for air. "You're a no-good, feckin' liar!"

"This sheet is going home to where it belongs," I said. "What is taking the T-men so long to get here? Usually they're prompt."

Liam looked around again. He took a breath and appeared to gather himself. He sat up in the chair, seemingly unruffled, and pointed at me.

"Do you think you can traipse through my town like you own it?" He bent over for air and came up again. "Dozens of men are under my command, dozens! You won't get out of Belfast alive, Sparhawk."

"I enjoyed showing you the bills." I held the sheet up again. "It was fun to rub your face in it."

"You are going to regret every word you said today."

"You're a failure, Liam." I rolled up the sheet and put it back in the tube. "You got your grandson killed, you got McAfee killed, you got Webb killed, and you lost a sheet of $100,000 bills. Only a complete fuck-up could accomplish those feats of failure."

"You're a dead man." He got up to leave. "Dead, I tell you!"

"Do you really think I'm afraid of you?" I stood next to Liam and looked down at him. "Get out of here before I swat you like a flea."

"You're feckin' dead!" He walked away.

§

I tapped the tube on the table, a roll of cardboard worth $3.2 million. Kenny Bowen came into the café and sat next to me. I handed him the cylinder.

"Do you think it worked?" he asked.

"We'll know in a day or two," I said. "I thought he might point a gun at me to take the money right here in the café. Then we'd be out two sheets of bills."

A man at the table behind me turned and said, "He wouldn't have gotten far."

It was Rat T. Kennedy, hiding in plain sight. He opened his windbreaker and showed me a concealed weapon. I wondered if it was the same gun he used to blow two holes in Phillip Webb's head.

"Hi, Rat," I said. "You have my back as usual."

Kenny said, "I take chances, but they're measured chances. Rat T. has a way of mitigating risk."

"I found that out firsthand," I said.

"If Liam tried to grab the money, we'd have stopped him." Kenny paused. "Well, Dermot, you set the hook."

"And a fine hook it was." I replied. "But as my bald Irish friend would say, it's not a fish 'til it's on the bank."

Kenny Bowen and Rat T. Kennedy left the Café Bar. A minute later my cousin Cam O'Hanlon came in. He'd been monitoring the scene from the magazine stand across the terminal.

A few days ago I had called Cam and asked him for help. Superintendent Hanson made the necessary arrangements with law enforcement in Northern Ireland, paving the way for Cam to come to Belfast. I wasn't going to risk losing a sheet of $100,000 bills no matter what precautions Kenny put in place. I also wasn't going to risk eating a bullet from Liam's gun. Cam sat with me.

"As it turned out, you didn't need me," he said.

"But I might have, and I might yet." I thought about Liam's threats. "I'm not out of Belfast, Cam, not by a long shot."

"I'm here until you leave." He turned to me. "Are you wearing the Kevlar vest?"

I tapped my chest with an extended thumb. "You bet I am."

VII.

Kenny called me at the Maryville House the moment I got in. The call surprised me because I had just talked to him at the airport. He asked me how O'Byrne reacted when I told him that Phillip Webb had murdered Kathleen on Liam McGrew's orders. Before I could answer, Kenny cut in and repeated the question. Kenny sounded hyper. He wasn't his usual cool self. When I got an opening, I spoke.

I told Kenny that I couldn't get a clear reading on O'Byrne's reaction, that he was a tough guy to figure out. Kenny pursued the topic. Did O'Byrne believe me when I told him about the link between Webb and Liam? I repeated that I didn't know whether he believed me or not. I found Kenny's questioning odd, almost slippery.

"What's going on?" I finally asked. "Is there something you're not telling me?"

"My mind is racing all over the place," he said. "Bottom line, I think I have something you can use."

"Can you be more specific?"

"Phillip Webb collected souvenirs."

"Okay, Webb collected souvenirs," I said, and I started to see where Kenny might be going. "What kind of souvenirs?"

"He saved objects from the people he killed, keepsakes of his dirty work."

"Right, keepsakes." I thought about Webb's dead body on the Northern Avenue Bridge, the back of his head blown off, the blood dripping through the grating. "I thought you said he had nothing on him."

"Webb had a flat in West London, in Mayfair, to be exact." Kenny was so excited he had to stop and catch his breath. "Nobody knew about the flat, not his family, not his colleagues in the British Army, nobody. It was his secret hideaway. After some extensive digging, Scotland Yard tracked it down."

"Is that where Webb kept the trophies, at his Mayfair flat?"

"Webb had souvenirs from Tullyverry. He had other things from a foiled IRA bombing campaign near Buckingham Palace." Kenny paused. "He also had a souvenir from O'Byrne's wife, some kind of a religious item."

"How do you know it belonged to her?" I asked.

"The name Kathleen O'Byrne is embroidered on it." He paused again. "The item was also stained with blood, probably her blood." Kenny continued. "The item is made of a fine woolen cloth, according to the lab boys at Scotland Yard, and it is speckled with dry blood. I think it could be useful."

"What a sick bastard."

I wasn't sure what Kenny had in mind. I doubted the lab could get usable DNA off it. Too much time had passed. And even if they got a viable reading, they'd still have to dig up Kathleen's body to get a tissue sample for comparison, if there was any tissue left after thirty years in the ground. I knew one thing. O'Byrne wouldn't fancy the idea of his wife getting exhumed.

"Wouldn't the blood be degraded by now?" I asked.

"The blood is useless for forensic testing," Kenny said. "Why do you care if the blood is degraded?"

"I assumed you were thinking of DNA testing," I said.

"I see the confusion," Kenny said. "No, not DNA testing, I was thinking of sending Kathleen's item to you, so you can show it to O'Byrne as physical evidence of her murder."

"You want me to show it to O'Byrne?"

"Scotland Yard found the item in Phillip Webb's flat, which proves that Webb murdered Kathleen."

"It sure does."

Kenny's idea might have been morbid, showing O'Byrne a souvenir from his wife's murder, but it was also smart.

I said, "You're saying the item will prove to O'Byrne once and for all that Kathleen was Webb's target all along. The item Webb took was a trophy for a good kill."

"Should I send it to you or not?" Kenny asked.

"Send it along," I said. "Can you send Webb's souvenirs from Tullyverry, too?"

"Consider it done," Kenny said. "But Tullyverry is ancient history."

"Not in Belfast it's not." Something was amiss. "Why did Scotland Yard give you the souvenirs? Isn't that stuff evidence?"

"It wasn't really Scotland Yard that found Webb's flat," he said. "A consulting group that works with Scotland Yard found it. And since nobody can say with certainty that Webb is dead, and since nobody can know for sure that the flat belonged to him, the consulting group was willing to be more flexible than they usually are with the evidence."

"Flexible?" Then it came to me. "You bribed them to get the items."

"I wouldn't call it a bribe," Kenny said. "I'd call it cooperation between interested parties. Do you have a problem with that?"

"Just get the stuff over to me."

Kenny told me that a courier would be delivering the evidence to the Maryville House. I asked him when it might get here.

"I'm a step ahead of you, Dermot. You'll get it today."

"Including the Tullyverry trophies?" I asked.

"Like I said, I'm a step ahead of you."

He hung up the phone.

An hour later Rat T. Kennedy delivered a sealed manila envelope to my room. He nodded and left without a word. I opened the parcel and emptied it on my bed. I saw various forms of withered identification. A driver's license, a library card, a passport, things like that, which presumably belonged to the Tullyverry victims. The items were cloudy and yellowing and tough to read. Some were burnt, some were torn. Clearly they had seen battle.

I then found the souvenir that had belonged to Kathleen O'Byrne, a blood-spattered necklace with the Carmelite scapulars. A third patch had been attached to the necklace with Kathleen's name sewn in gold needlepoint. It looked similar to the scapulars that Aunt Bridget had given to me, except mine had a Saint Bridget's Cross on it. It must be an Irish thing, the scapulars.

I put everything back in the envelope and dozed off on the bed. I had no sooner fallen asleep when my phone rang. It was O'Byrne. He said that he wanted to see me, that he had important news. I told him to come by whenever he wanted.

VIII.

When O'Byrne arrived at the Maryville House, he called Sparhawk's room from the front desk and told him that he was downstairs. He then sat in a leather club chair and waited. Moments later Sparhawk came into the lobby carrying a manila envelope. He sat down across from O'Byrne, who smiled.

"Your plan worked," O'Byrne said. "I tailed Liam for two days, and by Jesus, he led me to the money. I couldn't believe his carelessness, his sloppy disregard for protocol. Not once did the eejit check over his shoulder, not that he would have spotted me if he had. I followed him out to the country, miles outside of Belfast to the farmlands, and that's where the damn fool hid the sheet of money. He stashed it in an old barn on his family farm. After Liam left the farmhouse, I went into the barn and took the sheet."

"Any trouble?" Sparhawk asked.

"Not a bloody lick," O'Byrne answered. "A teenage boy could have done it."

"Unless that teenage boy was Alroy McGrew," Sparhawk said. "Don't sell yourself short. You did well. Let's make the exchange."

Sparhawk handed O'Byrne a cashier's check for $320,000, ten percent of the sheet's worth. O'Byrne handed Sparhawk a canister containing the sheet of money. He asked Sparhawk to look inside it, which Sparhawk did, and the towering Yank nodded his approval.

"The deal is done," Sparhawk said to O'Byrne. "Now you can leave Northern Ireland. You can get out of Belfast and never look back."

"I only wish Kathleen could join me." O'Byrne cleared his throat and looked away. "I suppose I'll have to go it alone. My godmother told me of a place in the Leeward Islands. The Emerald Isle of the Caribbean she called it, the island of Montserrat."

"Never heard of it," Sparhawk admitted. "Sounds tropical."

"Aye, it is indeed. Montserrat is part of the West Indies, the Lesser Antilles chain, but you're probably not interested in a geography lesson." He said this with anticipation in his voice. "I'll be packing my bags any day now."

"I need to ask you something." Sparhawk shifted his weight. "Did you believe me when I told you that Liam ordered Kathleen's murder?"

"I believed that your man on the phone told you that, yes." O'Byrne answered.

"But you have doubts as to whether it's true."

"Most of life is filled with doubts, don't you think?" O'Byrne said. "We rarely get definitive answers."

"I hate to show you this," Sparhawk said, "but I think it's important you see it."

He handed O'Byrne the manila envelope.

"What is this?" O'Byrne emptied the envelope on a low table and picked up the scapulars. His eyes riveted onto the bloody patches and his breathing turned to panting. "Where the feck did you get this? It belonged to Kathleen. Bridie gave it to her on our wedding day."

"I thought it was hers," Sparhawk said.

"Where the hell did you get it?" O'Byrne's eyes flooded to two pools of blue. He touched his chest, feeling his own scapulars.

"Scotland Yard found this stuff in Phillip Webb's flat in Mayfair," Sparhawk answered. "Webb collected souvenirs from the people he killed."

"Webb killed Kathleen," O'Byrne said with resignation in his voice, not wanting to believe it. "Webb really did kill her."

"Yes, he did." Sparhawk looked at the Carmelite scapulars. "Webb killed her and took the necklace as a memento."

"And Webb was in cahoots with Liam," O'Byrne conceded. "They were partners in her murder."

"Yes, they were," Sparhawk said. "Their relationship went back forty years."

"What are the other things, the identification tags and such?" asked O'Byrne.

"Souvenirs from the raid at Tullyverry," Sparhawk told him. "ID cards from the dead rebels, more of Webb's mementos."

"Proving that Liam told Webb about Tullyverry," O'Byrne admitted.

O'Byrne rose from the chair and slowly walked to the men's room. He came back a few minutes later, with his eyes stinging red and his hand clutching Kathleen's scapulars. He sat down and gathered his emotions. He told Sparhawk that he now believed that Liam McGrew had hired Phillip Webb to murder Kathleen.

"I'm sorry you had to find out this way." Sparhawk extended open hands as a sign of condolence. "You've been loyal to Liam your whole life."

The two men sat quietly. Tourists checked in, tourists checked out, and the staff hustled to serve them. There were bursts of laughter and hugs of joy and reunions of distant families. Sparhawk and O'Byrne didn't belong there. They didn't fit in. O'Byrne clutched Kathleen's necklace again.

"Jesus had Judas Iscariot, the colonists had Benedict Arnold, and I have Liam McGrew. I feel the fool for not seeing it sooner." O'Byrne sniffled. "Before you leave, I'll be needing a few things from you."

"Name it," Sparhawk said.

"I'll be needing the name and address of Mr. H." O'Byrne cleared his throat. "Can you give me that, Dermot?"

Sparhawk wrote the information on hotel stationery and handed it to O'Byrne. He asked O'Byrne what else he needed.

"I'd like the men's belongings from Tullyverry," O'Byrne said. "And I'd like to keep Kathleen's scapulars."

Sparhawk pushed the items across the table to O'Byrne.

O'Byrne said, "Go home to Boston, Dermot. Let me deal with Liam. Everything will go better if you go home. Will you do that for me?"

Sparhawk hemmed and hawed, as the Americans like to say. He didn't like the idea of leaving Belfast until he settled the matter with

Liam, and he told O'Byrne so. O'Byrne assured Sparhawk that he didn't have to worry about Liam any longer, and that he was going to take care of everything. He guaranteed it.

O'Byrne then said, "If you hadn't noticed, I have a score to settle with Liam myself. He killed my wife. This is my territory, my people. Please go home."

"Okay, I'll go," said Sparhawk.

IX.

I stepped outside the Maryville House after O'Byrne left the lobby and breathed in the misty air. Once my head cleared, I called Cam O'Hanlon, who was staying in the room next to mine. He answered right away. I asked him to meet me in the lobby when he got the chance. Cam told me to turn around, and when I did, I saw him standing ten feet away from me. We went into the lobby and sat in club chairs.

"I wanted to keep an eye on you and O'Byrne," he said. "I know you trust him, but you never know. I noticed that he got pretty upset."

"He sure did," I said. "I showed him a necklace that belonged to his murdered wife. The memory of it hit him hard."

"What's the next move?" Cam asked.

"O'Byrne wants me to go home to Boston," I said. "He told me that he could handle everything from here on in. He has a plan."

Cam and I stopped talking until a couple of tourists walked past us. The woman carried a folded map. The man had a hundred-dollar bill in his hand. Neither of them spoke with a brogue. They stood in front of the hotel, and a taxi pulled over to pick them up. It must be nice to be a tourist in Belfast, and not a hunted man.

"What about Liam McGrew?" Cam asked. "He still wants to kill you."

"O'Byrne's plan covers Liam," I said. "He guaranteed my safety."

"Are you okay with that?" Cam asked. "You're placing a lot of faith in a man you barely know."

"I know I am," I said. "But for some reason I trust him."

"You're a good judge of character." Cam kicked out his legs and slumped in the chair. "You said that O'Byrne wants you to leave Belfast."

"He does." I thought about the conversation with O'Byrne and felt pretty good about it. "For once in my life, I'm going to take someone's advice. We're out of here, Cam. I'll book a flight for tomorrow."

"Smart move," Cam said.

"I sure hope so."

CHAPTER THIRTEEN

I.

O'Byrne drank flat stout from a thick mug inside the Valhalla House, an ancient Belfast taproom located across the street from Slattery's Pub. He sat on a high stool at a wavy window and watched the afternoon traffic go by. The parade of cars put him in a hypnotic state. A car slowed to a stop in front of Slattery's, breaking O'Byrne's trance. Two tweed-capped men got out and glanced up and down the street. One of the men was IRA Army Council member Salty McBrine. With his lips hardly moving, he whispered into the other man's ear. The man shielded his mouth, pretending to be rubbing his nose, and whispered something back. They went into the pub. O'Byrne left the Valhalla House to join them.

Once inside Slattery's, O'Byrne nodded to Salty, who barely nodded back. O'Byrne recognized the other man as Chuck Race, an IRA soldier and fellow inmate at the Maze, a man O'Byrne had bonded with during the hunger strikes and the dirty protests. Chuck's hair was still mostly blond.

"He's out back," O'Byrne said.

O'Byrne led Salty and Chuck to the back room. And there in the bleakness sat Liam McGrew. He occupied his customary chair and drank his customary drink, his red blotch looking pale, his oxygen tank churning air. Liam swallowed some Irish whiskey and invited the men to have a seat. He offered them Jameson and they accepted his offer. He poured three generous glassfuls. "No sense skimping," Liam said to his guests, and he handed one to Salty, one to O'Byrne, and one to Chuck. After a nasty belch, Liam commenced his oration.

"I thank ye all for joining me on this, shall we say, most inauspicious occasion. I asked you here today to clear the air, to set the record straight on some gross misunderstandings, and I might add, to refute some ugly rumors that are circling my head like ravenous buzzards."

"What needs to be refuted?" Salty asked.

Liam McGrew nodded grimly with the face of a man wrongly accused, a man forced to restore his honor and reputation.

"First, there is the issue of money," Liam said. "A whopping opportunity came our way, a chance to reap millions, but I had to be careful. This particular opportunity had to be handled with the utmost delicacy, lest we squander the moment and lose the commission. Discretion! I had to be smart." Liam upped the tank pressure and gulped his drink. "I was dealing with an important man, a partner from the States who is sympathetic to our cause. Everything had to be hush-hush."

"Tell me what happened," Salty said, now leaning forward.

Was Salty buying into this heap of shite, O'Byrne wondered.

"We were hired to pull off a heist," Liam started. "Thanks to my lifelong comrade, O'Byrne, the heist went without a hiccup, not a hitch to be had. We were paid two million American dollars for services rendered, but alas, I was struck down with illness and hospitalized at Musgrave." After another swallow he added, "I nearly died, I did. Thus I never paid tribute to the larger cause—the fight for freedom!"

Salty McBrine looked at Chuck and O'Byrne, and then he turned back to Liam McGrew. "Are you ready to make payment now, Liam?"

"Aye, indeed I am," he said. "I am hale and hearty and prepared to pay my allotment. That is one of the reasons I asked for this meeting today, to feather the nest of the Irish cause with an influx of much-needed cash, cash I shall gladly furnish."

"That sounds reasonable to me," Salty said. He looked around the table to the other men. "Do you have concerns on this matter, Chuckie? How about you, O'Byrne? Any questions for Liam?"

O'Byrne said, "What about the money from the museum job twenty years ago? What happened to *that* money? And what happened to the paintings?"

"Ah, the museum job, what a fine piece of work that was. You were brilliant on that job, O'Byrne, brilliant, I say! Never has a man performed so valiantly."

"What happened to the money and the paintings?" O'Byrne persisted.

"The money and paintings were worth a hefty fortune," he said. "Obviously, I paid tribute to the council. I gave a portion and a handsome portion it was."

"Is that true, Salty?" O'Byrne asked. "Did Liam pay tribute on the museum job?"

"Salty wouldn't know." Liam interrupted. "Salty wasn't on the Army Council at that time. I gave the money to McCoy."

"McCoy?" O'Byrne said. "McCoy is dead."

"Indeed, he is," Liam said. "I was greatly saddened by McCoy's passing. His funeral was a dreadful affair. I barely got through the reading the family asked me to do."

Salty McBrine drank Jameson. "Any other questions?" He waited. "I find Liam's explanation on the money matter plausible, well within the realm of reason. After all, he was sick in the hospital. As for the museum matter, McCoy is no longer with us, so I'll be taking Liam at his word that he made payment. What else is on your plate, Liam?"

Liam bowed his head like a sinner confessing a wrong.

"I ordered an execution," he said, as his shoulders sagged lower.

"An execution?" Salty growled. "You need permission for an execution. You ignored Army protocol. This is an egregious offense."

"If the hit were here in Ireland, I would have asked your permission, Salty. But it wasn't in Ireland. It was in the States, and there were extenuating circumstances."

"What extenuating circumstances?"

"My grandson was murdered in Boston by a man named Dermot Sparhawk." Liam answered. "I was enraged by the murder and ordered a hit on Sparhawk. I ordered it because Sparhawk killed my Alroy."

"I see." Salty's tone softened.

Liam seized on the shift in Salty's demeanor and continued. "I acted on emotion when I learned of Alroy's death. I lost my composure and lashed out on my own, never seeking your permission."

"I am sorry to hear about Alroy," Salty said.

"I hope you can forgive my recklessness. I have never done anything like this before, acting without Army approval."

Salty paused for another swig of whiskey and placed the glass on the table.

"I understand your wanting revenge, but why didn't you come to us?"

"I wasn't thinking straight, Salty." Liam spoke sheepishly, playing the mourning grandfather. "I jumped the gun."

"We have serious problems with splinter groups killing people in our name," Salty said, but not with much force. "You know of the problems we've had."

"Aye, I do indeed, but nobody in Boston knows that Alroy was with us. No one there knows he was in the IRA," Liam said.

"Is that true, O'Byrne?" asked Salty.

"No one in Boston knows Alroy's identity, let alone his link to the IRA."

Liam grabbed the momentum.

"Oh, this Sparhawk fellow is a sneaky cad, a twister of facts, a charlatan of the first order." Liam shook his head and snorted. "He filled O'Byrne's head with lies about me, but I don't blame O'Byrne for believing him, for Sparhawk is a master of deception. His parlor tricks would fool the devil himself."

"Do you know this man Sparhawk?" Salty asked O'Byrne.

"Aye, I know him."

Salty said, "Go on, Liam."

"After Sparhawk hunted down and murdered my Alroy, I ordered William McAfee to kill him." Liam wiped his eyes with his shirtsleeves. "And then Sparhawk went and killed McAfee, too, shot him to death in a filthy car lot in Boston."

"Mac is dead?" Salty said. "Why didn't you tell me this? McAfee is my wife's cousin's son. He's family. Why didn't you come to me?"

"I didn't want to bother you, Salty." Liam sniffled. "On top of that, I felt it was my fault. If only I had planned better. If only Sparhawk hadn't proved to be such a formidable foe. It was my fault, all of it."

"Easy now, Liam, you lost your grandson."

"What about Phillip Webb?" O'Byrne interjected. "Tell us about him."

"Who is Phillip Webb?" Salty asked.

"Thank you for bringing him up, O'Byrne." Liam adjusted the tube and inhaled air. "I would now like to address the matter of Phillip Webb if I may."

"I'm listening," Salty said.

"Phillip Webb is a British Army Intelligence officer, a man I've been cultivating for many years. He provided crucial intelligence that saved Irish lives." Liam paused. "Of course, handling a man like Webb is a ticklish undertaking, but I always kept a step ahead of him, for he is a crafty sort. You'd expect that from a Brit."

O'Byrne said, "You mean he *was* a crafty sort. Phillip Webb is dead. Sparhawk killed him in Boston."

"Three men dead in Boston?" Salty put his drink to the side. "You hired a Brit to do our bidding?"

"He was on our side." Liam filled his glass and drank. "Espionage is a cunning game, as you well know. I played Webb, played him like a Donegal fiddle, and then I used him to get information to advance the cause."

"Like Tullyverry?" O'Byrne said.

"What about Tullyverry?" asked Salty, who turned to face O'Byrne. "What the feck are you talking about?"

"Liam set us up at Tullyverry," O'Byrne said. "He told Phillip Webb about the gun shipments. He told Webb the time and place."

"I saved lives at Tullyverry!" Liam reached for a stick that was no longer there. "I alerted you, O'Byrne. You'd be dead if not for me."

"You wanted me alive so I could keep robbing for you," O'Byrne said. "It had nothing to do with the cause."

"Falsehoods!" Liam heaved for oxygen. "Canards!"

Salty said, "The Brits killed my brother at Tullyverry."

"And many more would have died if I hadn't intervened." Liam shook his fist. "O'Byrne is lying. Sparhawk corrupted him."

Salty said, "I've never known O'Byrne to lie about Army matters."

"Don't you see what's happening?" Liam implored. "It's Sparhawk."

Salty asked O'Byrne, "Can you prove that Liam betrayed us at Tullyverry?"

"I talked to our friend in Boston, the man in the armaments business," O'Byrne said. "I asked him about Tullyverry. I asked him if the British navy chased after him at Tullyverry. The Brits captured two ships that night."

"And sank another, and gunned down our soldiers on the coast, including my brother," Salty said. "What did our friend say?"

"He said that Liam had warned him about Tullyverry a week in advance," O'Byrne said. "An entire feckin' week before the raid. Our friend never bothered to load his ship he got such early warning. Call him. He'll tell you himself."

Salty said to Chuck, "You know our friend in Boston. Check it out."

Chuck left the room.

O'Byrne kept it going. "Liam had to throw Webb a bone, something important that Webb could give to his commanders. Liam gave him Tullyverry."

"You bounder!" Liam gasped.

"Tullyverry was Webb's greatest triumph," O'Byrne said. "The Queen honored him with a medal. He became a national hero, albeit under the radar."

"Smears, treacheries!" Liam groaned. "Don't believe him."

Chuck returned. "Our friend in Boston corroborated O'Byrne's story. He had a week's notice on Tullyverry, and he got the notice from Liam McGrew."

O'Byrne said, "Phillip Webb collected souvenirs from the people he killed."

"What?" Salty exclaimed.

"Webb had souvenirs from Tullyverry." O'Byrne laid what was left of the identification cards on the round table. "I just got my hands on these death pelts. They were in Phillip Webb's flat in Mayfair."

"What are they?" Salty picked one up. "Wait a goddamn minute. This is my brother's ID. And identifications from the other casualties at Tullyverry." Salty stood up and cracked Liam in the face with a backhander, knocking off the oxygen tube. "You murdered my brother! You feckin' traitor!"

"He also murdered my wife." O'Byrne dangled the bloody scapulars in the air. "Webb's souvenir from Kathleen's murder."

Liam scrambled for the tube and put it back in his nose. "No, no." Blood dripped from his mouth. Fighting for air, he said, "It's not true."

Chuck Race held a gun to Liam's head and took Liam's weapon away from him and put it in his pocket.

Salty said, "Tell me the rest of it, O'Byrne."

"Liam and Webb were partners in crime. Why would a decorated British Army officer fly to Boston to kill Dermot Sparhawk? To avenge the death of Alroy McGrew? Nay! Webb wouldn't give a damn about Alroy. To advance the Irish fight for freedom in the North? Not a chance. Webb went to Boston because Liam bribed him to go to Boston. He promised Webb a share of the $100,000 bills."

"What $100,000 bills?" Salty asked.

Liam twisted the knob and sucked air but couldn't speak.

Salty said, "Go on, O'Byrne."

O'Byrne told him about the World's Fair of Money, and Mr. H, and the killings of Alroy, Mac, and Webb.

Salty said, "It seems that Sparhawk took care of Webb for us, so I won't be needing to concern myself with that situation. What about the man who hired Liam in the first place, the American? This Mr. H."

"You'd be talking about Halloran," O'Byrne said. "He lives outside of Boston."

"Where can I find him?"

O'Byrne gave Salty the address.

"Liam the traitor," Salty said, as Liam sat gagging for air. "A feckin' tout."

O'Byrne said, "'Tis better to have fifty enemies outside the house than one within."

Salty's pupils dilated, growing as big and as black as eight balls. He pulled out a Luger and shot Liam in the head. He fired a second round into his heart, not that it was still pumping. The gunshots were lovely and loud, gunshots of revenge.

"Clean it up, Chuckie," Salty said. "And get Slattery to help."

§

O'Byrne walked along the Falls Road, grateful for the air that cleansed the scent of cordite from his nostrils. He hoped he never smelled it again, or witnessed a man's face blown off again, or heard footsteps following him again. He was done. He looked to the Ulster sky and said, "It's over, Kathleen."

CHAPTER FOURTEEN

I.

The flight touched down in Boston at six in the evening. Cam and I walked down the ramp and into the terminal. When we reached US Customs, an agent came up to us. Cam showed her his badge. She glanced at it but paid it little mind. She looked at her phone and then at me.

"Dermot Sparhawk?" she asked

"Yes," I answered.

"May I see your passport?"

I gave her my passport. She examined it, flipped it over a couple of times, handed it back and told me to follow her. Cam walked with me. She escorted us to a gate and told us to go through, never checking the items we were carrying.

She said, "The US Attorney's Office called Customs today and asked us to expedite your reentry into the country. Consider yourself expedited, Mister Sparhawk."

"Thank you," I said.

"Thank Maddy Savitz," she said, and went back to her post.

On the other side of the gate I was greeted by Rat T. Kennedy, the man who killed Phillip Webb on the Northern Avenue Bridge. I introduced Rat to Cam. They looked at each other like pit bulls. I thought I saw Rat T.'s hair bristle. Cam said he'd talk to me later and left for the cabstand. Rat T. told me to follow him.

Lugging the only bag I had taken with me on the trip, along with a canister of cash, I followed Rat T. to an SUV that was idling in the pickup area. Another man, who also looked like he could do some business with a gun, was leaning against the side of the vehicle. He opened the rear door for me and shut it once I got in. Rat T. hopped into the passenger seat. The other man drove us out of the airport. When we hit the Expressway, Rat T. said to the driver, "Greenburg's Nightspot, Columbus Ave." The driver nodded once. That was all the instruction he needed.

We stopped in front of Greenburg's. Rat T. jumped out, looked up and down Columbus Ave, and opened the door for me. It was the first time in my life I felt like a big shot. We walked to the club's entrance, and that's where he stopped.

"This is as far as I go. I'll keep watch out here," He jutted his jaw in a hard guy's salute. "I heard you did some nice work for Kenny. I'll be seeing you around."

"Thanks for saving my ass on the bridge." I said to him.

Rat T. nodded once and stood guard like a sentry.

I went into Greenburg's to meet Kenny Bowen, but he hadn't arrived yet. Ruth Greenburg, the club's owner, took me to a table. She smelled of springtime lilacs after a long cold winter, a smell good enough to bottle.

"You're looking good tonight, Dermot," she said, throwing me off guard. I was surprised that she remembered my name. I was even more surprised that she thought I looked good.

"So do you," I said in a feeble attempt to be suave. She laughed at me. I finally got a laugh.

Ruth's dark eyes mesmerized me. Her eyelids opened and closed like a gateway to something private, and she was the gatekeeper. Nobody got in without her say-so. Her figure was the stuff of Marvel Comics, almost a caricature in dimension, with a svelte waistline, exaggerated hips, and shapely breasts that defined her blouse. But it was her locomotion more than her proportions that drew the stares, the way she moved her parts. Ruth snapped me out of my daze when she said, "I know you don't drink liquor. I recommend the Yemen Arabian Mocha coffee, just brewed."

"I'll have a pot."

The house pianist, Zack Sanders, came into the room dressed in a black tuxedo. He sat on a padded bench and settled himself at the Steinway grand. After a few practice scales, he played one of those swing tunes that everyone knows but no one can name. A waitress delivered the coffee. I opened a package of Effie's Oatcakes to go with it. Victory is not only sweet, but sweet to savor. Red Auerbach would light a cigar, the Beatles would take a bow, Orville Wright would fly a figure eight, and I ate Effie's Oatcakes. I was tapping my toe to the beat of the song when Kenny Bowen came in and sat next to me.

"Your Belfast ploy succeeded," he said.

"I had plenty of support." I handed him the canister. "I paid my Irish friend a full ten percent of that sheet."

"I'm amazed at your resources and your generosity." After Kenny examined the contents of the tube, he took a leather portfolio from his briefcase and opened it on the table. Inside the portfolio were gilded-edged checks. With theatrical flair he uncapped a fountain pen, filled in a check, tore it out, blew on the ink, and handed it to me, saying, "Nice work, Dermot."

"Thanks." I looked at the amount. "This can't be right."

"Is there a problem?" he asked.

"The amount is wrong. I recovered a hundred and twenty-eight $100,000 bills, which comes to $12.9 million." I was no math whiz, but ten percent of that number is roughly $1.3 million. "This check is for more than twenty million."

"The money you recovered was insured at market value, not face value. Each bill is worth $1.6 million. The four sheets are worth roughly $205 million. Do the math, I paid you ten percent."

"Market value?"

"What's your next move, a waterfront beach house down the Cape? A mountain villa in the Berkshires?"

What would I do down the Cape, watch waves roll in? Listen to seagulls? I'd rather dodge bullets in the projects.

"Montserrat," I said. "I owe an Irishman some money."

§

The next day I deposited the check. My hand shook as I handed it to the bank teller. She looked at the check and then at me.

"I know," I said. "I can't believe it either."

Back in Charlestown I bought the Boston newspapers and went to the Grasshopper Cafe for breakfast. After I finished my first cup of coffee I looked at the *Herald*. The headline said: "Billionaire Slain in Weston Mansion." The subhead read: "Two Men Shot in Head." Below the headline was a picture of Halloran's estate, along with pictures of Halloran and Kloosmann. Kloosmann's photo was a mugshot.

The article speculated that Halloran might have been involved in the drug trade and other illegal ventures. Why else would he be killed gangland style? The story went on to say that Karl Kloosmann, the second victim, had a lengthy criminal record in Ohio, a fact that bolstered the paper's premise that Halloran had engaged in illicit activities. Neither paper mentioned Belfast or the Irish Republican Army or the World's Fair of Money.

"Halloran and Kloosmann got their Irish comeuppance," I muttered.

"What was that?" the waitress asked. "Irish coffee?"

"Just talking to myself, Lynne," I said.

That evening I drove to Dorchester to conclude some unfinished business with a feisty cocktail waitress. I parked in front of the Blarney Stone and went inside and found Delia waiting on a table. When I approached her, she rolled her eyes.

"I thought I saw the last of you." She didn't sound angry when she said it. "What now, another twenty questions?"

"No more questions." I handed her an envelope. "Thanks for the help."

Inside the envelope was a check for five hundred thousand dollars. The information Delia provided proved to be pivotal in solving the case. Without it I never would have known about the Belfast connection, and for that she deserved to be rewarded.

"Hey, Dermot," Delia said, holding the envelope in her hand. "My friend Angel is interested in you."

"Who is Angel?"

"The bartender at Caffé Bella." She winked.

I should have given her a million.

EPILOGUE

I flew into Montserrat on an island hop and rented a car at the airport. After two days of searching the Emerald Isle of the Caribbean, I located O'Byrne at a waterfront cottage in the town of Hell's Gate. Finding O'Byrne was no great feat. Fewer than six thousand people inhabited Montserrat, a number that wouldn't fill the bleachers at Fenway Park.

I pulled into a short driveway that was paved with crushed oyster shells and knocked on the screen door of a pink stucco house. The door rattled but no one answered. I went around back and found O'Byrne lazing in a chaise lounge. He was ten feet from the shoreline holding a fishing rod. A canvas sailor's cap covered his bald head. Sunburnt skin flaked on his neck, and dry sea salt speckled his forearms.

"Catch anything?" I asked.

"For the love of Pete." O'Byrne got off the chaise. "It's good to see you, Dermot, better than you know. What brings you to nature's paradise, certainly not the bright lights and the action?"

"I have news from Boston."

"Nothing bad, I hope."

"Not as far as I'm concerned," I said, staring at the green ocean. "Halloran and Kloosmann are dead, both shot in the head point-blank."

"Mr. H and K," O'Byrne said. "I never met Mr. H."

"You didn't miss much."

"I dealt with K, God rest his soul." O'Byrne looked to the water. "I didn't like him very much, but he treated me fairly enough, I suppose. No doubt the lads in Belfast had a hand in this."

"The police have no leads."

"I don't suppose they ever will." O'Byrne picked up a flat stone and skimmed it on the water's surface. "I was wondering about something whilst sitting here wetting a line. Why did Liam warn our mutual friend in Charlestown about Tullyverry? Why did he warn Jackie, but not me? What was so special about Jackie that Liam tipped him off a week ahead of time?"

"I can venture a guess, but it's only a guess," I said.

"Well, don't keep me in suspense."

"Money," I said. "I'm guessing that Jackie *was* the middleman between Liam and Halloran. And if Jackie was the middleman, Liam would need him alive and out of jail to conduct business."

"A middleman, you say."

"Jackie linked Liam to Halloran's lucrative thefts," I said. "I can't see any other reason for Liam to warn Jackie, except money, but it's only a guess."

"And a good guess it is, I'm sad to say." O'Byrne actually looked sad. "Everything with Liam was money."

"Speaking of which, I owe you something."

"You don't owe me a blessed thing." He reeled in the line and set the rod on the sand. "I have my freedom. I've gone to confession. Kathleen and Bridie begged me to confess my sins and now I have. Thanks to you and Bridie, I have a new start."

"Who's Bridie?"

"My godmother," he said, "and a saint she was."

"I wish I had the chance to meet her." I handed O'Byrne an envelope with a check for five million dollars inside. "Open it later."

He tossed it on the chaise lounge.

"The water is tepid down here, nothing like the icy currents of the Irish Sea. Take a dip, will you?" He smiled at me with sunshine on his face. "Look at me, wearing Bermuda shorts and a tank top. I've never worn shorts in my life."

"You'll get used to it," I said.

O'Byrne doffed his hat and waded into the Caribbean. I followed him into the turquoise deep. We were up to our necks in it, twenty yards off shore, treading water and letting the soft whitecaps slap our face. After a time, probably seconds before our fingers pruned, we splashed toward the beach. We stood ankle deep in seawater, glistening in salty residue and basking in a spirit of unspoken joy, and then we stared at each other.

"I cannot believe it," O'Byrne said.

"Neither can I."

I looked at the Carmelite scapulars around O'Byrne's neck. They were exactly like the ones around my neck. Everything made sense.

"Tossy," I said.

"Aye, 'tis."